Praise for *Drive Your Plow Over the Bones of the Dead*

"A marvelously weird and fablelike mystery . . . Authors with Tokarczuk's vending machine of phrasing . . . and gimlet eye for human behavior . . . are rarely also masters of pacing and suspense. But even as Tokarczuk sticks landing after landing . . . her asides are never desultory or a liability. They are more like little cuts—quick, exacting and purposefully belated in their bleeding. . . . This book is not a mere whodunit: It's a philosophical fairy tale about life and death that's been trying to spill its secrets. Secrets that, if you've kept your ear to the ground, you knew in your bones all along."

—*The New York Times Book Review*

"A paean to nature . . . a sort of ode to Blake . . . [and] a lament . . . Does Tokarczuk transcend Blake? Arguable—perhaps."   —NPR

"*Drive Your Plow* is exhilarating in a way that feels fierce and private, almost inarticulable; it's one of the most existentially refreshing novels I've read in a long time."   —*The New Yorker*

"One of the funniest books of the year."   —*The Guardian*

"While it adopts the straightforward structure of a murder mystery, [the book features] macabre humor and morbid philosophical interludes [that] are distinctive to its author . . . [and an] excellent payoff at the finale. . . . As for Ms. Tokarczuk, there's no doubt: She's a gifted, original writer, and the appearance of her novels in English is a welcome development."

—*The Wall Street Journal*

"[A] winding, imaginative, genre-defying story. Part murder mystery, part fairy tale, *Drive Your Plow* is a thrilling philosophical examination of the ways in which some living creatures are privileged above others."   —*Time*

"A brilliant literary murder mystery."   —*Chicago Tribune*

"Reading this novel, I sometimes had the unsettling sensation that I was being told a fairy story from the perspective of the witch. . . . Her insistence that animal suffering matters is itself a kind of spell. The opposite idea is so firmly woven into our culture that reversing it would be a kind of magic."

—*The New Republic*

"Sometimes the opening sentence of a first-person narrative can so vividly capture the personality of its speaker that you immediately want to spend all the time you can in their company. That's the case with . . . *Drive Your Plow*

Also by Olga Tokarczuk

Flights

RIVERHEAD
BOOKS

New York

DRIVE YOUR PLOW OVER THE BONES OF THE DEAD

—— ✕ ——

Olga Tokarczuk

Translated by Antonia Lloyd-Jones

RIVERHEAD BOOKS
An imprint of Penguin Random House LLC
penguinrandomhouse.com

First published as *Prowadź swój pług przez kości umarłych*
by Wydawnictwo Literackie, Kraków
English-language edition first published by Fitzcarraldo Editions, London
First American edition published by Riverhead Books, 2019

A portion of this book was published, in different form, in *Granta* (138, *Journeys*) in 2017.

Riverhead and the R colophon are registered trademarks of Penguin Random House LLC.

The Library of Congress has catalogued the Riverhead hardcover edition as follows:

Names: Tokarczuk, Olga, 1962- author. | Lloyd-Jones, Antonia, translator.
Title: Drive your plow over the bones of the dead : a novel / Olga Tokarczuk ;
translated by Antonia Lloyd-Jones.
Other titles: Prowadź swój pług przez kości umarłych. English
Description: First American edition. | New York, New York : Riverhead Books, 2019.
Identifiers: LCCN 2018038235 (print) | LCCN 2018043363 (ebook) |
ISBN 9780525541356 (ebook) | ISBN 9780525541332 (hardcover)
Classification: LCC PG7179.O37 (ebook) | LCC PG7179.O37 P7613 2019 (print) |
DDC 891.8/537—dc23
LC record available at https://lccn.loc.gov/2018038235

First Riverhead hardcover edition: August 2019
First Riverhead trade paperback edition: August 2020
Riverhead trade paperback ISBN: 9780525541349

Printed in the United States of America
1 3 5 7 9 10 8 6 4 2

Book design by Cassandra Garruzzo

CONTENTS

DRIVE YOUR
PLOW
OVER THE
BONES
OF THE
DEAD

I.

Now Pay Attention

Once meek, and in a perilous path,
The just man kept his course along
The vale of death.

I am already at an age and additionally in a state where I must always wash my feet thoroughly before bed, in the event of having to
be removed by an ambulance in the Night.

Had I examined the Ephemerides that evening to see what was
happening in the sky, I wouldn't have gone to bed at all. Meanwhile I
had fallen very fast asleep; I had helped myself with an infusion of
hops, and I also took two valerian pills. So when I was woken in the
middle of the Night by hammering on the door—violent, immoder-
ate and thus ill-omened—I was unable to come round. I sprang up
and stood by the bed, unsteadily, because my sleepy, shaky body
couldn't make the leap from the innocence of sleep into wakefulness.
I felt weak and began to reel, as if about to lose consciousness. Unfortunately this has been happening to me lately, and has to do with my
Ailments. I had to sit down and tell myself several times: I'm at home,

it's Night, someone's banging on the door; only then did I manage to control my nerves. As I searched for my slippers in the dark, I could hear that whoever had been banging was now walking around the house, muttering. Downstairs, in the cubbyhole for the electrical meters, I keep the pepper spray Dizzy gave me because of the poachers, and that was what now came to mind. In the darkness I managed to seek out the familiar, cold aerosol shape, and thus armed, I switched on the outside light, then looked at the porch through a small side window. There was a crunch of snow, and into my field of vision came my neighbor, whom I call Oddball. He was wrapping himself in the tails of the old sheepskin coat I'd sometimes seen him wearing as he worked outside the house. Below the coat I could see his striped pajamas and heavy hiking boots.

"Open up," he said.

With undisguised astonishment he cast a glance at my linen suit (I sleep in something the Professor and his wife wanted to throw away last summer, which reminds me of a fashion from the past and the days of my youth—thus I combine the Practical and the Sentimental) and without a by-your-leave he came inside.

"Please get dressed. Big Foot is dead."

For a while I was speechless with shock; without a word I put on my tall snow boots and the first fleece to hand from the coat rack. Outside, in the pool of light falling from the porch lamp, the snow was changing into a slow, sleepy shower. Oddball stood next to me in silence, tall, thin and bony like a figure sketched in a few pencil strokes. Every time he moved, snow fell from him like icing sugar from pastry ribbons.

"What do you mean, dead?" I finally asked, my throat tightening, as I opened the door, but Oddball didn't answer.

He generally doesn't say much. He must have Mercury in a reticent sign, I reckon it's in Capricorn or on the cusp, in square or maybe in opposition to Saturn. It could also be Mercury in retrograde—that produces reserve.

We left the house and were instantly engulfed by the familiar cold, wet air that reminds us every winter that the world was not created for Mankind, and for at least half the year it shows us how very hostile it is to us. The frost brutally assailed our cheeks, and clouds of white steam came streaming from our mouths. The porch light went out automatically and we walked across the crunching snow in total darkness, except for Oddball's headlamp, which pierced the pitch dark in one shifting spot, just in front of him, as I tripped along in the Murk behind him.

"Don't you have a flashlight?" he asked.

Of course I had one, but I wouldn't be able to tell where it was until morning. It's a feature of flashlights that they're only visible in the daytime.

Big Foot's cottage stood slightly out of the way, higher up than the other houses. It was one of three inhabited all year round. Only he, Oddball and I lived here without fear of the winter; all the other inhabitants had sealed their houses shut in October, drained the water from the pipes and gone back to the city.

Now we turned off the partly cleared road that runs across our hamlet and splits into paths leading to each of the houses. A path trodden in deep snow led to Big Foot's house, so narrow that you had to set one foot behind the other while trying to keep your balance.

"It won't be a pretty sight," warned Oddball, turning to face me, and briefly blinding me with his headlamp.

I wasn't expecting anything else. For a while he was silent, and then, as if to explain himself, he said: "I was alarmed by the light in his kitchen and the dog barking so plaintively. Didn't you hear it?"

No, I didn't. I was asleep, numbed by hops and valerian.

"Where is she now, the Dog?"

"I took her away from here—she's at my place, I fed her and she seemed to calm down."

Another moment of silence.

"He always put out the light and went to bed early to save money, but this time it continued to burn. A bright streak against the snow. Visible from my bedroom window. So I went over there, thinking he might have got drunk or was doing the dog harm, for it to be howling like that."

We passed a tumbledown barn and moments later Oddball's flashlight fetched out of the darkness two pairs of shining eyes, pale green and fluorescent.

"Look, Deer," I said in a raised whisper, grabbing him by the coat sleeve. "They've come so close to the house. Aren't they afraid?"

The Deer were standing in the snow almost up to their bellies. They gazed at us calmly, as if we had caught them in the middle of performing a ritual whose meaning we couldn't fathom. It was dark, so I couldn't tell if they were the same Young Ladies who had come here from the Czech Republic in the autumn, or some new ones. And in fact why only two? That time there had been at least four of them.

"Go home," I said to the Deer, and started waving my arms. They twitched, but didn't move. They calmly stared after us, all the way to the front door. A shiver ran through me.

Meanwhile Oddball was stamping his feet to shake the snow off his boots outside the neglected cottage. The small windows were sealed with plastic and cardboard, and the wooden door was covered with black tar paper.

THE WALLS IN THE HALL WERE STACKED WITH FIREWOOD FOR THE stove, logs of uneven size. The interior was nasty, dirty and neglected. Throughout there was a smell of damp, of wood and earth—moist and voracious. The stink of smoke, years old, had settled on the walls in a greasy layer.

The door into the kitchen was ajar, and at once I saw Big Foot's body lying on the floor. Almost as soon as my gaze landed on him, it leaped away. It was a while before I could look over there again. It was a dreadful sight.

He was lying twisted in a bizarre position, with his hands to his neck, as if struggling to pull off a collar that was pinching him. Gradually I went closer, as if hypnotized. I saw his open eyes fixed on a point somewhere under the table. His dirty vest was ripped at the throat. It looked as if the body had turned on itself, lost the fight and been killed. It made me feel cold with Horror—the blood froze in my veins and I felt as if it had withdrawn deep inside my body. Only yesterday I had seen this body alive.

"My God," I mumbled, "what happened?"

Oddball shrugged.

"I can't get through to the Police, it's the Czech network again."

I pulled my cell phone from my pocket and tapped out the number I knew from the television—997—and soon after an automated Czech voice responded. That's what happens here. The signal wanders, with no regard for the national borders. Sometimes the dividing line between operators parks itself in my kitchen for hours on end, and occasionally it has stopped by Oddball's house or on the terrace for several days. Its capricious nature is hard to predict.

"You should have gone higher up the hill behind the house," I belatedly advised him.

"He'll be stiff as a board before they get here," said Oddball in a tone that I particularly disliked in him—as if he had all the answers. He took off his sheepskin coat and hung it on the back of a chair. "We can't leave him like that, he looks ghastly. He was our neighbor, after all."

As I looked at Big Foot's poor, twisted body I found it hard to believe that only yesterday I'd been afraid of this Person. I disliked him. To say I disliked him might be putting it too mildly. Instead I should say that I found him repulsive, horrible. In fact I didn't even regard him as a human Being. Now he was lying on the stained floor in his dirty underwear, small and skinny, limp and harmless. Just a piece of matter, which some unimaginable processes had reduced to a fragile object, separated from everything else. It made me feel sad, horrified, for even someone as foul as he was did not deserve death. Who on earth does? The same fate awaits me too, and Oddball, and the Deer outside; one day we shall all be nothing more than corpses.

I glanced at Oddball, in the hope of some consolation, but he was already busy making the rumpled bed, a shakedown on a dilapidated folding couch, so I did my best to comfort myself. And then it occurred to me that in a way Big Foot's death might be a good thing. It had freed him from the mess that was his life. And it had freed other living Creatures from him. Oh yes, suddenly I realized what a good thing death can be, how just and fair, like a disinfectant, or a vacuum cleaner. I admit that's what I thought, and that's what I still think now.

Big Foot was my neighbor, our houses were only half a kilometer apart, yet I rarely had anything to do with him. Fortunately. Instead I used to see him from afar—his diminutive, wiry figure, always a little unsteady, would move across the landscape. As he went along, he'd mumble to himself, and sometimes the windy acoustics of the Plateau would bring me snippets of this essentially simple, unvarying monologue. His vocabulary mainly consisted of curses, onto which he tacked some proper nouns.

He knew every scrap of this terrain, for it seems he was born here and never went further than Kłodzko. He knew the forest well— what parts of it he could use to earn money, what he could sell and to whom. Mushrooms, blueberries, stolen timber, brushwood for kindling, snares, the annual off-road vehicle rally, hunting. The forest nurtured this little goblin. Thus he should have respected the forest, but he did not. One August, when there was a drought, he set an entire blueberry patch ablaze. I called the fire brigade, but not much could be saved. I never found out why he did it. In summer he would wander about with a saw, cutting down trees full of sap. When I politely admonished him, though finding it hard to restrain my Anger, he replied in the simplest terms: "Get lost, you old crone." But more crudely than that. He was always up to a bit of stealing, filching, fiddling, to make himself extra cash; when the summer residents left a flashlight or a pair of pruning shears in the yard, Big Foot would instantly nose out an opportunity to swipe these items, which he could then sell off in town. In my view he should have received several Punishments by now, or even been sent to prison. I don't know how he got away with it all. Perhaps there were some angels watching over him; sometimes they turn up on the wrong side.

I also knew that he poached by every possible means. He treated the forest like his own personal farm—everything there belonged to him. He was the pillaging type.

He caused me many a sleepless Night. I would lie awake out of helplessness. Several times I called the Police—when the telephone was finally answered, my report would be received politely, but nothing else would happen. Big Foot would go on his usual rounds, with a bunch of snares on his arm, emitting ominous shouts. Like a small, evil sprite, malevolent and unpredictable. He was always slightly drunk, and maybe that prompted his spiteful mood. He'd go about muttering and striking the tree trunks with a stick, as if to push them out of his way; he seemed to have been born in a state of mild intoxication. Many a time I followed in his tracks and gathered up the primitive wire traps he'd set for Animals, the nooses tied to young trees bent in such a way that the snared Animal would be catapulted up to hang in midair. Sometimes I found dead Animals—Hares, Badgers and Deer.

"We must shift him onto the couch," said Oddball.

I didn't like this idea. I didn't like having to touch him.

"I think we should wait for the Police," I said. But Oddball had already made space on the folding couch and was rolling up the sleeves of his sweater. He gave me a piercing look with those pale eyes of his.

"You wouldn't want to be found like that, would you? In such a state. It's inhuman."

Oh yes, the human body is most definitely inhuman. Especially a dead one.

Wasn't it a sinister paradox that now we had to deal with Big Foot's body, that he'd left us this final trouble? Us, his neighbors whom he'd never respected, never liked, and never cared about?

To my mind, Death should be followed by the annihilation of

matter. That would be the best solution for the body. Like this, annihilated bodies would go straight back into the black holes whence they came. The Souls would travel at the speed of light into the light. If such a thing as the Soul exists.

Overcoming tremendous resistance, I did as Oddball asked. We took hold of the body by the legs and arms and shifted it onto the couch. To my surprise I found that it was heavy, not entirely inert, but stubbornly stiff instead, like starched bed linen that has just been through the mangle. I also saw his socks, or what was on his feet in their place—dirty rags, foot wrappings made from a sheet torn into strips, now gray and stained. I don't know why, but the sight of those wrappings hit me so hard in the chest, in the diaphragm, in my entire body, that I could no longer contain my sobbing. Oddball cast me a cold, fleeting glance, with distinct reproach.

"We must dress him before they arrive," said Oddball, and I noticed that his chin was quivering too at the sight of this human misery (though for some reason he refused to admit it).

So first we tried to remove his vest, dirty and stinking, but it adamantly refused to be pulled over his head, so Oddball took an elaborate penknife from his pocket and cut the material to pieces across the chest. Now Big Foot lay half-naked before us on the couch, hairy as a troll, with scars on his chest and arms, covered in tattoos, none of which made any sense to me. His eyes squinted ironically while we searched the broken wardrobe for something decent to dress him in before his body stiffened for good and reverted to what it really was—a lump of matter. His torn underpants protruded from under brandnew silvery tracksuit bottoms.

Cautiously I unwound the repulsive foot wrappings, and saw his feet. They astonished me. I have always regarded the feet as the most intimate and personal part of our bodies, and not the genitals, not the heart, or even the brain, organs of no great significance that are too highly valued. It is in the feet that all knowledge of Mankind lies hidden; the body sends them a weighty sense of who we really are and how we relate to the earth. It's in the touch of the earth, at its point of contact with the body that the whole mystery is located—the fact that we're built of elements of matter, while also being alien to it, separated from it. The feet—those are our plugs into the socket. And now those naked feet gave me proof that his origin was different. He couldn't have been human. He must have been some sort of nameless form, one of the kind that—as Blake tells us—melts metals into infinity, changes order into chaos. Perhaps he was a sort of devil. Devilish creatures are always recognized by their feet—they stamp the earth with a different seal.

These feet—very long and narrow, with slender toes and shapeless black nails—looked prehensile. The big toe stood slightly apart from the rest, like a thumb. They were thickly coated in black hair. Had anyone seen the like before? Oddball and I exchanged glances.

In the near-empty wardrobe we found a coffee-colored suit, slightly stained, but obviously rarely worn. I had never seen him in it. Big Foot always went about in thick felt boots and threadbare trousers, with which he wore a checked shirt and a quilted waistcoat, whatever the time of year.

DRESSING THE DEAD MAN WAS LIKE A FORM OF CARESS. I DOUBT HE ever experienced such tenderness in life. We held him up gently by the arms and pulled the clothing onto him. As his weight rested on my chest, after a wave of quite natural disgust that made me feel nauseous, it suddenly occurred to me to hug this body, to pat it on the back, to soothe it by saying: don't worry, it'll be all right. But on account of Oddball's presence I did no such thing. He might have thought I was being perverse.

My aborted gestures changed into thoughts, and I began to feel sorry for Big Foot. Perhaps his mother had abandoned him, and he'd been unhappy throughout his miserable life. Long years of unhappiness cause a Person worse degradation than a fatal illness. I never saw any visitors at his place, no family or friends had ever appeared. Not even the mushroom pickers stopped outside his house to chat. People feared and disliked him. It seems he only kept company with hunters, but even that was a rare event. I'd say he was about fifty years old; I'd have given a lot to see his eighth house, and whether Neptune and Pluto were conjoined in there by some aspect, with Mars somewhere in the Ascendant, for with that jag-toothed saw in his sinewy hands he reminded me of a predator that only lives in order to sow death and inflict suffering.

To pull on his jacket, Oddball raised him to a sitting position, and that was when we noticed that his large, swollen tongue was trapping something in his mouth, so after a brief hesitation, clenching my teeth with disgust and withdrawing my hand several times, I gently took hold of the something by its tip, and saw that what I had between my fingers was a little bone, long and thin, and sharp as a dagger. A throaty gurgle and some air emerged from the dead mouth, making a soft whistle, exactly like a sigh. We both leaped back from the corpse, and I'm sure Oddball felt the same thing as I did: Horror. Especially seconds later, when dark red, almost black blood appeared in Big Foot's mouth. A sinister trickle came flowing out of it.

We froze on the spot, terrified.

"Well, I never," said Oddball, his voice quavering. "He choked. He choked on a bone, the bone stuck in his throat, the bone got caught in his throat, he choked," he nervously repeated. And then, as if to calm himself down, he said: "Back to work. It's no pleasure, but our duties to our neighbors aren't always going to be pleasant."

I could see that he had put himself in charge of this night shift, and I fell in line behind him.

We fully abandoned ourselves to the thankless task of squeezing Big Foot into the coffee-colored suit and placing him in a dignified position. It was a long time since I had touched anyone else's body, never mind a dead one. I could feel the inertia rapidly flowing into it as it grew more rigid by the minute; that was why we were in such haste. And by the time Big Foot was lying there in his Sunday best, his face had finally lost all human expression—now he was a corpse, without a doubt. Only his right index finger refused to submit to the traditional pose of politely clasped hands but pointed upward, as if to catch our attention and put a brief stop to our nervous, hurried efforts. "Now pay attention!" said the finger. "Now pay attention, there's something you're not seeing here, the crucial starting point of a process that's hidden from you, but that's worthy of the highest attention. Thanks to it we're all here in this place at this time, in a small cottage on the Plateau, amid the snow and the Night—I as a dead body, and you as insignificant, aging human Beings. But this is only the beginning. Only now does it all start to happen."

THERE WE STOOD IN THE COLD, DAMP ROOM, IN THE FROSTY VACuum prevailing at this dull, gray time of night, and it crossed my mind that the thing that leaves the body sucks a piece of the world after it, and no matter how good or bad it was, how guilty or blameless, it leaves behind a great big void.

I looked out of the window. Dawn was breaking, and idle snowflakes were gradually starting to fill the nothingness. They were falling slowly, weaving their way through the air and spinning on their own axis like feathers.

By now Big Foot had gone, so it was hard to feel any pity or resentment toward him. All that remained was his body, lifeless, clothed in the suit. Now it looked calm and satisfied, as if the spirit were pleased to be finally free of the matter, and the matter were pleased to be finally free of the spirit. In this short space of time a metaphysical divorce had occurred. The end.

We sat down in the open kitchen doorway, and Oddball reached for a half-drunk bottle of vodka that was standing on the table. He found a clean shot glass and filled it—first for me, then himself. Through the snowy windows, dawn was gradually flowing in, milk-white like hospital lightbulbs, and in its glow I saw that Oddball was unshaven; his stubble was just as white as my hair, the faded striped pajamas protruding from under his sheepskin coat were not buttoned, and the coat itself was soiled with every imaginable sort of stain.

I swallowed a large shot of vodka, which warmed me from inside.

"I think we've done our duty by him. Who else would have done it?" said Oddball, more to himself than to me. "He was a wretched little bastard, but so what?"

He poured himself another shot and drank it in one, then shook with disgust. He plainly wasn't used to it.

"I'm going to make that call," he said, and went outside. I reckoned he must be feeling faint.

I stood up, and started scanning the terrible mess in the hope of finding Big Foot's identity card. I wanted to know his date of birth, in order to check his Score.

On a table covered with worn-out oilcloth I saw a roasting tin containing burned pieces of an Animal; in a saucepan next to it there was some stagnant beetroot soup, coated in a film of white fat. A slice of bread cut from a loaf, butter in gold foil. On the floor, covered with torn linoleum, some more Animal remains lay scattered; they'd fallen from the table, along with a plate, a glass and some broken biscuits. All this was crushed and trodden into the dirty floor.

Just then, on a tin tray on the windowsill, I caught sight of something that my brain took quite a while to recognize, in its efforts to shy away; it was a cleanly severed Deer's head. Beside it lay four little trotters. The half-open eyes must have been closely following our labors throughout.

Oh yes, it was one of those starving Young Ladies that naively let themselves be lured in winter by frozen apples, are caught in snares and die in torment, strangled by the wire.

As I slowly became aware of what had happened here, I was gradually filled with Horror. He had caught the Deer in a snare, killed her, then butchered, roasted and eaten her body. One Creature had devoured another, in the silence and stillness of the Night. Nobody had protested, no thunderbolt had struck. And yet Punishment had come upon the devil, though no one's hand had guided death.

Quickly, with trembling hands I gathered the remains, those poor little bones, into one spot, in a heap, to bury them later on. I found an old shopping bag, and one after another, I put those little bones inside this plastic shroud. Then I carefully placed the head in the shopping bag too.

So eager was I to know Big Foot's date of birth that I nervously began to search for his identity card—on the sideboard, among some papers, pages from a calendar and newspapers, then in the drawers; that is where documents are kept in rural homes. And indeed there it was—in tattered green covers, surely out of date by now. In the picture Big Foot was twenty-something, with a long, asymmetrical face and squinting eyes. He wasn't a pretty sight, not even then. With the stub of a pencil I wrote down the date and place of birth. Big Foot was born on December 21, 1950. Right here.

And I should add that there was something else in that drawer as well: a wad of photographs, quite new, in color. I flicked through them, just out of habit, but one of them caught my attention. I looked at it more closely, and was about to lay it aside. It took me a while to understand what I was looking at. Suddenly total silence fell, and I found myself right in the middle of it. I stared at the picture. My body tensed, I was ready to do battle. My head began to spin, and a dismal wailing rose in my ears, a roar, as if from over the horizon an army of thousands was approaching—voices, the clank of iron, the creak of wheels in the distance. Anger makes the mind clear and incisive, able to see more. It sweeps up the other emotions and takes control of the body. Without a doubt Anger is the source of all wisdom, for Anger has the power to exceed any limits.

With shaking hands I put the photographs in my pocket, and at once I heard everything moving forward, the world's engines firing up and its machinery taking off—a door creaked, a fork fell to the floor. Tears flowed from my eyes.

Oddball was standing in the doorway.

"He wasn't worth your tears."

His lips were pursed as he focused on tapping out the number.

"Still the Czech operator," he said. "We'll have to go up the hill. Are you coming with me?"

We quietly closed the door behind us and set off, wading through the snow. On the hilltop, Oddball began turning on his own axis with a cell phone in each outstretched hand, seeking a signal. The whole of the Kłodzko Valley lay before us, bathed in the silver, ashen glow of dawn.

"Hello, son," said Oddball into the phone. "I didn't wake you up, did I?"

A muffled voice gave an answer that I couldn't understand.

"It's that our neighbor's dead. I think he choked on a bone. Just now. During the night."

The voice at the other end spoke again.

"No. I'm just about to call. There wasn't any signal. Mrs. Duszejko and I have already dressed him, you know, my other neighbor"—at this point he cast a glance at me—"so he wouldn't stiffen . . ."

I heard the voice again, sounding more nervous.

"Well, anyway, he's in a suit now . . ."

Then the Person at the other end started gabbling at length, so Oddball held the phone away from his ear, casting it a look of distaste.

Afterward we called the Police.

II.

Testosterone Autism

A dog starv'd at his Master's Gate
Predicts the ruin of the State.

I was grateful to him for inviting me home for a hot drink. I felt completely drained, and the thought of having to return to my cold, empty house made me feel sad.

I said hello to Big Foot's Dog, who had been resident at Oddball's for the past few hours. She recognized me and was clearly pleased to see me. She wagged her tail—by now she'd probably forgotten about the time when she'd run away from me. Some Dogs can be silly, just like people, and this Dog was certainly one of them.

We sat in the kitchen at a wooden table, so clean that you could lay your cheek on it. And that is what I did.

"Are you tired?" he asked.

Everything in here was clean and bright, warm and cozy. What a joy it is in life when you happen to have a clean, warm kitchen. It has never happened to me. I have never been good at keeping order around me. Too bad—I'm reconciled to it by now.

Before I'd had time to look around, I had a glass of tea in front of me. It was in a sweet little metal basket with a handle, and it was on a saucer. There were sugar lumps in the sugar bowl—a sight that reminded me of happy childhood hours, and really did improve my rather dismal mood.

"Perhaps we shouldn't have moved him," said Oddball, and opened a drawer in the table to fetch out some small teaspoons.

The Dog stayed close to Oddball's feet, as if refusing to let him out of the orbit of her small, emaciated body.

"You'll knock me over," he told her with gruff affection. I could see it was the first time he'd ever had a Dog, and he wasn't sure how to behave.

"What are you going to call her?" I asked, as the first sips of tea warmed me from the inside, and the tangle of emotions caught in my throat began to melt a little.

Oddball shrugged.

"I don't know, maybe Fly, or Tray."

I didn't say anything, but I didn't like it. Those names didn't suit this Dog, considering her personal history. Something else would have to be thought up for her instead.

What a lack of imagination it is to have official first names and surnames. No one ever remembers them, they're so divorced from the Person, and so banal that they don't remind us of them at all. What's more, each generation has its own trends, and suddenly everyone's named Magdalena, Patryk, or—God forbid—Janina. That's why I try my best never to use first names and surnames, but prefer epithets that come to mind of their own accord the first time I see a Person.

I'm sure this is the right way to use language, rather than tossing about words stripped of all meaning. Oddball's surname, for instance, is Świerszczyński—that's what it says on his front door, with the letter "Ś" in front of it. Is there really a first name that starts with the letter Ś? He has always introduced himself as "Świerszczyński," but he can't expect us to twist our tongues trying to pronounce it. I believe each of us sees the other Person in our own way, so we should give them the name we consider suitable and fitting. Thus we are polyonymous. We have as many names as the number of people with whom we interact. My name for Świerszczyński is Oddball, and I think it reflects his Attributes well.

But now, as I gazed at the Dog, the first thing that occurred to me was a human name, Marysia. Maybe because of the orphan in the classic children's story—she was so emaciated.

"She wouldn't be called Marysia, would she?" I asked.

"Possibly," he replied. "Yes, I think that's right. Her name's Marysia."

The naming of Big Foot occurred in a similar way. It was quite straightforward—it suggested itself to me when I saw his footprints in the snow. To begin with, Oddball had called him "Shaggy," but then he borrowed "Big Foot" from me. All it means is that I chose the right name for him.

Unfortunately, I couldn't choose a suitable name for myself. I regard the one that's written on my identity card as scandalously wrong and unfair—Janina. I think my real name is Emilia, or Joanna. Sometimes I think it's something like Irmtrud too. Or Bellona. Or Medea.

Meanwhile Oddball avoids calling me by my name like the plague. That means something too. Somehow he always finds a way to address me as "you."

"Will you wait with me until they get here?" he asked.

"Sure," I readily agreed, and realized I'd never have the courage to call him "Oddball" to his face. When you're such close neighbors, you don't need names to address each other. Whenever I see him weeding his small garden as I'm passing by, I don't need his name to speak to him. It's a special degree of familiarity.

OUR HAMLET CONSISTS OF A FEW HOUSES SITUATED ON THE Plateau, far from the rest of the world. The Plateau is a distant geological cousin of the Table Mountains, their remote harbinger. Before the war our settlement was called Luftzug, meaning "current of air," and nowadays it's still called that unofficially, because we don't have an official name. All you can see on the map is a road and a few houses, no letters. It's always windy here, as waves of air come pouring across the mountains from west to east from the Czech Republic. In winter the wind becomes violent and shrill, howling in the chimneys. In summer it scatters among the leaves and rustles—it's never quiet here. Many people can afford to have one house in the city, their year-round, official home, and another—a sort of frivolous, childish one—in the country. And that's how these houses look as well—childish. Small and squat, with steep roofs and tiny little windows. They were all built before the war and they're all positioned exactly the same way: long walls facing east and west, one short wall facing south, and the other, with an adjoining barn, facing north. Only the Writer's house is a little more eccentric—it has terraces and balconies built onto it on every side.

It's no surprise that most people leave the Plateau in winter. It's hard to live here from October to April, as I know very well. Every year heavy snow falls here, and the wind carves drifts and dunes out of it. Recent climatic changes have made everything warmer, but not our Plateau. Quite the contrary, especially in February, when the snow is heavier and stays put for longer. Several times over the winter the temperature drops to minus twenty, and the season only ends for good in April. The road is poor, the frost and snow destroy whatever the local council tries to repair with its limited expenditure. To reach the asphalt you must drive four kilometers on a dirt road full of potholes, but in any case there's nothing to be gained from the effort— the bus to Kudowa leaves each morning from down the hill and comes back in the afternoon. In summer, when the few pallid local children have school holidays, the buses don't run at all. In the village there's a highway that changes it imperceptibly, like a magician's wand, into the suburbs of a small town. Should you so wish, you could drive along that highway to Wrocław or to the Czech Republic.

But there are some for whom these conditions are ideal. There'd be lots of Hypotheses to put forward if we wanted to amuse ourselves by looking into it. Psychology and sociology would have plenty of potential lines of inquiry to suggest, but I don't find the subject in the least bit interesting.

For example, Oddball and I show a bold face to the winter. In any case, what a silly phrase: "show a bold face"; in fact we belligerently stick out our lower jaws, like those men on the bridge in the village. If provoked with some unflattering phrase, they respond aggressively: "What do you mean by that? Eh?" In a way, we provoke the winter too, but it ignores us, just like the rest of the world. Old eccentrics. Pathetic hippies.

Here the winter does a beautiful job of wrapping everything in white cotton wool, and shortens the day to the utmost, so that if you

OLGA TOKARCZUK

make the mistake of staying up too late at night, you might awake in the Gloom of the following afternoon, which—I frankly admit—has been happening to me more and more often since last year. Here the sky hangs over us dark and low, like a dirty screen, on which the clouds are fighting fierce battles. That's what our houses are for—to protect us from the sky, otherwise it would pervade the very inside of our bodies, where, like a little ball of glass, our Soul is sitting. If such a thing exists.

I don't know what Oddball does through the dark months, because we're not in very close contact, though I won't hide it—I would have hoped for more. We see each other once every few days, and when we do, we exchange a few words in greeting. We didn't move here for the purpose of inviting each other to tea. Oddball bought his house a year after I bought mine, and it looks as if he'd decided to start a new life, like anyone whose ideas and means for the old one have run out. Apparently he worked at a circus, but I don't know if he was an accountant there, or an acrobat. I prefer to think he was an acrobat, and whenever he limps, I imagine that long ago, in the beautiful 1970s, during a special act, something happened that caused his hand to miss the bar, and he fell from a height onto the sawdust-sprinkled floor. But on further reflection, I must admit that accountancy isn't such a bad profession, and the fondness for order that's typical of the accountant inspires my approval and total respect. Oddball's fondness for order is plain to see in his small front yard: the firewood for the winter lies piled in ingenious cords arranged in a spiral. The result is a neat stack of golden proportions. Those cords of his could be regarded as a local work of art. I find it hard to resist their beautiful spiral order. Whenever I pass that way, I always stop a while to admire the constructive cooperation of hands and mind, which in such a trivial thing as firewood expresses the most perfect motion in the Universe.

The path in front of Oddball's house is so very neatly graveled that it looks like a special kind of gravel, a collection of identical pebbles, handpicked in a rocky underground factory run by hobgoblins. Every fold of the clean curtains hanging in the windows is exactly the same width; he must use a special device for that. And the flowers in his garden are neat and tidy, standing straight and slender, as if they'd been to the gym.

Now, as Oddball bustled about in his kitchen, I could see how tidily the glasses were lined up in his dresser, and what a spotless cloth lay over the sewing machine. So he even had a sewing machine! Shamefully I pressed my hands between my knees. It was a long time since I had devoted any special care to them. Oh well, I have the courage to admit that my fingernails were quite simply dirty.

As he fetched the teaspoons, for a brief moment his drawer was revealed to me, and I couldn't tear my eyes away from it. It was wide and shallow like a tray. Inside, carefully arranged in separate compartments, lay all sorts of cutlery and other Utensils needed in the kitchen. Each one had its place, though most of them were quite unfamiliar to me. Oddball's bony fingers purposefully chose two teaspoons that soon came to rest on willow-green napkins right beside our teacups. A little too late, unfortunately, for I had already drunk my tea.

It was hard to have a conversation with Oddball. He was a man of very few words, and as it was impossible to talk, one had to keep silent. It's hard work talking to some people, most often males. I have a Theory about it. With age, many men come down with testosterone autism, the symptoms of which are a gradual decline in social intelligence and capacity for interpersonal communication, as well as a reduced ability to formulate thoughts. The Person beset by this Ailment becomes taciturn and appears to be lost in contemplation. He develops an interest in various Tools and machinery, and he's drawn to the Second World War and the biographies of famous people, mainly politicians and villains. His capacity to read novels almost entirely vanishes; testosterone autism disturbs the character's psychological understanding. I think Oddball was suffering from this Ailment.

But that day at dawn it was hard to demand eloquence of anyone. We were utterly dispirited.

On the other hand, I felt great relief. Sometimes, when one thinks more broadly, ignoring one's usual mental preferences, and considers instead the sum total of a Person's deeds, one might conclude that their life is not a good thing for others. I think anyone would say that I'm right about this.

I asked for another glass of tea, but purely to have the chance to stir it with the lovely spoon.

"I once reported Big Foot to the Police," I said.

For a moment Oddball stopped drying the biscuit plate.

"Because of the dog?" he asked.

"Yes. And the poaching. I sent letters complaining about him too."

"And what happened?"

"Nothing."

"Are you trying to say it's a good thing that he's dead?"

———

LAST YEAR, BEFORE CHRISTMAS, I MADE MY WAY TO THE LOCAL administration to report the matter in person. Until then I had written letters. Nobody had ever answered them, though there is in fact a legal obligation to respond to citizens' inquiries. The police station turned out to be small, resembling the single-family houses built in the communist era out of materials rustled up from here and there—shoddy and sad. And so was the atmosphere prevailing inside too. The walls, coated with oil paint, were covered in sheets of paper, all of them headed "Public Notice"; incidentally, what a dreadful phrase. The Police use lots of extremely off-putting words, such as "cadaver" or "cohabitee."

In this temple of Pluto, first a young man sitting behind a wooden barrier tried to get rid of me, and then his older superior tried to do the same. I wanted to see the Commandant, and I insisted; I was sure that eventually they'd both lose patience and usher me into his presence. I had to wait a long time; I was afraid the grocery store would close before I left, and I still had to do my shopping. Until at last Dusk fell, which meant it was about four o'clock, and I'd been waiting for more than two hours.

Finally, just before the office was due to close, a young woman appeared in the corridor and said: "You can come in, madam."

By now I was rather lost in thought, so I found it hard to come to my senses. Gradually I gathered my wits as I headed after the woman for an audience upstairs, where the Police Commandant had his office.

The Commandant was an obese man of about my age, but he

addressed me as if I were his mother, or even his grandmother. He cast me a fleeting glance and said: "Sit yourself down."

And sensing that this form of address revealed his rural origins, he cleared his throat and corrected himself: "Take a seat, madam."

I could almost hear his thoughts—to his mind I was definitely a "little old lady," and once my accusatory speech was gathering strength, a "silly old bag," "crazy old crone," or "madwoman." I could sense his disgust as he watched my movements and cast (negative) judgment on my taste. He didn't like my hairstyle, or my clothes, or my lack of subservience. He scrutinized my face with growing dislike. But I could tell a lot about him too—I could see he was hot-tempered, that he drank too much and had a weakness for fatty foods. During my oration his large bald head gradually reddened from the back of his neck to the top of his nose, and visible knots of dilated blood vessels appeared on his cheeks, like an unusual army tattoo. He must have been accustomed to giving orders and being obeyed, and was easily carried away by Anger. A Jovian personality.

I could also tell that he didn't understand everything I was saying—firstly, for the obvious reason that I was using arguments alien to him, but also because he had a limited vocabulary. And that he was the type of Person who despises anything he can't understand.

"He poses a threat to many Creatures, human and animal," I concluded my complaint about Big Foot, in which I had described my observations and suspicions.

The Commandant wasn't sure if I was making fun of him, or if he was dealing with a madwoman. There were no other possibilities. I saw the blood briefly flood his face—he was undoubtedly the pyknic type, who will eventually die of a stroke.

"We had no idea he's been poaching. We'll see to it," he said through clenched teeth. "Please go home, and don't worry about it. I know him well."

"All right," I said in a conciliatory tone.

But he was on his feet by now, leaning his hands on the desk, a sure sign that the audience was at an end.

Once we have reached a certain age, it's hard to be reconciled to the fact that people are always going to be impatient with us. In the past, I was never aware of the existence and meaning of gestures such as rapidly giving assent, avoiding eye contact, and repeating "yes, yes, yes" like clockwork. Or checking the time, or rubbing one's nose— these days I fully understand this entire performance for expressing the simple phrase: "Give me a break, you old bag." I have often wondered: Would a strapping, handsome young man be treated like that if he were to say the same things as I do? Or a buxom brunette?

He must have been expecting me to leap from my chair and leave the room. But I had one more, equally important thing to report to him, forcing him to sit down again.

"That Man locks his Dog in the shed all day. It's not heated, so the Dog howls in there because of the cold. Can the Police deal with this by taking the Dog away from him, and punishing him as an example?"

He looked at me for a while in silence, and the feature I had ascribed to him at the start, calling it disdain, was now clearly visible on his face. The corners of his mouth drooped, and his lips pouted slightly. I could also see that he was making an effort to control his facial expression. He covered it with a lame smile, revealing his large, nicotine-stained teeth.

"That's not a matter for the Police, madam," he said. "A dog is a dog. The countryside is the countryside. What do you expect? Dogs are kept in kennels and on chains."

"I am simply informing the Police that the man is committing evil. Where am I to go, if not to the Police?"

He laughed throatily.

"Evil, you say? Maybe you should go to the priest!" he quipped, pleased with his own sense of humor, but he plainly realized that I did not find his joke amusing, because his face at once became serious again. "There's probably a society for the care of animals, or something of the kind somewhere. You'll find them in the phone book. The League for the Protection of Animals—that's where you should go. We're the Police for people. Please call them in Wrocław. They have some sort of animal wardens there."

"In Wrocław?" I exclaimed. "How can you say that? These are the responsibilities of the local Police—I know the law."

"Oh!" he said, smiling ironically. "So now you're going to tell me what my responsibilities are, eh?"

In my mind's eye I could see our troops drawn up on the plain, ready for battle.

"Yes, I'm only too happy to do so," I said, gearing up for a longer speech.

In panic, he glanced at his watch and curbed his dislike for me.

"Yes, all right, we'll look into it," he said indifferently, and started to put the papers from his desk into a briefcase. He had escaped me.

At this point it occurred to me that I didn't like this man. More than that: I felt a sudden surge of hatred toward him, as sharp as a knife.

He stood up again decisively, and I noticed that his leather uniform belt was too short to encompass his enormous belly. Out of shame this belly was trying to hide itself lower down, in the uncomfortable, forgotten vicinity of his genitals. His shoelaces were undone; he must have kicked his shoes off under his desk. Now he had to squeeze into them at high speed.

"May I know your date of birth?" I asked politely, already by the door.

He stopped in surprise.

"What do you want it for?" he asked suspiciously, holding the door open for me.

"I calculate Horoscopes," I replied. "Would you like one? I can draw it up for you."

An amused smile flashed across his face.

"No, thank you. I'm not interested in astrology."

"You'll know what to expect in life. Wouldn't you like that?"

At that point he glanced knowingly at the policeman sitting behind the reception desk, and with an ironic smile, as if taking part in a jolly children's game, he gave me all his details. I wrote them down, said thank you and, pulling up my hood, headed for the exit. In the doorway I heard them snorting with laughter, and the very words I had predicted: "Crazy madwoman."

THAT EVENING, JUST AFTER DUSK, BIG FOOT'S DOG began to bay again. The air had turned blue, sharp as a razor. The deep, dull howling filled it with alarm. Death is at the gates, I thought. But then death is always at our gates, at every hour of the day and Night, I told myself. For the best conversations are with yourself. At least there's no risk of a misunderstanding. I stretched out on the couch in the kitchen and lay there, unable to do anything but listen to that piercing wail. Several days earlier, when I had gone to Big Foot's house to intervene, that brute had refused to let me in, but had simply told me not to interfere in other people's business. In fact, he had let the Dog out for a few hours afterward, but later on he'd locked her in the dark shed again, so that Night she'd howled again.

There I lay, on the couch in the kitchen, trying to think about something else, but of course it was no use. I could feel an itching, pulsating energy seeping into my muscles—just a little more and it would blow my legs off from inside.

I leaped up, put on my boots and jacket, fetched a hammer and a metal bar, and every other Tool that fell into my hands. Minutes later, breathless, I was standing outside Big Foot's shed. He wasn't in, the lights were off, and there was no smoke rising from the chimney. He'd locked up the Dog and disappeared. Who could say when he'd be back? But even if he had been at home, I'd have done the same. After a few minutes' work, I was bathed in sweat, but had managed to get the wooden door open—the boards on either side of the lock came loose, and I was able to slide the bolt. Inside it was dark and damp; some rusty old bikes had been tossed in here, and there were some plastic barrels and other rubbish lying about. The Dog was standing on a pile of planks, tied to the wall by a string around her neck. What else immediately caught my eye was a pile of excrement— clearly she'd always had to relieve herself in the same spot. She wagged her tail uncertainly. She looked at me with moist eyes, joyfully. I cut off the string, took her in my arms and we went home.

I didn't yet know what I was going to do. Sometimes, when a

Person feels Anger, everything seems simple and obvious. Anger puts things in order and shows you the world in a nutshell; Anger restores the gift of Clarity of Vision, which it's hard to attain in any other state.

I put her down on the kitchen floor and was amazed how very small and slight she was. Judging by her voice, by that dismal howling, one might have expected a Dog the size of a Spaniel at least. But she was one of those local Dogs, known as a Table Mountains Uglymutt, because they're not very attractive. They're small, with thin, often crooked legs, a gray-and-brown coat, a tendency to gain weight, and above all with a visible overbite. Let's just say this nocturnal songstress wasn't blessed with beauty.

She was anxious, trembling all over. She drank half a liter of warm milk, which made her belly round as a ball, and I also shared some bread and butter with her. I hadn't been expecting a Guest, so my fridge was glaringly empty. I spoke to her soothingly, I gave her an account of my every move, and she watched me questioningly, clearly baffled by such a sudden change of circumstances. Then I lay down on the couch, suggesting to her at the same time that she too should find herself a place to rest. Finally she squeezed under the radiator and fell asleep. As I didn't want to leave her alone for the Night in the kitchen, I decided to stay put on the couch.

I slept fitfully; evidently there was still agitation roaming around my body, and it brought down continual dreams about stoked-up ovens belching heat, never-ending boiler rooms with hot, red walls. The flames locked in the ovens were roaring to be released, wanting that instant to spring onto the world with a monstrous explosion and burn everything to ashes. I think these dreams may be a symptom of the night fever that's connected with my Ailments.

———————

I AWOKE BEFORE DAWN, WHEN IT WAS STILL COMPLETELY DARK. My neck had gone stiff from sleeping in an uncomfortable position. The Dog was standing by my headrest, insistently staring at me, and pitifully whining. Groaning, I got up to let her out—all that milk she had drunk was finally in need of an outlet. A gust of damp, cold air that smelled of earth and putrefaction blew in through the open door—as if from the grave. The Dog ran outside like a shot and had a pee, comically raising her back leg in the air, as if she couldn't decide if she were a Dog or a Bitch. Then she glanced at me sorrowfully—I can boldly say that she looked me deep in the eyes—and raced off toward Big Foot's house.

And so she went back to her Prison.

That was the last I'd seen of her. I'd called her, annoyed at letting myself be led up the garden path so easily, and helpless in the face of the sinister workings of bondage. I'd started to put on my boots, but that terrible gray morning alarmed me. Sometimes I feel as if we're living inside a tomb, a large, spacious one for lots of people. I looked at the world wreathed in gray Murk, cold and nasty. The prison is not outside, but inside each of us. Perhaps we simply don't know how to live without it.

A few days later, before the heavy snow fell, I saw a police car outside Big Foot's house. I admit that I was pleased to see it. Yes, I had the satisfaction of knowing that the Police had finally called on him. I played two games of patience, both of which came out right. I imagined they'd arrest him, bring him out in handcuffs, confiscate his supplies of wire, and take away his saw (this particular Tool should require the same sort of permit as a gun, for it wreaks Havoc among the plants). But the car drove away without Big Foot, Dusk fell rapidly, and the snow began to fall. Locked up again, the Dog howled all evening. Next morning, the first thing I saw on the beautiful, spotless white ground was Big Foot's unsteady footprints and yellow trails of urine around my silver Spruce.

ALL THIS CAME BACK TO ME WHILE WE WERE SITTING IN ODDBALL'S kitchen. And my Little Girls.

As he listened to my story, Oddball made soft-boiled eggs, which he served in china egg cups.

"I don't share your trust in the authorities," he said. "One has to do everything oneself."

I'm not sure what exactly he meant by this.

III.

Perpetual Light

Whate'er is Born of Mortal Birth
Must be consumed with the Earth.

When I came home, it was already light and I was entirely off my guard, because once again I imagined I could hear the patter of my Little Girls on the hall floor, that I'd see their inquiring gazes, their furrowed brows, their smiles. And at once my body was gearing up for the welcoming rituals, for affection.

But the house was deserted. Winter whiteness was pouring through the windows in soft waves, and the vast open space of the Plateau was insistently pushing its way inside. I stored the Deer's head in the garage, where it was cold, and topped up the wood-burning stove. I went to bed in my clothes, and slept like the dead.

"Mrs. Duszejko, Janina."

And after a pause, again, louder: "Mrs. Duszejko, Janina, Janina."

A voice in the hall awoke me. Low, male and tentative. Someone was there, calling me by my detested first Name. I was doubly annoyed: for once again my sleep had been disturbed, and secondly, I was being called by that Name, which I do not like and do not accept. I was given it by chance, without a second thought. That's what happens when a Person fails to consider the meaning of Words, and of Names in particular, but uses them blindly. I never let anyone call me "Janina."

I got up and brushed down my clothing, which was looking rumpled—after all, I'd slept in it for two Nights—and peeped out of the room. In the hall, in a pool of melted snow, stood two men from the village. Both were tall, with broad shoulders and moustaches. They had come inside because I hadn't locked the door, and perhaps for that reason they had a justified sense of guilt.

"Would you please come over to the cottage?" said one of them in a deep voice.

They smiled apologetically, and I noticed that they had identical teeth. I recognized them—they worked as lumberjacks. I'd seen them at the village shop.

"I've only just come back from there," I muttered.

They said the Police hadn't arrived yet, and they were also waiting for the priest—the roads had been snowed in during the Night; even the road to the Czech Republic and Wrocław was impassable, and the container trucks were stuck in long traffic jams. But news travels quickly about the neighborhood, and some of Big Foot's friends had come on foot. It was nice to hear that he did have some friends. It looked to me as if the adverse weather conditions were improving their mood. It's easier to cope with a snowstorm than a death.

I followed them, trudging through the fluffy, pure white snow. It was fresh, and the low winter Sun gave it a blush. The men were wearing thick rubber boots with felt uppers, which is the only winter fashion for the men around here. Using their wide soles, they trod out a small tunnel for me.

SEVERAL OTHER MEN WERE STANDING OUTSIDE THE COTTAGE, smoking cigarettes. They bowed hesitantly, avoiding eye contact. The death of someone you know is enough to deprive anyone of self-confidence. They all had the same look on their faces—of ritual solemnity and formal ceremonial grief. They spoke to each other in muffled tones. Whoever had finished smoking went inside.

All of them, without exception, had moustaches. They stood gloomily around the folding couch where the body lay. Now and then the door opened and new men arrived, bringing snow and the metallic smell of frost into the room. Most of them were former state-farm workers, now on benefits, though occasionally employed to fell trees. Some of them had gone to work in England, but soon returned, scared of being in a foreign place. Or they doggedly ran small, unprofitable farms that were kept alive by subsidies from the European Union. There were only men in the cottage. The room was steamy with their breath, and now I could smell a faint whiff of ingested alcohol, tobacco and damp clothing. They were casting furtive, rapid glances at the body. I could hear sniffling, but I don't know if it was just the cold, or if in fact tears had sprung to the eyes of these great big men, but finding no outlet there, were flowing into their noses. Oddball wasn't there, or anyone else I knew.

One of the men took a handful of flat candles in little metal cups from his pocket and gave them to me with such an overt gesture that

I automatically accepted them, but I wasn't entirely sure what I was meant to do with them. Only after a lengthy pause did I realize what he had in mind. Ah, yes—I was to position the candles around the body and light them; things would become solemn and ceremonial. Maybe their flames would allow the tears to flow and soak into the bushy moustaches. And that would bring them all relief. So I bustled about with the candles, thinking that many of them must have the wrong idea about my involvement. They took me for the mistress of ceremonies, for the chief mourner, for once the candles were burning, they suddenly fell silent and fixed their sad gazes on me.

"Please begin," a man whom I thought I knew from somewhere whispered to me.

I didn't understand.

"Please start singing."

"What am I to sing?" I asked, genuinely alarmed. "I don't know how to sing."

"Anything," he said, "best of all 'Eternal Rest.'"

"Why me?" I asked in an impatient whisper.

At this point the man standing closest to me replied firmly: "Because you're a woman."

Oh, I see. So that's the order of the day. I didn't know what my gender had to do with singing, but I wasn't going to rebel against tradition at a time like this. "Eternal Rest." I remembered that hymn from funerals I had attended in my childhood; as an adult I never went to them. But I'd forgotten the words. It turned out, however, that all I had to do was mumble the beginning and a whole chorus of deep voices instantly joined in with my feeble one, producing a hesitant polyphony which was out of tune but gathered strength with every repetition. And suddenly I felt relief myself, my voice gained confidence and soon I had remembered the simple words about the Perpetual Light that, as we believed, would enfold Big Foot as well.

We sang like that for about an hour, the same thing over and over, until the words ceased to have any meaning, as if they were pebbles in the sea, tossed eternally by the waves, until they were round and as alike as two grains of sand. It undoubtedly gave us respite, and the corpse lying there became more and more unreal, until it was just an excuse for this gathering of hardworking people on the windy Plateau. We sang about the real Light that exists somewhere far away, imperceptible for now, but that we shall behold as soon as we die. Now we can only see it through a pane of glass, or in a crooked mirror, but one day we shall stand face-to-face with it. And it will enfold us, for it is our mother, this Light, and we came from it. We even carry a particle of it within us, each of us, even Big Foot. So in fact death should please us. That's what I was thinking as I sang, though in actual fact I have never believed in any personalized distribution of eternal Light. No Lord God is going to see to it, no celestial accountant. It would be hard for one individual to bear so much suffering, especially an omniscient one; in my view they would collapse under the burden of all that pain, unless equipped in advance with some form of defense mechanism, as Mankind is. Only a piece of machinery could possibly carry all the world's pain. Only a machine, simple, effective and just. But if everything were to happen mechanically, our prayers wouldn't be needed.

When I went outside, I saw that the moustachioed men who had summoned the priest were now greeting him in front of the cottage. The priest hadn't been able to drive all the way here—his car was stuck in a snowdrift, so they'd had to bring him here by tractor. Father Rustle (as I privately called him) brushed off his cassock, and gratefully jumped to the ground. Without looking at anyone, at a fast pace he went inside. He passed so close that his scent enveloped me— a mixture of eau de Cologne and smoldering fireplace.

I noticed that Oddball was extremely well organized. In his sheepskin work coat, like the master of ceremonies, he was pouring coffee from a large Chinese thermos into plastic cups and handing them out to the mourners. So there we stood outside the house, and drank hot, sweetened coffee.

A LITTLE LATER THE POLICE ARRIVED. THEY DIDN'T DRIVE, BUT walked up, because they'd had to leave their car on the asphalt—they didn't have winter tires.

There were two policemen in uniform and one in plain clothes, in a long black coat. By the time they reached the cottage in their snow-caked boots, panting heavily, we had all come outside. In my view, we were showing courtesy and respect toward the authorities. Both uniformed policemen were standoffish and very formal, visibly seething with rage because of the snow, the long journey and the general circumstances of the case. They brushed off their boots and disappeared into the house without speaking. Meanwhile, quite out of the blue, the fellow in the black coat came up to me and Oddball.

"Good morning. Hello, madam, hi, Dad."

He said, "Hi, Dad," and he said it to Oddball.

I would never have expected Oddball to have a son in the Police, and in such a funny black coat as well.

Disconcerted, Oddball introduced us rather awkwardly, but I didn't register Black Coat's official name, for at once they stepped aside, and I heard the son scolding his father: "For the love of God,

Dad, why did you touch the body? Haven't you seen the films? Everyone knows that whatever may have happened, you don't touch the body until the Police arrive."

Oddball defended himself weakly, as if rendered helpless by talking to his son. I'd have thought it would be the other way around, and that a conversation with his own child could only give him extra strength.

"He looked dreadful, Son. You'd have done just the same. He'd choked on something, he was all twisted and dirty . . . He was our neighbor, you know—we couldn't just leave him on the floor that way, like, like . . ." he said, searching for the right words.

"An Animal," I specified, going up to them; I couldn't bear the way Black Coat was dressing down his father. "He choked on a bone from a Deer he'd poached. Vengeance from beyond the grave."

Black Coat cast me a fleeting glance and addressed his father: "Dad, you could be charged with obstructing the inquiry. You too, madam."

"You must be joking! That'd be the limit. And with a son who's the local prosecutor."

The son decided to put an end to this embarrassing conversation.

"All right, Dad. You'll both have to make statements later on. They might have to do an autopsy."

He gave Oddball an affectionate pat on the arm, a gesture that included domination, as if he were saying: There, there, old boy, I'll take matters into my own hands now.

Then he disappeared into the dead man's cottage. Without waiting for any sort of resolution, I went home, frozen through, and with a sore throat. I had had enough.

From my windows I saw a snowplow locally known as "the Belarussian" driving up from the direction of the village. Thanks to the path it cleared, toward evening a hearse was able to drive up to Big Foot's cottage—a long, low, dark vehicle, with black curtains veiling its windows. But only to drive up. At around four o'clock, just before Dusk, when I went out onto the terrace, I noticed a black shape moving along the road in the distance—it was the men with moustaches, bravely pushing the hearse with their friend's body back toward the village, to his eternal rest in Perpetual Light.

—✕—

Usually I have the television on all day, from breakfast onward. I find it soothing. When there's a winter fog outside, or after only a few hours of daylight the Dawn imperceptibly fades into the Dusk, I start to believe there's nothing out there. You look outside, but the windowpanes merely reflect the inside of my kitchen, the small, cluttered center of the Universe.

Hence the television.

I have a large choice of programs; one day Dizzy brought me an aerial that looks like an enamel bowl. There are several dozen channels, but that's too many for me. Even ten would be too many. Or even two. In fact I only watch the weather channel. Since finding it, I'm happy to say I have everything I need, and I have no idea where the remote control has gone.

So from morning onward I'm kept company by pictures of weather fronts, lovely abstract lines on maps, blue ones and red ones, relentlessly approaching from the west, from over the Czech Republic and Germany. They carry the air that Prague was breathing a short while ago, maybe Berlin too. It flew in from the Atlantic and crept across the whole of Europe, so one could say we have sea air up here, in the mountains. I particularly love it when they show maps of pressure, which explain a sudden resistance to getting out of bed or an ache in the knees, or something else again— an inexplicable sorrow that has just the same character as an atmospheric front, a moody *figura serpentinata* within the Earth's atmosphere.

I find the satellite pictures and the curvature of the Earth very moving. So is it true that we live on the surface of a sphere, exposed to the gaze of the planets, left in a great void, where after the Fall the light was smashed to smithereens and blown apart? It is true. We should remember that every day, for we do tend to forget. We believe we are free, and that God will forgive us. Personally I think otherwise. Finally, transformed into tiny quivering photons, each of our deeds will set off into Outer Space, where the planets will keep watching it like a film until the end of the world.

As I make myself coffee, they are usually reading the weather forecast for skiers. They show a bumpy world of mountains, slopes and valleys, with a capricious layer of snow—the Earth's rough skin is only whitened here and there by snowfields. In spring the skiers are replaced by allergy sufferers, and the picture takes on color. Soft lines establish the danger zones. Where there is red, nature's attack is the fiercest. All winter it has been dormant, waiting to assail Mankind's immune system, fragile as filigree. One day it will get rid of us entirely in this way. Before the weekend, weather forecasts for drivers appear, but their world is reduced to the few rare lines marking this country's motorways. I find this division of people into three groups— skiers, allergy sufferers and drivers—very convincing. It is a good, straightforward typology. Skiers are hedonists. They are carried down the slopes. Whereas drivers prefer to take their fate in their hands, although their spines often suffer as a result; we all know life is hard. Whereas the allergy sufferers are always at war. I must surely be an allergy sufferer.

I wish there was a channel about the stars and planets as well. "The Cosmic Impact Channel." This sort of viewing would also consist of maps; it would show lines of influence and fields of planetary strikes. "Mars is starting to rise above the ecliptic, and this evening it will cross the belt of Pluto's influence. Please leave your car in the garage or a covered parking lot, please put away the knives, be careful going down into the cellar, and until the planet passes through the sign of Cancer, we appeal to you to avoid bathing and chickening out of family quarrels," the slender, ethereal presenter would say. We would know why the trains were late today, why the postman's Fiat Cinquecento got stuck in the snow, why the mayonnaise didn't come out right, or why the headache suddenly went of its own accord, without any pills, as unexpectedly as it came. We would know the right time to start dyeing our hair, and when to hold a wedding.

AT NIGHT I OBSERVE VENUS, CLOSELY FOLLOWING THE TRANSItions of this beautiful Damsel. I prefer her as the Evening Star, when she appears as if out of nowhere, as if by magic, and goes down behind the Sun. A spark of eternal light. It is at Dusk that the most interesting things occur, for that is when simple differences fade away. I could live in everlasting Dusk.

IV.

999 Deaths

He who Doubts from what he sees
Will ne'er Believe, do what you Please.
If the Sun & Moon should Doubt
They'd immediately Go out.

The next day I buried the Deer's head in my graveyard by the house. I placed almost everything that I had taken from Big Foot's house into a hole in the ground. I hung the shopping bag, on which there were still bloodstains, on the branch of a plum tree, in memoriam. At once some snow fell into it, and that night the freezing temperature changed it into ice. I toiled for ages to dig an adequate pit in the frozen, stony soil. The tears froze on my cheeks.

As usual, I laid a stone on the grave. There were already quite a number of these stones in my graveyard. Here lay: an old Tomcat, whose carcass I found in the cellar when I bought this house, and a She-Cat, semi-feral, who died after giving birth along with her Little Ones. A Fox, killed by forest workers who claimed it was rabid, several Moles and a Deer from last winter mauled to death by Dogs.

Those are just some of the Animals. The ones that I found dead in the forest, in Big Foot's snares, I merely moved to another spot, so that at least someone could feed on them.

From the graveyard, nicely situated by the pond, on a very gentle hillside, I think the entire Plateau was on view. I'd like to lie here too, and take care of everything from here, forever.

TWICE A DAY I MADE THE EFFORT TO GO ON A TOUR OF MY ESTATE. I had to keep an eye on Luftzug, as I had agreed to do so. I would go in turn to each of the houses left in my care, and finally I'd climb the hill as well to take in our entire Plateau at a single glance.

From this perspective, things could be seen that weren't visible at close range: round here, in winter, the prints in the snow documented every move. Nothing could escape this register—as diligently as a chronicler the snow recorded the footsteps of Animals and people, and immortalized the infrequent tracks of car wheels. I'd carefully inspect our roofs, in case a cornice of snow had formed that might later tear off a gutter or—God forbid—come to a halt against the chimney, get stuck at some point and slowly melt, letting water trickle under the roof tiles and into the house. I'd carefully inspect the windows to check they were intact, and that I hadn't neglected anything during my previous visit, or left a light on, perhaps; I'd also monitor the yards, doors, gates, sheds and wood stores.

I was the caretaker for my neighbors' properties while they devoted themselves to winter jobs and amusements in the city—I spent the winter here for them, protected their houses against the cold and damp, and minded their fragile possessions. In this way I relieved them of taking part in the Darkness.

———————

UNFORTUNATELY, MY AILMENTS WERE ONCE AGAIN MAKING THEIR presence known. In fact they always intensified as a result of stress and other unusual occurrences. Sometimes all it took was a disturbed Night's sleep for everything to start tormenting me. My hands would shake, and I'd feel as if a current were coursing through my limbs, as if an invisible electric net were wrapped around my body and someone were inflicting minor Punishments on me, at random. And then a sudden, painful cramp would seize my shoulder or my legs. Now I could feel my foot going entirely numb, stiffening and tingling. As I walked, I dragged it behind me, limping. And there was more: for months my eyes had never ceased to water; my tears would flow for no reason, out of the blue.

I decided that today, despite the pain, I'd go up the slope and survey the world from above. Everything was sure to be in its place. Maybe that would calm me down, loosen my throat, and I'd feel better. I wasn't at all sorry about Big Foot. But as I was passing his cottage from afar, I thought of his dead hobgoblin's body in the coffee-colored suit, and then the bodies of all my acquaintances came to my mind, alive and happy in their homes. And I thought of myself too, of my foot, and of Oddball's thin, wiry body; it all seemed shot through with appalling sorrow, quite unbearable. As I gazed at the black-and-white landscape of the Plateau I realized that sorrow is an important word for defining the world. It lies at the foundations of everything, it is the fifth element, the quintessence.

The scenery that opened before me was composed of shades of black and white, and of trees woven together in lines along the boundaries between the fields. In places where the grass had not been cut, the snow had failed to blanket the fields in a uniform plane of white. Blades of grass were poking through its cover; from a distance it looked as if a large hand had begun to sketch an abstract pattern, by practicing some short strokes, fine and subtle. I could see the beautiful geometric shapes of fields, strips and rectangles, each with a different texture, each with its own shade, sloping at different angles toward the rapid winter Dusk. And our houses, all seven, were scattered here like a part of nature, as if they had sprung up with the field boundaries, and so had the stream and little bridge across it—it all seemed carefully designed and positioned, perhaps by the very same hand that had been sketching.

I too could have sketched a map from memory. On it our Plateau would have the shape of a fat crescent moon, enclosed on one side by the Silver Mountains—a fairly small, fairly low range that we share with the Czech Republic—and on the other, Polish side, by the White Hills. There is only one settlement on it—ours. The village and the town lie below, to the northeast, just like all the rest. The difference in levels between the Plateau and the rest of the Kłodzko Valley isn't great, but it's enough for one to feel slightly higher up here, looking at everything from above. The road climbs laboriously from below, and fairly gently from the north, but the descent from the Plateau on the eastern side ends quite steeply, which in winter can be dangerous. During harsh winters the Roads Authority, or whatever that agency is called, closes this road to traffic. And then we drive down it illegally, at our own risk. Assuming we have good cars, of course. In fact I'm talking about myself. Oddball only has a moped, and Big Foot had his own two feet. We call this steep stretch the Pass. There's also a stony precipice nearby, but anyone who thinks it's a natural feature would be mistaken, for it's the remains of an old quarry, which used to take bites out of the Plateau and would surely have consumed the whole thing eventually in the avid mouths of its diggers. They say there are plans to start it up again, at which point we shall vanish from the face of the Earth, devoured by Machines.

Over the Pass, a dirt road that's only drivable in summer leads to the village. To the west our road joins another, bigger one, but not yet the highway. On this road lies a village that I like to call Transylvania, because of its general atmosphere. There's a church, a shop, some broken ski lifts and a youth club. The horizon is high, so eternal Dusk prevails there. That's my impression of the place. At the very end of the village there's a side road as well, leading to the Fox farm, but I prefer not to go in that direction.

Past Transylvania, just before the slip road onto the motorway we have a sharp bend, on which accidents often occur. Dizzy named it Ox Heart Corner, because he once saw a box of offal fall off a truck coming from the slaughterhouse that belongs to a local bigwig, and cows' hearts were spilled across the road; or so he claims. I find it rather a gruesome story, and I'm not convinced that he didn't just imagine the whole thing. Dizzy tends to be oversensitive on some topics. The surfaced road connects the towns in the Valley. On a fine day, from our Plateau the road is visible, and so are Kudowa and Lewin threaded along it, and far off to the north you can even see Nowa Ruda, Kłodzko and Ząbkowice, which before the war was called Frankenstein.

Now that world is far away. I usually drove my Samurai to town across the Pass. Beyond it, one could turn left and drive up to the border, which meandered capriciously, making it easy to step across it without noticing. I often crossed it inadvertently when out that way on my daily rounds. But I also liked to cross it on purpose, deliberately stepping to and fro. A dozen times, or several dozen times. I'd amuse myself like that for half an hour—playing the game of crossing the border. It gave me pleasure, because I could remember the time when it wasn't possible. I love crossing borders.

THE FIRST HOUSE ON MY TOUR OF INSPECTION BELONGED TO THE Professor and his wife. It was my favorite—small and simple. A silent, solitary house with white walls. They were rarely here; instead it was their children who turned up with their friends, and the wind would carry their noisy voices. With its shutters open, illuminated and filled with loud music, the house seemed a little dazed and bewildered. One could say that those gaping window holes made it look rather empty-headed. It recovered as soon as they left. Its weak point was a steep roof. The snow would slide down it and lie against the northern wall until May, letting the damp seep inside. So I had to shift the snow, which is always a hard and thankless task. In spring my job was to take care of the small garden—plant some flowers and see to the ones already growing in the stony scrap of earth outside the house. This I did with pleasure. Occasionally, minor repairs were needed, so I would call the Professor and his wife in Wrocław, they'd transfer money to my account, and then I'd have to hire the laborers myself and keep an eye on the work.

This winter I'd noticed that a fairly large family of Bats had taken up residence in their cellar. One time I'd had to go in there because I thought I could hear water dripping down below. There'd be a problem if a pipe had cracked. And I saw them sleeping in a tight cluster, up against the stone ceiling; they hung there without moving, yet I couldn't help feeling that they were watching me in their sleep, that the glare of the lightbulb was reflected in their open eyes. I whispered farewell to them until spring, and without finding any evidence of damage, I tiptoed back upstairs.

Meanwhile there were Martens breeding in the Writer woman's house. I didn't give any of them names, as I could neither count them nor tell them apart. Their special Characteristic is being difficult to spot—they're like ghosts. They appear and disappear at such speed that one can't be sure one has really seen them. Martens are beautiful Animals. I could have them in my coat of arms, should the need arise. They seem to be light and innocent, but that is just an appearance. In fact they're cunning and menacing Creatures. They wage their minor wars with Cats, Mice and Birds. They fight among themselves. At the Writer's house they'd squeezed in between the roof tiles and the attic insulation, and I suspect they were wreaking havoc, destroying the mineral wool and gnawing holes in the wooden boards.

The Writer usually drove down in May, in a car packed to the roof with books and exotic foods. I would help her to unload it, because she had a bad back. She went about in an orthopedic collar; it seems she had had an accident in the past. Or perhaps her spine was ruined by writing. She looked like a survivor from Pompeii—as if she were entirely coated in ash. Her face was ash-gray, including her lips, and her eyes were gray, and so was her long hair tightly gathered into a small bun on the top of her head. If I hadn't known her so well, I'm sure I would have read her books. But as I did know her, I was afraid to open them. What if I found myself described in them in a way that I couldn't fathom? Or my favorite places, which for her are something completely different from what they are to me? In a way, people like her, those who wield a pen, can be dangerous. At once a suspicion of fakery springs to mind—that such a Person is not him- or herself, but an eye that's constantly watching, and whatever it sees it changes into sentences; in the process it strips reality of its most essential quality—its inexpressibility.

She spent time here until the end of September. She didn't come out of the house much; just now and then, when despite our wind the heat became sticky and unbearable, she would lay her ashen body on a deckchair and stay there in the Sun without moving, going even grayer. If only I could have seen her feet, perhaps it would have turned out that she was not a human Being either, but some other form of life. A water nymph of the *logos*, or a sylph. Sometimes her girlfriend came to see her, a strong, dark-haired woman who wore brightly colored lipstick. She had a birthmark on her face, a little brown mole, which I believe to mean that at the hour of her Birth Venus was in the first house. Then they cooked together, as if they had suddenly remembered their atavistic family rituals. Several times last summer I ate with them: spicy soup with coconut milk, and potato pancakes with chanterelles. They cooked well—it was tasty. The girlfriend was very affectionate toward the Gray Lady and looked after her as if she were a child. She clearly knew what she was doing.

The smallest house, below a damp copse, had recently been bought by a noisy family from Wrocław. They had two obese, pampered children, teenagers, and a grocery store in the Krzyki district. The house was going to be rebuilt and transformed into a miniature Polish manor—one day they'd add columns and a porch, and at the back there'd be a swimming pool. So their father told me. But first it had all been enclosed by a precast concrete fence. They paid me handsomely, and asked me to look inside every day, to make sure no one had broken in. The house itself was old, in bad shape, and looked as if it wanted to be left in peace to carry on decomposing. This year, however, there was a revolution in store for it—heaps of sand had already been delivered and piled outside the gate. The wind was always blowing off its plastic cover, and replacing it cost me a major effort. They had a small spring on their land, and were planning to make fish ponds there, and to build a brick barbecue. Their family name was Weller. I spent a long time wondering if I should give them a name of my own, but then I realized that this was one of the two cases known to me where the official surname fitted the Person. They really were the people from the well—they'd fallen into it long ago and had now arranged their lives at the bottom of it, thinking the well was the entire world.

The final house, right by the road, was a rental home. It was usually hired by young couples with children, the type in search of nature for the weekend. Sometimes lovers rented it. Occasionally there were suspicious sorts too, who got drunk in the evening and spent the whole Night shouting drunkenly, then slept until noon. They all passed through our hamlet like shadows. Just for a weekend. Here today, gone tomorrow. The small, impersonally refurbished cottage belonged to the richest Person in the neighborhood, who owned property in every valley and on every plain. The fellow was named Innerd— and that was the other instance where the name fitted its owner perfectly. Apparently he had bought the house because of the land it occupied. Apparently he bought the land to turn it into a quarry one day. Apparently the whole Plateau is fit to be a quarry. Apparently we're living on a gold mine here, gold that's known as granite.

I had to make quite an effort to take care of it all. And the little bridge too—I had to check it was in one piece, and that the water hadn't washed away the brackets that were fixed onto it after the last flood. And that the water hadn't made any holes. At the end of my tour, I would take a final look around, and I should have felt happy that everything was there. After all, it could just as well not have been. There could have been nothing but grass here—large clumps of wind-lashed steppe grass and the rosettes of thistles. That's what it could have been like. Or there could have been nothing at all—a total void in outer space. But perhaps that would have been the best option for all concerned.

As I wandered across the fields and wilds on my rounds, I liked to imagine how it would all look millions of years from now. Would the same plants be here? And what about the color of the sky? Would it be just the same? Would the tectonic plates have shifted and caused a range of high mountains to pile up here? Or would a sea arise, removing all reason to use the word "place" amid the idle motion of the waves? One thing's for sure—these houses won't be here; my efforts are insignificant, they'd fit on a pinhead, just like my life as well. That should never be forgotten.

Then, if I went beyond our bounds, the landscape changed. Here and there exclamation marks stuck out of the ground, sharp needles piercing the scenery. Whenever my gaze caught on them, my eyelids began to quiver; the eye cut itself on those wooden structures erected in the fields, on their boundaries, or at the edge of the forest. In total there were eight of them in the Plateau, I knew the exact figure, for I'd had dealings with them in the past, like Don Quixote with the windmills. They were knocked together out of wooden beams, set crosswise; they consisted entirely of crosses. These grotesque figures had four legs and a cabin with embrasures on top. Pulpits, for hunting. This name has always amazed and angered me. For what on earth was taught from that sort of pulpit? What sort of gospel was preached? Isn't it the height of arrogance, isn't it a diabolical idea to call a place from which one kills a pulpit?

I can still see them. I squint, as a way of blurring their shape and making them disappear. I only do it because I cannot bear their presence. But the truth is that anyone who feels Anger, and does not take action, merely spreads the infection. So says our Blake.

As I stood there, gazing at the pulpits, I could turn around at any moment to take gentle hold of the sharp, jagged line of the horizon as if it were a strand of hair. To look beyond it. Over there is the Czech Republic. The Sun flees over there, once it has seen enough of these atrocities. There my Damsel goes down for the Night. Oh yes, Venus goes to bed in the Czech Republic.

THIS IS HOW I'D SPEND MY EVENINGS: I'D SIT AT THE BIG KITCHEN table and devote myself to my favorite occupation. Here on the table sat the laptop Dizzy gave me, though I only ever used a single program. Here were my Ephemerides, some notepaper, and a few books. The dry muesli that I nibble while working, and a small pot of black tea; I don't drink any other kind.

In fact I could have done all the calculations by hand, and perhaps I'm a little sorry that I didn't. But who still uses a slide rule nowadays?

Though if I ever had to calculate a Horoscope in the desert, with no computer, no electricity or Tools of any kind, I could do it. All I would need are my Ephemerides, and therefore if anyone were suddenly to ask me (though sadly no one ever will) which book I would take to a desert island, my answer would be: *The Complete Ephemerides, 1920–2020.*

I was curious to know if the date of a Person's death can be seen in their Horoscope. Death in a Horoscope. What does it look like? How does it manifest itself? Which planets play the role of the Fates?

Down here, in the world of Urizen, the laws apply. From the starry sky down to moral conscience. These are strict laws, without mercy and without exception. As there is an order of Births, why should there not be an order of Deaths?

In all these years I have gathered 1,042 dates of birth and 999 dates of death, and my minor research is still in progress. A project without funding from the European Union. A kitchen table project.

I HAVE ALWAYS BELIEVED THAT ASTROLOGY SHOULD BE LEARNED through practice. It is solid knowledge, to a large extent empirical and just as scientific as psychology, let's say. One must closely observe a few people from one's own environment, and match moments in their life with the planetary system. One must also monitor and analyze the same Events in which various people participate. One will soon notice that similar astrological patterns describe similar incidents. That's when one's initiation occurs—oh yes, order does exist, and it is within reach. The stars and planets establish it, while the sky is the template that sets the pattern of our lives. Extensive study will make it possible to guess the arrangement of the planets in the sky from tiny details here on Earth. An afternoon storm, a letter that the postman has pressed into a crack in the door, a broken lightbulb in the bathroom. Nothing is capable of eluding this order. It works on me like alcohol, or one of those new drugs that, so I imagine, fill a person with pure delight.

One must keep one's eyes and ears open, one must know how to match up the facts, see similarity where others see total difference, remember that certain events occur at various levels or, to put it another way, many incidents are aspects of the same, single occurrence.

And that the world is a great big net, it is a whole, where no single thing exists separately; every scrap of the world, every last tiny piece, is bound up with the rest by a complex Cosmos of correspondences, hard for the ordinary mind to penetrate. That is how it works. Like a Japanese car.

Dizzy, who's prone to effusive digressions on the topic of Blake's bizarre symbolism, has never shared my passion for Astrology. That's because he was born too late. His generation has Pluto in Libra, which somewhat weakens their vigilance. And they think they can balance hell. I don't believe they'll manage it. They may know how to design projects and write applications, but most of them have lost their vigilance.

I grew up in a beautiful era, now sadly in the past. In it there was great readiness for change, and a talent for creating revolutionary visions. Nowadays no one still has the courage to think up anything new. All they ever talk about, round the clock, is how things already are, they just keep rolling out the same old ideas. Reality has grown old and gone senile; after all, it is definitely subject to the same laws as every living organism—it ages. Just like the cells of the body, its tiniest components, the senses, succumb to apoptosis. Apoptosis is natural death, brought about by the tiredness and exhaustion of matter. In Greek this word means "the dropping of petals." The world has dropped its petals.

But something new is bound to follow, as it always has—isn't that a comical paradox? Uranus is in Pisces, but when it moves into Aries, a new cycle will begin and reality will be born again. In spring, in two years' time.

Studying Horoscopes gave me pleasure, even while I was discovering these orders of death. The motion of the planets is always hypnotic, beautiful, impossible to halt or hasten. I like considering the fact that this order goes far beyond the time and place of Janina Duszejko. It's good to be able to rely on something totally.

And thus: to determine natural death we examine the positions of the hyleg, in other words the heavenly body that sucks vital energy from the Cosmos for us. For daytime births it is the Sun, for nocturnal ones it is the Moon, and in some cases the ruler of the Ascendant is the hyleg. Death usually ensues when the hyleg reaches some radically inharmonious aspect with the ruler of the eighth house or with the planet positioned within it.

In considering the risk of violent death, I had to take note of the hyleg, its house and the planets situated within this house. In doing so I paid attention to which of the harmful planets—Mars, Saturn or Uranus—was stronger than the hyleg, and was creating a negative aspect with it.

That day I sat down to work and pulled from my pocket a crumpled piece of paper on which I had written down Big Foot's details, to check if his death had come for him at the right time. As I was tapping out his date of birth, I cast an eye at the piece of paper, and saw that I'd written his details down on a page from a hunting calendar, headed "March." There was a table featuring the figures of Animals that could be hunted in March.

The Horoscope sprang up before me on the screen, and for an hour it held my gaze captive. First of all I looked at Saturn. Saturn in a fixed sign is often a signifier of death by suffocation, choking or hanging.

For two evenings I labored over Big Foot's Horoscope, until Dizzy called and I had to dissuade him from the idea of visiting me. His valiant old Fiat 126 would get bogged down in the mushy snow. Let that golden boy translate Blake at home in his workers' hostel. Let him develop English negatives to produce Polish sentences in the darkroom of his mind. It would be better if he came on Friday—then I would tell him the whole story, and present as proof the precise configuration of the stars.

I must be very careful. Now I shall dare to say this: I'm not a good Astrologer, unfortunately. There's a flaw in my character that obscures the image of the distribution of the planets. I look at them through my fear, and despite the semblance of cheerfulness that people naively and ingenuously ascribe to me, I see everything as if in a dark mirror, as if through smoked glass. I view the world in the same way as others look at the Sun in eclipse. Thus I see the Earth in eclipse. I see us moving about blindly in eternal Gloom, like May bugs trapped in a box by a cruel child. It's easy to harm and injure us, to smash up our intricately assembled, bizarre existence. I interpret everything as abnormal, terrible and threatening. I see nothing but Catastrophes. But as the Fall is the beginning, can we possibly fall even lower?

In any case, I know the date of my own death, and that lets me feel free.

V.

A Light in the Rain

Prisons are built with stones of Law,
Brothels with bricks of Religion.

A thump, a distant bang, as if someone in the next room had clapped an inflated paper bag.

I sat up in bed with a terrible foreboding that something bad was happening, and that this noise might be a sentence on someone's life. More of them followed, so I hurriedly started to dress, though not entirely conscious. I came to a halt in the middle of the room, tangled in my sweater, suddenly feeling helpless—what was I to do? As usual on such days the weather was beautiful; the weather god clearly favors hunters. The Sun was dazzlingly bright, it had only just risen, and still red from the effort, was casting long, sleepy shadows. I went outside, and again I felt as if my Little Girls were running out ahead of me, straight into the snow, thrilled that the day had come, showing their joy so openly and shamelessly that I was bound to be infected by it. I'd throw them a snowball, they'd take it as a green light for all sorts of high jinks and immediately be off on their chaotic chases, in which the pursuer suddenly turns into the pursued, so the reason for the race changes from one second to the next, and finally their joy becomes so great that there's no way to express it other than by running around the house like mad.

Again I felt tears on my cheeks—perhaps I should go and see Doctor Ali about it. He's a dermatologist, but he knows about everything and understands it all. My eyes must be really sick.

As I strode toward the Samurai, I unhooked the shopping bag filled with ice from the plum tree and manually felt the weight of it. *"Die kalte Teufelshand,"* a distant memory came back to me from the past. Is it *Faust?* The cold fist of the devil. The Samurai started up first time, and, as if it knew my state of mind, obligingly set off across the snow. The spades and the spare wheel rattled in the back. It was hard to localize where the shots were coming from; they were bouncing off the wall of the forest, amplifying. I drove toward the Pass, and about two kilometers beyond the precipice I saw their cars—swanky jeeps and a small truck. There was a man standing by them, smoking a cigarette. I accelerated and drove straight past this encampment. The Samurai clearly knew what I was thinking, because it enthusiastically splashed wet snow in all directions. The man ran a few meters after me, waving his arms, probably trying to stop me. But I took no notice of him.

Then I saw them, walking in loose line formation. Twenty or thirty men in green uniforms, in army camouflage and those idiotic hats with feathers in them. I stopped my car and ran toward them. Soon I recognized several of them. And they saw me too. They looked at me in amazement and exchanged amused glances.

"What the hell is going on here?" I shouted.

One of them, a helper, came up to me. It was one of the two moustachioed men who'd come to fetch me on the day of Big Foot's death.

"Mrs. Duszejko, please don't come any closer, it's dangerous. Please move away from here. We're shooting."

I waved my hands in front of his face.

"No, it's you who should get out of here. Otherwise I'll call the Police."

Another one detached himself from the line formation and came up to us; I didn't know him. He was dressed in classic hunting gear, with a hat. The line of men moved on, pointing their shotguns ahead of them.

"There's no need, madam," he said politely. "The Police are already here." He smiled patronizingly. Indeed, I could see the potbellied figure of the Commandant in the distance.

"What is it?" someone shouted.

"Nothing, it's just the old lady from Luftzug. She wants to call the Police," he said, with a note of irony in his voice.

I felt hatred toward him.

"Mrs. Duszejko, please don't be foolish," said Moustachio amicably. "We really are shooting here."

"You've no right to shoot at living Creatures!" I shouted at the top of my voice. The wind tore the words from my mouth and carried them across the entire Plateau.

"It's all right, please go home. We're just shooting pheasants," Moustachio reassured me, as if he didn't understand my protest. The other man added in a sugary tone: "Don't argue with her, she's crazy."

At that point I felt a surge of Anger, genuine, not to say Divine

Anger. It flooded me from inside in a burning-hot wave. This energy made me feel great, as if it were lifting me off the ground, a mini Big Bang within the universe of my body. There was fire burning within me, like a neutron star. I sprang forward and pushed the Man in the silly hat so hard that he fell onto the snow, completely taken by surprise. And when Moustachio rushed to his aid, I attacked him too, hitting him on the shoulder with all my might. He groaned with pain. I am not a feeble girl.

"Hey, hey, woman, is that the way to behave?" His mouth was twisted in pain as he tried to catch me by the hands.

Just then the Man who'd been standing by the cars ran up from behind—he'd clearly driven after me—and grabbed me in a vise-like grip.

"I'll escort you to your car," he said into my ear, but that wasn't his plan at all; instead he pulled me backward, making me fall over.

Moustachio tried to help me to my feet, but I pushed him away in disgust. I didn't have a chance.

"Don't upset yourself, madam. We're within the law."

That's what he said: "within the law." I brushed off the snow and headed for my car. Trembling with anger, I kept stumbling. Meanwhile the line of hunters had disappeared into the low brushwood, young willows on boggy terrain. Soon after that I heard shots again; they were shooting at the Birds. I got into the car and sat still, with my hands on the steering wheel, but it was a while before I was capable of moving.

I drove home, weeping out of helplessness. My hands were shaking, and now I knew this would end badly. With a sigh of relief, the Samurai stopped outside the house, as if it were on my side in everything. I pressed my face against the steering wheel. The horn responded sadly, like a summons. Like a cry of mourning.

MY AILMENTS APPEAR TREACHEROUSLY; I NEVER KNOW WHEN they're coming. And then something happens inside my body, my bones begin to ache. It's an unpleasant ache, sickening—that's the word I'd use. It continues incessantly, it doesn't stop for hours, sometimes days on end. There's no hiding from this pain, there are no pills or injections for it. It must hurt, just as a river must flow and fire must burn. It spitefully reminds me that I consist of physical particles, which are slipping away by the second. Perhaps one could get used to it? Learn to live with it, just as people live in the cities of Auschwitz or Hiroshima, without ever thinking about what happened there in the past. They simply live their lives.

But after these pains in my bones come pains in my stomach, intestine, liver, everything we have inside, without cease. Glucose is capable of soothing it for a while, so I always carry a small bottle of it in my pocket. I never know when an Attack will occur, or when I will feel worse. Sometimes it's as if I'm composed of nothing but symptoms of illness, I am a phantom built out of pain. Whenever I find it hard to know what to do with myself, I imagine I have a zip fastener in my belly, from my neck to my groin, and that I'm slowly undoing it, from top to bottom. And then I pull my arms out of my arms, my legs out of my legs, and take my head off my head. As I extract myself from my own body, it falls off me like old clothes. Underneath them I'm finer, soft, almost transparent. I have a body like a Jellyfish, white, milky, phosphorescent.

This fantasy is the only thing capable of bringing me relief. Oh yes, then I am free.

—✕—

Toward the end of the week, on Friday, I asked Dizzy to come later than usual, for I was feeling sick enough to have decided to go to the doctor.

I sat in the queue in the waiting room and remembered how I had met Doctor Ali.

Last year, the Sun had burned me again. I must have looked rather pitiful, because the terrified nurses on reception took me straight into the ward. They told me to wait there, and as I was hungry, I fetched some biscuits sprinkled with coconut out of my bag and tucked into them. Shortly after, the doctor appeared. He was pale brown, like a walnut. He looked at me and said: "I like coconut *baskets* too."

That made me warm to him at once. He turned out to have a special Characteristic—like many people who have learned Polish in adult life, he swapped some words for completely different ones.

"I'll soon see what's *wailing* you," he said this time.

This Man treated my Ailments very thoroughly, and not just the ones affecting my skin. His dark face was always calm. Taking his time, he would tell me convoluted anecdotes while carefully checking my pulse and blood pressure. Oh yes, he certainly went far beyond the duties of a dermatologist. Ali, who came from the Middle East, had very traditional, reliable methods for curing skin diseases—he'd tell the ladies at the pharmacy to prepare some unusually elaborate ointments and lotions, time-consuming to make and including many ingredients. I guessed the local pharmacists didn't like him for this reason. His mixtures had startling colors and shocking smells. Perhaps he believed that the cure for an allergic rash had to be just as spectacular as the rash itself.

Today he closely examined the bruises on my arms as well.

"How did this happen?"

I made light of the matter. Just a small knock has always been enough to give me a red mark for a month. He also looked down my throat, felt my lymph nodes and listened to my lungs.

"Would you please give me something to anesthetize me?" I said. "There must be some sort of drugs. I'd like that. To stop me from feeling anything, or worrying, to let me sleep. Is that possible?"

He started writing out the prescriptions. He contemplated each one at length, chewing the tip of his pen; finally he handed me a whole wad of them, and each medicine was to be made to order.

— ✗ —

I returned home late. It had been dark for a long time now, and since yesterday a foehn wind had been blowing, so the snow was melting rapidly, and dreadful sleet was falling. Luckily the stove had not gone out. Dizzy was late too, for once again it was impossible to drive up our road because of the softened, slippery snow. He left his little Fiat where the asphalt ended and came on foot, soaked through and frozen to the marrow.

Dizzy, official name Dionizy, showed up at my house every Friday, and as he came straight from work, I would make dinner that day. As I am alone the rest of the week, I make a large pot of soup on Sunday, and heat it up daily until Thursday, when I eat dry provisions from the kitchen cupboard, or a pizza Margherita in town.

Dizzy has a nasty allergy, so I can't give free rein to my culinary imagination. I have to cook for him without using dairy products, nuts, peppers, eggs or wheat, which greatly limits our menu. Especially as we don't eat meat. Sometimes, when he'd been recklessly tempted by something unsuitable for him, his skin would be covered in an itchy rash, and little blisters filled with water. Then he'd start to scratch uncontrollably, and the scratched skin would change into festering wounds. So it was better not to experiment. Even Ali and his mixtures weren't capable of calming Dizzy's allergy. Its nature was mysterious and perfidious—the symptoms varied. No one had ever managed to catch it in the act with any test.

From his tatty backpack Dizzy pulled an exercise book and a battery of colored pens, at which he cast impatient glances throughout our meal; then, once we'd eaten every last scrap and were sipping black tea (the only kind that finds favor with us), he reported on what he had managed to do that week. Dizzy was translating Blake. Or so he had decided, and until now he had been rigorously pursuing his aim.

Once, long ago, he had been my pupil. Now he had reached the age of thirty, but in fact he was no different in any way from the Dizzy who had accidentally locked himself in the lavatory during his secondary-school graduation English exam, as a result of which he had failed it. He'd been too embarrassed to call for help. He'd always been slight, boyish, or even girlish, with small hands and soft hair.

It's strange that fate brought us together again many years after that unfortunate exam, here in the marketplace in town. I saw him one day as I was coming out of the post office. He was on his way to collect a book he had ordered via the Internet. Unfortunately, I must have changed a lot, because he didn't instantly recognize me, but stared at me with his mouth open, blinking.

"Is it you?" he finally whispered, sounding surprised.

"Dionizy?"

"What are you doing here?"

"I live near here. What about you?"

"So do I, Mrs. Duszejko."

Then we spontaneously threw ourselves into each other's arms. It turned out that while working in Wrocław as an IT specialist for the Police, he'd failed to avoid some reorganization and restructuring. He'd been offered a job in the provinces, and even guaranteed temporary accommodation at a hostel until he found himself a proper apartment. But Dizzy hadn't found one, and was still living at the local workers' hostel, a vast, ugly, concrete block where all the noisy tour groups stopped on their way to the Czech Republic, and businesses held their team-building events, with drunken parties until dawn. Dizzy had a large room in there, with a vestibule and a shared kitchen upstairs.

Now he was working on *The Book of Urizen*, which seemed to me far harder than the earlier ones, *Proverbs of Hell* and the *Songs of Innocence*, with which I had devotedly helped him. In fact I hadn't found it easy, for I couldn't make head or tail of the beautiful, dramatic images that Blake conjured up in words. Did he really think like that? What was he describing? Where is that? Where is it happening, and when? Is it a fable or a myth?—I kept asking Dizzy these questions.

"It's happening all the time and everywhere," he'd say with a gleam in his eye.

ONCE HE'D FINISHED A PASSAGE, HE'D SOLEMNLY READ EACH LINE to me and wait for my comments. Sometimes I felt that I was only understanding the individual words, but failing to grasp their meaning. I wasn't entirely sure how to help him. I didn't like poetry; all the poems ever written seemed to me unnecessarily complicated and unclear. I couldn't understand why these revelations weren't recorded properly—in prose. Then Dizzy would lose patience and become exasperated. I liked teasing him this way.

I don't think I was particularly helpful to him. He was far better than I was, his intelligence was faster, digital, I'd say; mine remained analog. He cottoned on quickly and was able to look at a translated sentence from a completely different angle, to leave aside unnecessary attachment to a word, but to bounce off it and come back with something completely new and beautiful. I always passed him the salt cellar, because I have a Theory that salt is very good for the transmission of nerve impulses across the synapses. And he learned to plunge a saliva-coated finger into it, and then lick off the salt. I had forgotten most of my English by now; swallowing the entire Wieliczka salt mine couldn't have helped me, and besides, I soon found such laborious work boring. I was at a complete loss.

How does one translate a rhyme that small children might use to start a game, instead of constantly reciting "Eeny meeny miny moe":

Every Night & every Morn
Some to Misery are Born

Every Morn & every Night
Some are Born to sweet delight,
Some are born to Endless Night.

This is Blake's most famous verse. It's impossible to translate it into Polish without losing the rhythm, rhyme and childlike brevity. Dizzy tried many times, and it was like solving a charade.

Now he'd had his soup; it warmed him so much his cheeks were flushed. His hair was full of static electricity from his hat, and he had a funny little halo around his head.

That evening we found it hard to focus on translation. I was tired and feeling very anxious. I couldn't think.

"What's wrong with you? You're absentminded today," said Dizzy.

I agreed with him. The pains were weaker but hadn't entirely left me. The weather was awful, windy and rainy. When the foehn wind blows it's hard to concentrate.

"What Demon hath form'd this abominable void?" asked Dizzy.

Blake suited the mood that evening: we felt as if the sky had sunk very low over the Earth, and hadn't left much space or much air for living Creatures to survive. Low, dark clouds had been scudding across the sky all day, and now, late in the evening, they were rubbing their wet bellies against the hills.

I tried persuading him to stay the Night, as he sometimes did—then I would make up a bed for him on the sofa in my small study, switch on the electric heater and leave the door open to the room where I slept—so that we could hear each other's breathing. But today he couldn't. Sleepily rubbing his brow, he explained that the police station was switching to a new computer system; I didn't really want to know the details, what mattered was that he had a lot of work to do as a result. He had to be on-site early in the morning. And there were the slushy roads to negotiate.

"How will you get there?" I fretted.

"Once I reach the asphalt I'll be fine."

I didn't like the idea of him going. I threw on two fleeces and a hat. We both had yellow rubber raincoats, making us look like dwarves. Under his coat, Dizzy wore a flimsy jacket that hung on him loosely; although we had tried to dry his boots on the radiator, they were still soaking wet. I walked with him to the dirt road, and I would have been happy to escort him to his car. But he didn't want me to. We said good-bye on the dirt road, and I was already heading for home when he shouted after me.

He was pointing toward the Pass. Something was shining over there, feebly. Strange.

I turned back.

"What can it be?" he asked.

I shrugged.

"Maybe someone's prowling over there with a flashlight?"

"Come on, let's check." He grabbed me by the hand and pulled me along, like a boy scout on the trail of a mystery.

"Now, at Night? Don't be silly, it's wet over there," I said, surprised by his obstinacy. "Perhaps Oddball lost a flashlight and it's lying over there, shining."

"That's not a flashlight," said Dizzy, and headed off.

I tried to stop him. I grabbed his hand, but all that was left in mine was his glove.

"Dionizy, no, let's not go there. Please."

Something must have taken possession of him, because he didn't react at all.

"I'm staying here," I said, trying to blackmail him.

"Fine, you go home, I'll go and check on my own. Maybe something's happened. Off you go."

"Dizzy!" I shouted angrily.

He didn't answer.

So I went after him, shining a light for us, picking out of the darkness clear patches in which every color had vanished. The clouds were so low that one could hook onto them and let oneself be carried away to a distant land, to the south, to warmer climes. There one could jump down straight into the olive groves, or at least the vineyards in Moravia, where delicious green wine is made. Meanwhile our feet were getting bogged down in the semi-liquid slush, as the rain tried to push its way under our hoods and slap us in the face repeatedly.

Finally we saw it.

In the Pass stood a car, a large off-road vehicle. All the doors were open, and a feeble inside light was shining. I remained a few meters away, afraid to approach it; I felt as if I were going to burst into tears at any moment like a child, out of fear and nervous strain. Dizzy took the flashlight from me and slowly approached the car. He lit up the interior. The car was empty. On the backseat lay a black briefcase, and there were some shopping bags too, maybe full of groceries.

"You know what," said Dizzy quietly, dragging out each syllable. "I recognize this car. It's our Commandant's Toyota."

Now he was sweeping the area immediately surrounding the car with the flashlight beam. It was standing at a point where the road turned left. On the right-hand side there was dense brushwood; before the war there had been a house and a windmill here. Now there were some overgrown ruins and a large walnut tree, to which the Squirrels came running in autumn from all over the neighborhood.

"Look," I said, "look what's on the snow!"

The flashlight picked out some strange tracks—masses of round spots the size of coins; they were absolutely everywhere, all around the car and on the road. And there were also the prints of men's boots with thick, ridged soles. They were clearly visible because the snow was melting and dark water was seeping into every footprint.

"Those are hoofprints," I said, kneeling and closely examining the small, round marks. "They're deer prints. Do you see?"

But Dizzy was looking the other way, toward a spot where the soggy snow had been trodden down, stamped completely flat. The beam of the flashlight glided on, toward the undergrowth, and shortly after I heard his cry. He was leaning over the top of an old well standing among the bushes, beside the road.

"Oh my God, oh my God, oh my God," he repeated mechanically, which threw me right off balance. Obviously no god was going to come and put things to rights.

"My God, there's someone here," he whined.

Lying in the shallow well there was a body, head down, twisted. Behind an arm, part of the face was visible, horrible, covered in blood, with its eyes open. A pair of boots were sticking up, hefty ones, with thick soles. The well had been filled in years ago and was shallow, just a pit. I myself had once covered it with branches to stop the Dentist's Sheep from falling in.

Dizzy kneeled down and touched the boots helplessly, stroking their uppers.

"Don't touch," I whispered.

My heart was thumping like mad. I felt as if any moment now the bloodstained head would turn toward us, the whites of the eyes would shine through the streams of caked blood, the lips would move and utter a word, and then the whole of this burly body would slowly scramble up again, come back to life, enraged by its own death, furious, and seize me by the throat.

"Perhaps he's still alive," said Dizzy mournfully.

I prayed that he was not.

There we stood, chilled to the bone and stricken with horror. Dizzy was trembling as if having a fit; I was worried about him. His teeth were chattering. We embraced each other, and Dizzy began to weep.

Water was pouring from the sky and streaming from the ground— it felt as if the earth were a vast sponge saturated in cold water.

"We'll catch pneumonia," said Dizzy, sniveling.

"Come away from there. Let's go and see Oddball, he'll know what to do. Let's get away from here. Let's not stop here," I suggested.

We headed back, clinging to each other clumsily like wounded soldiers. I could feel my head burning with sudden, anxious thoughts, I could almost see them steaming in the rain, changing into a white cloud and joining the black ones. As we walked along, slipping on the sodden ground, words came to my lips that I urgently wanted to share with Dizzy. I longed to say them aloud, but for the moment I couldn't bring them out. They were eluding me. I didn't know where to start.

"Jesus Christ," sobbed Dizzy. "It's the Commandant, I saw his face. It was him."

I had always cared about Dizzy very much, and I didn't want him to take me for a lunatic. Not him. Once we had reached Oddball's house, I plucked up my courage and decided to go ahead and tell him what I was thinking.

"Dizzy," I said, "it's Animals taking revenge on people."

Dizzy always believes me, but this time he wasn't listening to me at all.

"It's not as strange as it sounds," I continued. "Animals are strong and wise. We don't realize how clever they are. There was a time when Animals were tried in court. Some were even convicted."

"What are you saying? What are you saying?" he gibbered vacantly.

"I once read about some Rats that were sued for causing a lot of damage, but the case was deferred because they never showed up for the hearings. Finally the court appointed them a defense lawyer."

"Christ, what are you on about?"

"I think it was in France, in the sixteenth century," I carried on. "I don't know how it ended and whether they were convicted."

Suddenly he stopped, gripped me tightly by the arms, and shook me.

"You're in shock. What on earth are you on about?"

I knew very well what I was saying. I decided to check the facts as soon as I had the chance.

ODDBALL LOOMED FROM BEHIND THE FENCE WEARING A HEAD-lamp. In its light his face looked weird and cadaverous.

"What's happened? Why are you walking about at night?" he asked in the tone of a sentry.

"The Commandant's over there, he's dead. By his car," said Dizzy, his teeth chattering, and pointed behind him.

Oddball opened his mouth and moved his lips without making a sound. I was starting to think he really had lost the power of speech, but after a long pause he said: "I saw that great big car of his today.

It was bound to end like that. He was driving under the influence. Have you called the Police?"

"Must we?" I asked, with Dizzy's agitation in mind.

"You've found a body. You're witnesses."

He went over to the phone, and soon after we heard him calmly reporting a man's death.

"I'm not going back there," I said, and I knew Dizzy wouldn't either.

"He's lying in a well. Feet up. Head down. Covered in blood. There are footprints everywhere. Tiny ones, like deer hooves," gabbled Dizzy.

"There'll be a fuss because it's a policeman," said Oddball drily. "I hope you didn't tread on the prints. You probably watch crime films, don't you?"

We went into his warm, bright kitchen, while he waited for the Police outside. We didn't exchange another word. We sat on the chairs like wax figures, motionless. My thoughts were racing like those heavy rain clouds.

The Police arrived in a jeep about an hour later. Last to get out of the car was Black Coat.

"Oh, hello, Dad, yes, I thought you'd be here," he said sarcastically, and poor Oddball was extremely embarrassed.

Black Coat greeted the three of us with a soldierly handshake, as if we were boy scouts and he were our team leader. We had just done a good deed, and he was thanking us. Though he cast a suspicious glance at Dizzy and asked: "Don't we know each other?"

"Yes, but only by sight. I work at the police station."

"He's my friend. He comes to see me on Fridays, because we're translating Blake together," I hastened to explain.

He looked at me with distaste and politely asked us to get into the police car with him. When we reached the Pass, the policemen cordoned off the area around the well with plastic tape and switched on floodlights. It was raining, and in the brilliant light the raindrops became long silver threads, like angel hair on a Christmas tree.

WE SPENT THE WHOLE MORNING AT POLICE HEADQUARTERS, ALL three of us, though in fact Oddball did not deserve to be there at all. He was alarmed, and I had a tremendous sense of guilt for dragging him into it.

We were interrogated as if we had murdered the Commandant with our own hands. Luckily they had an unusual coffee machine at this police station that also made hot chocolate. I liked it very much, and it instantly put me to rights, although in view of my Ailments I should have been more cautious.

By the time we were taken home it was well past noon. The stove had gone out, so I toiled away to relight it.

I fell asleep on the couch. Fully dressed. I hadn't brushed my teeth. I slept like the dead, and shortly before dawn, when the darkness was still at full strength outside, I suddenly heard a strange noise. I thought the central-heating furnace had stopped working, and that its gentle hum had ceased. I threw on a coat and went downstairs. I opened the door to the boiler room.

There stood my Momma, in a flowery summer frock, with a handbag slung over her shoulder. She was anxious and confused.

"For God's sake, what are you doing here, Momma?" I shouted in surprise.

She opened her mouth as if to answer, and tried moving her lips for a while, but did not produce any sound. Then she gave up. Her eyes roamed fitfully across the walls and ceiling of the boiler room. She didn't know where she was. Once again she tried to say something, and once again she gave up.

"Momma," I whispered, trying to catch her fugitive gaze.

I was angry with her, for she had died a long time ago, and that's not how long-gone mothers should behave.

"How did you end up here? This is no place for you," I began to reproach her, but I was overcome by intense grief. She cast me a frightened look, then her eyes began to wander the walls, totally confused.

I realized that I had unintentionally brought her here from somewhere else—it was my fault she was here.

"Be off with you, Momma," I said gently.

But she wasn't listening to me; perhaps she couldn't even hear me. Her gaze refused to stop on me. Exasperated, I slammed the boiler room door shut, and then stood on the other side, listening. All I could hear was rustling, something like the scratching of Mice or Woodworm in the timber.

I returned to the sofa. In the morning it all came back to me as soon as I awoke.

VI.

Trivia and Banalities

The wild deer, wand'ring here & there
Keeps the Human Soul from Care.

Oddball was probably made for a life of solitude, just as I was, but there was no way for our separate solitudes to be united. After these dramatic events everything went back to its old ways. Spring came, so Oddball energetically set about cleaning, and in the seclusion of his workshop was sure to be getting various Tools ready, which he'd use in the summer to make my life unpleasant—such as an electric saw, a garden shredder, and the gadget I hated most of all—a lawn mower.

Sometimes during my ritual daily rounds I would see his slim, hunched figure, but always from afar. Once I even waved to him from the hilltop, but he didn't answer. Perhaps he hadn't noticed me.

In early March I had another, acute Attack, and the thought crossed my mind of calling Oddball or shambling over there to knock at his door. My stove had gone out, but I hadn't enough strength to go down to the boiler room, which had never been a pleasure. I promised myself that when my clients came to visit their houses in the summer I would tell them that unfortunately I wasn't going to take the job on again next year. And that this might be my last year here. Perhaps before next winter I would have to move back to my little apartment on Więzienna Street in Wrocław, right by the university, from where one can watch the River Oder for hours on end as it hypnotically, insistently pumps its waters northward.

Luckily Dizzy came by and got the old stove going again. He went to the woodshed and fetched a wheelbarrow full of logs saturated with March damp that gave off a lot of smoke, but little warmth. From a jar of pickled gherkins and the remains of some vegetables he managed to make a delicious soup.

I lay up for several days, subdued by my body's rebellions. I patiently endured fits of numbness in my legs, and the unbearable sensation of fire burning within them. I pissed red, and can confirm that a toilet bowl filled with red liquid is a dreadful sight. I drew the curtains, for I could not bear the bright March light reflected off the snow. Pain lashed my brain.

I have a Theory. It's that an awful thing has happened—our cerebellum has not been correctly connected to our brain. This could be the worst mistake in our programming. Someone has made us badly. This is why our model ought to be replaced. If our cerebellum were connected to our brain, we would possess full knowledge of our own anatomy, of what was happening inside our bodies. Oh, we'd say to ourselves, the level of potassium in my blood has fallen. My third cervical vertebra is feeling tension. My blood pressure is low today, I must move about, and yesterday's egg salad has sent my cholesterol level too high, so I must watch what I eat today.

We have this body of ours, a troublesome piece of luggage, we don't really know anything about it and we need all sorts of Tools to find out about its most natural processes. Isn't it scandalous that last time a doctor wanted to check what was happening in my stomach he made me have a gastroscopy? I had to swallow a thick tube, and it took a camera to reveal the inside of my stomach to us. The only coarse and primitive Tool gifted us for consolation is pain. The angels, if they really do exist, must be splitting their sides laughing at us. Fancy being given a body and not knowing anything about it. There's no instruction manual.

Unfortunately, the mistake was made at the very start, as were other errors too.

Luckily my sleep cycle was changing again; I'd nod off at dawn and wake in the afternoon, which may have been a natural defense against the daylight, against the day in general and everything that belonged to it. I'd wake up—or maybe it was all in a dream—and I'd hear my Little Girls' footsteps pattering on the stairs, as if everything that had happened lately were just a tiresome hallucination prompted by fever. And those were beautiful moments.

In my somnolent state I also thought about the Czech Republic. The border would appear in my mind, and that gentle, beautiful country beyond it. Over there, everything is lit up by the Sun, gilded with light. The fields breathe evenly at the foot of the Table Mountains, surely created purely for the purpose of looking pretty. The roads are straight, the streams are clear, Mouflons and Fallow Deer graze in pens by the houses, Leverets frolic in the corn, and little bells are tied to the combines as a gentle way of scaring them off to a safe distance. The people aren't in a hurry, and don't compete against each other all the time. They don't go chasing after pipe dreams. They're happy with who they are and what they have.

The other day Dizzy told me that in a small bookshop in the Czech town of Náchod he found a nice edition of Blake, so let us now imagine that these good people, who live on the other side of the border, and who speak to each other in a soft, childlike language, come home from work in the evenings, light a fire in the hearth and read Blake to one another. And perhaps, if he were still alive, seeing all this, Blake would say that there are some places in the Universe where the Fall has not occurred, the world has not turned upside down and Eden still exists. Here Mankind is not governed by the rules of reason, stupid and strict, but by the heart and intuition. The people do not indulge in idle chatter, parading what they know, but create remarkable things by applying their imagination. The state ceases to impose the shackles of daily oppression, but helps people to realize their hopes and dreams. And Man is not just a cog in the system, not just playing a role, but a free Creature. That's what was passing through my mind, making my bedrest almost a pleasure.

Sometimes I think that only the sick are truly healthy.

THE FIRST DAY I FELT BETTER I PUT ON SOME CLOTHES AND, hounded by a sense of duty, went on my usual round. I was as weak as a potato sprout grown in darkness in the cellar.

It turned out that the melting snow had torn off a gutter at the Writer's house, and now water was pouring straight down the wooden wall. Dry rot guaranteed. I called her, but of course she wasn't at home, maybe she was out of the country. Which meant that I would have to deal with the gutter myself.

It's a complete mystery that every challenge triggers vital forces within us. I really did feel better—only my left leg was still racked with pain, like an electric current, so I was walking on it stiffly, as if it were a prosthesis. But once I had to move the ladder, I stopped worrying about my Ailments. I forgot about the pain.

I stood on that ladder for about an hour with my arms raised, unsuccessfully struggling to replace the gutter in its semicircular supports. On top of that, one of them had broken off and must be lying somewhere in the deep snow piled against the house. I could have waited for Dizzy, who was coming by that evening with a new quatrain and the shopping, but Dizzy is fragile, he has small, girlish hands, and to put it plainly, he's a bit scatterbrained. I say this with all due love and respect for him. It's not an imperfection on his part. There are more than enough traits and Characteristics in this world for each of us to be richly endowed, I thought to myself.

And from the ladder I viewed the changes that the thaw had brought to the Plateau. Here and there, especially on the southern and eastern slopes, dark patches had appeared—there the winter was withdrawing its army, but it was still holding out on the field boundaries and below the forest. The entire Pass was white. Why is plowed land warmer than grassland? Why does the snow melt faster in the forest? Why do rings appear in the snow around tree trunks? Are trees warm?

I put these questions to Oddball, whom I had gone to ask for help with the Writer's gutter. He gave me a baffled look but didn't answer. As I was waiting for him, I examined his diploma for taking part in the mushroom-picking contest organized each year by the "Penny Buns" Mushroom Pickers' Society.

"I didn't know you were so good at picking mushrooms," I said.

He smiled gloomily without speaking, in his usual way.

He led me into his workshop, which was like a doctor's office—there were all sorts of drawers and little shelves, with a Tool on each one, a special Tool, designed to perform one particular task. He spent ages rummaging in a box until finally he extracted a piece of flattened aluminum wire, twisted into a ring that wasn't quite closed.

"Hose clamp," he said.

Slowly, word by word, as if battling progressive paralysis of the tongue, he confessed that he hadn't talked to anyone for several weeks, and evidently his capacity to articulate speech had waned. Finally, hawking as he spoke, he also told me that Big Foot had died choking on a bone. Apparently the autopsy had proved it was an unfortunate accident. He knew this from his son.

I burst into laughter.

"I thought the Police were capable of more astute discoveries than that. The fact that he'd choked was obvious at first glance . . ."

"Nothing's obvious at first glance," he snapped with uncharacteristic vigor, causing the remark to stick in my mind.

"You know what I think about it, don't you?" I said.

"What?"

"You remember the Deer that were standing outside his house when we got there? They murdered him."

He stared in silence at the hose clamp in his hand.

"How?"

"How, how. I don't know exactly. Maybe they just gave him a fright while he was so barbarously eating their sister."

"Are you trying to say it was collusion? The deer conspired against him?"

For a while I didn't answer. He seems to need plenty of time to gather his thoughts, and then absorb them. He should eat more salt. As I have said, salt is good for quick thinking. He was also slow putting on his snow boots and sheepskin coat.

As we were walking across the wet snow I said: "And what about the Commandant in the well?"

"What's your question? Do you want to know what the cause of his death was? I don't know. He didn't say."

He meant Black Coat, of course.

"No, no, I know what the cause of his death was."

"What was it?" he asked, as if he couldn't care less.

So I didn't answer immediately, but waited until we were crossing the little bridge to the Writer's house.

"The same."

"You mean he choked on a bone?"

"Don't mock. I mean the Deer killed him."

"Hold the ladder," he said in reply.

He climbed the rungs and tinkered with the gutter, while I expounded my Theory. I had a witness—Dizzy. Dizzy and I knew the most, for we had been first on the scene of the incident and we had seen things the Police couldn't see later on. When the Police arrived it was dark and wet. The snow was melting before our eyes, erasing the most vital thing of all—those strange prints around the well, lots of them, hundreds, maybe more—small and round, as if a herd of Deer had surrounded a Person.

Oddball listened, but didn't answer, this time because he was holding screws in his mouth. So I carried on—saying that maybe at first the Commandant had been driving along, and then for some reason he had stopped. Maybe a Deer, one of the killers, had feigned illness, pretended to be sick, and he'd been pleased to find some wild game. Then, when he got out of the car, they'd surrounded him and started pushing him toward the well . . .

"His head was covered in blood," said Oddball from above, once he had driven in the final screw.

"Yes, because he hit it falling into the well."

"There," he said after a long silence, and began to descend the ladder.

Indeed, the gutter was firmly fixed on the aluminum hose clamp. The old one was sure to be found a month from now when the snow had melted.

"Try to keep your theory to yourself. It's highly improbable and it could do you harm," said Oddball, and headed straight for home without looking at me.

It occurred to me that like everyone else, he took me for a madwoman, and it hurt my feelings.

Tough. As it says in Blake: "Opposition is true friendship."

———✖———

I was summonsed for another interrogation by a registered letter the Postman brought. As he'd had to scramble up to the Plateau all the way from town, he was annoyed with me and did not fail to show it.

"People shouldn't be allowed to live so far away," he said at the front door. "What do you gain by hiding away from the world like this? It'll catch up with you anyway." There was spiteful satisfaction in his voice. "Sign here, please, a letter from the Prosecution Service."

Oh dear, he hadn't been among my Little Girls' best friends. They'd always made it very plain to him that they didn't like him.

"Well, what's it like living in an ivory tower, above the heads of lesser mortals, with your nose in the stars?" he asked.

That's what I dislike most of all in people—cold irony. It's a very cowardly attitude to mock or belittle everything, never be committed to anything, not feel tied to anything. Like an impotent man who can't experience pleasure himself, but will do all he can to ruin it for others. Cold irony is Urizen's basic weapon. The armaments of impotence. At the same time the ironists always have a world outlook that they proclaim triumphantly, though if one starts badgering and questioning them about the details, it turns out to consist of nothing but trivia and banalities. I would never venture to call someone a stupid person, and I wasn't going to condemn the Postman out of hand. I told him to sit down and I made him coffee, the sort Postmen like—strong, unfiltered, in a glass. I also offered him some gingerbread that I baked before Christmas; I was hoping it hadn't gone stale and he wouldn't break his teeth on it.

He took off his jacket and sat at the table.

"I've delivered a lot of these invitations lately—it must be to do with the Commandant's death," he said.

I was curious to know whom else the Prosecution had summonsed, but I didn't let it show. The Postman waited for my question, which never came. He fidgeted on his chair and slurped his coffee. But I knew how to manage silence.

"For instance I've delivered these invitations to all his pals," he said at last.

"Oh, yes," I said indifferently.

"They're all birds of a feather," he began slowly, hesitantly, but it was obvious that he was getting into his stride and would find it hard to stop. "They've grabbed power. Where did they get those fancy cars and houses? Someone like Innerd, for instance? Can you believe he made a fortune out of the slaughterhouse?" He meaningfully tugged on his lower eyelid, revealing his mucous membrane. "Or the fox farm? All that's just a cover, Mrs. Duszejko."

For a while we were silent.

"Apparently they were part of the same clique. Someone must have helped him into that well, I know that much," added the Postman with great satisfaction.

His need to speak ill of his neighbors was so great that there was no need to draw him out.

"Everyone knows they played poker for high stakes. And as for that new restaurant of his, Casablanca, it's a brothel for the white slave trade."

I thought he was exaggerating.

"Apparently they were smuggling luxury cars from abroad. Stolen ones. Someone told me—I won't say who—that he saw a beautiful BMW driving along the dirt roads at daybreak. What on earth was it doing there?" he asked rhetorically, surely expecting me to faint in amazement after all these revelations.

Much of what he was saying was certainly pure fiction.

"They took enormous bribes. Where did they get cars like the Commandant's, for instance? On a police salary? You'll say power goes to the head in a nasty way, and you'll be right. A man loses all sense of decency. They've sold off Poland for a song. I knew the Commandant for years. He used to be an ordinary militiaman—he joined the force to avoid going to the glassworks, like the rest. I used to play soccer with him twenty years ago. But these days he didn't even recognize me. How much our roads diverge in life . . . I'm a common postman, while he's a big police chief. I drive a Fiat Cinquecento, he drives a Jeep Cherokee."

"Toyota," I said. "A Toyota Land Cruiser."

The Postman sighed heavily, and suddenly I felt sorry for him, for once upon a time he must have been one of the innocent too, but now his heart was flooded with bile. His life must be hard indeed. And it must have been all the bitterness that was making him so angry.

"God made Man Happy and Rich, but cunning made the innocent poor," I quoted Blake, more or less. Anyway, that's what I think.

Except that I place the word "God" in quotation marks.

—✖—

When Dizzy arrived that afternoon, he'd caught a cold. We were now working on *The Mental Traveller*, and right at the start a dispute arose over whether we should translate the English word "mental" as *mentalny*—"mental" in the literal sense, meaning "of the mind"—or *duchowy*—more like "spiritual." Sneezing, Dizzy read out the original text:

> I travel'd through a Land of Men,
> A land of Men & Women too,
> And heard & saw such dreadful things
> As cold Earth wanderers never knew.

First, we each wrote out our own translation, in the trochaic meter more natural to Polish verse, then we compared them, and started to wind our ideas together. It was a bit like a game of logic, a complicated form of Scrabble.

Over Human Lands I wandered,
Lands of Men and also Women,
Seeing, hearing Things so fearful,
Such as no mind ever summoned.

Or:

Through the World of Man I journeyed,
Realms of Men as well as Women,
Hearing, seeing sights so awful,
No pure soul would ever dream on.

Or:

Throughout the World of Men I wandered,
Crossing Realms of Men and Women,
What I saw and heard was ghastly,
Such as None would ever dream on.

"Why have we insisted on putting the word 'women' at the end?" I asked. "What if we made it: 'Men's and Women's Land'? Then the rhyme would be with 'land.' 'Hand,' or 'stand,' for instance."

Dizzy said nothing, chewed his fingers and at last triumphantly suggested:

As I wandered human countries,
Men's and women's shared domain,
Dreadful things did I encounter,
Horrors none on Earth had seen.

I didn't like the word "domain," but now we were up and running, and by ten o'clock the whole poem was done. Then we ate parsnips roasted in olive oil. And rice with apples and cinnamon.

After this splendid supper, instead of probing the subtleties of the poem, somehow we found ourselves returning to the case of the Commandant. Dizzy was very well informed about what the Police knew. After all, he had access to the entire police network. Of course he didn't know everything. The inquiry into the Commandant's death was being conducted by a higher authority. Besides, Dizzy was sworn to strict professional confidentiality, but not with regard to me. What could I possibly do with a secret, even of the highest importance? I don't even know how to gossip. So he usually confided in me a lot.

For example, they knew by now that the Commandant had died of a blow to the head, probably when he fell with force into the half-collapsed well. They had also discovered that he was under the influence of alcohol, which should have cushioned his fall, because people are more supple when they're drunk. At the same time, the blow to the head looked too mighty for an ordinary fall into a well. He would have to have fallen from a height of several meters. Yet no other possible explanation had been found. The blow was to his temple. There was no potential murder weapon. And no clues. Some bits of trash had been collected—candy wrappers, shopping bags, old cans, and a used condom. The weather had been awful, and the special team had arrived late. There was a strong wind, it was raining, and the thaw was advancing at lightning speed. We both remembered that Night very well. Photographs had been taken of the strange marks on the ground—deer hoofprints, as I continued to maintain. But the Police weren't sure if those tracks had been there at all, and if they were, whether they had any connection with the death. In those conditions it had been impossible to confirm. And the human footprints weren't distinct either.

But there had also been a revelation, which was that the Commandant had twenty thousand zlotys on him, in a gray envelope tucked under his trouser belt. The money was evenly divided into two wads secured with elastic bands. This had puzzled the investigators the most. Why hadn't the murderer taken it? Didn't he know about it? And what if it was the killer who gave him the money? And what for? If it's not clear what a crime is about, it's sure to be about money. So they say, but I think that's a gross simplification.

There was also a version involving an unfortunate accident, which seemed rather far-fetched. The idea was that in a drunken state he had been looking for a place to hide the cash, but had fallen into the well and been killed.

Yet Dizzy was adamant that it must have been Murder.

"Every instinct is telling me. We were the first on the scene. Do you remember the sense of crime that was hanging in the air?"

I had exactly the same feeling.

VII.

A Speech to a Poodle

A Horse misused upon the Road
Calls to Heaven for Human blood.

The Police harassed us all several times more. In law-abiding fashion, we presented ourselves for questioning, and took the opportunity to see to various things in town—we bought seeds, applied for an EU grant, and once we went to the cinema. For we always went together, even if only one of us was being questioned. Oddball admitted to the Police that he had heard the Commandant's car whining and wheezing as it drove past our houses that afternoon. He said that the Commandant always drove along the side roads when he was drunk, so he hadn't been particularly surprised. The policemen who took his statements must have been embarrassed.

Unfortunately I could not confirm what Oddball had said, although I very much wanted to.

"I was at home, I didn't hear any cars, nor did I see the Commandant.

I must have been topping up the stove in the boiler room, and noises from the road aren't audible in there."

And I soon stopped caring about it, though for the past few weeks the entire district had talked of nothing else, coming up with ever more elaborate theories. I simply did my best to ward off my thoughts on the matter—are there so few deaths around that one should take an obsessive interest in this one?

I went back to one of my Inquiries. This time I carefully analyzed the television schedule for as many channels as I could and studied the correlation between the contents of the films being broadcast and the configuration of the Planets on a given day. The mutual connections between them were highly distinct and plain to see. I had often wondered if the people who did the television programming were trying to display to us their extensive astrological knowledge. Or perhaps they just arranged the schedule unconsciously, unaffected by this vast store of knowledge. It could in fact be true that the correlations exist outside us, but that we pick them up quite unconsciously. For the time being I had limited my research to a small scale, only covering a few titles. For instance, I had noticed that a film entitled *The Medium*, very strange and thrilling, had been shown on television when the transiting Sun was entering an aspect with Pluto and the Planets in Scorpio. The film was about the desire for immortality and how to take possession of the human will. There was talk in it about states bordering on death, sexual obsession, and other Plutonic matters.

I succeeded in observing similar conformities with regard to the *Alien* films, set on a spaceship. Here subtle dependencies between Pluto, Neptune and Mars came into play. As soon as Mars was in aspect to these two Slow Planets at the same time, the television showed a repeat of one of the *Alien* films. Isn't that fascinating?

Coincidences of this kind are astonishing. I have enough empirical material to write an entire book about it. But for the time being I made do with a short essay, which I sent to several weeklies. I don't think anyone will publish it, but perhaps someone will Reflect on it.

IN MID-MARCH, ONCE I WAS FEELING COMPLETELY WELL AGAIN, I set off on a wider round, meaning that I didn't limit myself to inspecting the houses that were left in my care, but chose to turn an even bigger circle, going all the way to the forest, then across the meadows to the highway, making a stop at the precipice.

At this time of year the world is at its most detestable. There are still large white patches of snow on the ground, hard and compacted, barely recognizable as the lovely, innocent fluff that falls at Christmas to our great joy. Now it's like a knife blade, like a metal surface. It's difficult to walk across, it traps the legs. If not for tall snow boots, it would wound the calves. The sky is low and gray—it looks as if you could reach out and touch it from the top of a small hill.

As I walked, I considered the fact that I wouldn't be able to go on living here forever, in this house on the Plateau, guarding the other houses. Eventually the Samurai would break down and there'd be no way to drive into town. The wooden steps would rot, snow would tear off the gutters, the stove would stop working, and one freezing-cold February the pipes would burst. And I would grow weaker too. My Ailments were destroying my body, gradually, relentlessly. Each year my knees ached more, and my liver was clearly no longer fit for purpose. After all, I've been alive a long time. That's what I was thinking, rather pitifully. But one day I would have to start giving it all some proper thought.

Just then I saw a fast and agile swarm of Fieldfares. These are Birds that I only ever see in a flock. They move nimbly, like one large piece of living fretwork in the air. I read somewhere that were a Predator to attack them, one of those languid Hawks that hover in the sky like the Holy Spirit, for instance, the Fieldfares will defend themselves. For as a flock they're capable of fighting, in a very special, perfidious way, and also of taking revenge—they swiftly soar into the air, then in perfect unison they defecate on their oppressor—dozens of white droppings land on the predator's lovely wings, soiling them, gluing them together, and coating the feathers in corrosive acid. This forces the Hawk to come to its senses, cease its pursuit and land on the grass in disgust. It may well die of revulsion, so badly polluted are its feathers. It spends the whole day cleaning them, and then the next day too. It doesn't sleep, it cannot sleep with such dirty wings. It's sickened by its own overwhelming stink. It's like a Mouse, like a Frog, like carrion. It can't remove the hardened excrement with its beak, it's freezing cold, and now the rainwater can easily pervade its glued-up feathers to reach its fragile skin. Its own kind, other Hawks shun it too. It seems to them leprous, infected by a vile disease. Its majesty has been injured. All this is unbearable for the Hawk, and sometimes the Bird will die.

Now the Fieldfares, aware of their strength in numbers, were frolicking in front of me, performing aerobatics.

I also watched a pair of Magpies, and was surprised they had ventured all the way to the Plateau. But I know that these Birds spread their range faster than others, and in the near future they'll be everywhere, as Pigeons are today. One for sorrow, two for joy. So they said when I was a child, but there were fewer Magpies then. Last autumn, after the nesting season, I would see hundreds of them flying off to their night roost. I wonder if that means joy multiplied.

I watched the Magpies as they bathed in a puddle of melted snow. They gave me sidelong glances, but clearly weren't afraid of me, for they boldly went on spattering the water with their wings and dipping their heads in it. Seeing their joy, no one could doubt how much fun a bath of this kind must be.

Apparently Magpies cannot live without frequent baths. What's more, they're intelligent and insolent. As everyone knows, they steal material for their nests from other Birds and carry off shiny objects to put in them. I have also heard that sometimes they make mistakes and take glowing cigarette butts to their nests; like this they become fire-raisers, and burn down the building on which they've built their nest. Our good old Magpie has a lovely name in Latin: *Pica pica*.

How great and full of life the world is.

Far in the distance I also saw a familiar Fox whom I call Consul—so refined and well-bred is he. He always wanders the same paths; the winter reveals his routes—straight as an arrow, purposeful. He's an old dog fox, he comes and goes from the Czech Republic—clearly he has business to attend to over here. I watched him through binoculars as he loped downhill at a light trot, following the tracks he'd left in the snow last time he came this way—perhaps to make his potential stalkers think he'd only done it once. It was like seeing an old friend. Suddenly I noticed that this time Consul had turned off the beaten track and before I knew it, he'd vanished in the brushwood growing on the field boundary. There was a hunting pulpit at that spot, and another one a few hundred meters further on. I'd had dealings with them in the past. The Fox was gone from my sight, and as I had nothing else to do, I walked along the edge of the forest after him.

Here there was a large, snow-coated field. In the autumn it had been plowed, and now lumps of half-frozen earth created a surface underfoot that was hard to walk across. I was just starting to regret my decision to follow Consul when suddenly, once I'd toiled a short way uphill, I saw what had attracted him—a large black shape on the snow, and dried bloodstains. Consul was standing a little higher up, gazing at me calmly, without fear, as if he were saying: "You see? You see? I've brought you here, but now you must deal with it." And off he ran.

I went closer and saw that the shape was a Wild Boar, not quite an adult, lying in a pool of brown blood. The surrounding snow had been scraped away, exposing the ground, as if the Animal had thrashed about in convulsions. I could see other tracks around it too—of Foxes, Birds and Deer. Lots of Animals had been here. They'd come to see the murder for themselves and to mourn the poor young Boar. I preferred to examine their tracks rather than look at its body. How many times can one look at a dead body? Is there no end to it? I felt a stab of pain in my lungs and found it hard to breathe. I sat down on the snow, and once again my eyes began to stream with tears. I could feel the huge, unbearable burden of my own body. Why couldn't I have gone in another direction, without following Consul? Why hadn't I ignored his gloomy paths? Must I be a witness to every Crime? The day would have turned out quite differently, other days too perhaps. I could see where the bullets had struck—in the chest and belly. I could see where the Boar had been heading—toward the border, to the Czech Republic, away from the new pulpits, which stood on the other side of the forest. It must have been shot from there, so it must have run on, wounded, just a little further, in its effort to escape to the Czech Republic.

Sorrow, I felt great sorrow, an endless sense of mourning for every dead Animal. One period of grief is followed by another, so I am in constant mourning. This is my natural state. I kneeled on the blood-stained snow and stroked the Boar's coarse hair, cold and stiff.

———✕———

"You have more compassion for animals than for people."

"That's not true. I feel just as sorry for both. But nobody shoots at defenseless people," I told the City Guard that same evening. "At least not these days," I added.

"True. We're a law-abiding country," confirmed the guard. He seemed good-natured and not very bright.

"Its Animals show the truth about a country," I said. "Its attitude toward Animals. If people behave brutally toward Animals, no form of democracy is ever going to help them, in fact nothing will at all."

At the Police station I had only submitted a report. They had brushed me off. They had handed me a sheet of paper and I had written the relevant facts on it. It occurred to me that the City Guard was also a public body responsible for law and order, so I had come here. I promised myself that if this didn't help, I'd go to the Prosecution Service. Next day. To Black Coat. And I'd report a Murder.

The handsome young man who looked a bit like Paul Newman had fetched a wad of papers out of a drawer and was now looking for a pen. A woman in uniform came in from the other room and placed a full mug in front of him.

"Would you like some coffee?" she asked me.

I nodded gratefully. I was chilled to the bone. My legs were aching again.

"Why didn't they take away the body? What do you think?" I asked, without expecting them to answer. They both seemed surprised by my visit and weren't entirely sure how to behave. I accepted a mug of coffee from the nice young woman and answered my own question.

"Because they didn't even know they'd killed it. They shoot at everything illegally, so they shot it too, and then forgot about it. They thought it was sure to fall somewhere in the bushes, and nobody would ever know they'd killed a Boar beyond the legal deadline." I extracted a printout from my bag and shoved it under the man's nose. "I've checked the dates. It's March now. Have a look, it's not legal to shoot a Boar now," I concluded with satisfaction, feeling sure that my reasoning was beyond reproach, though from the logical point of view it would be hard to convince me that on February 28 you may kill someone, but the next day you may not.

"I'm sorry, madam," replied Paul Newman, "but this isn't really within our jurisdiction. Why don't you go and report the matter to the vet? He'll know what's done in such cases. Maybe the boar was rabid?"

I put down my mug with a thump.

"No, it's the killer who was rabid," I cried, because I know that argument well; the Slaughter of Animals is often justified by the fact that they may have been rabid. "It had been shot through the lungs, it must have died in agonies; they shot it, and they thought it had run away alive. Besides, the vet is one of them, he hunts too."

The man cast a helpless glance at his female colleague.

"What do you expect us to do?"

"Set the wheels in motion. Punish the culprits. Change the law."

"That's too much. You can't want all those things," he said.

"Oh yes I can! And I'm the one to define what I can want," I shouted furiously.

He was confused; the situation was slipping from his control.

"All right, all right. We'll report it formally."

"To whom?"

"First we'll ask the Hunters Association for an explanation. Let them have their say."

"And this isn't the first instance, because I found a Hare's skull with a bullet hole in it on the other side of the Plateau. Do you know where? Very near the border. Now I call that copse the Site of the Skull."

"They might have lost one of their hares."

"Lost!" I shrieked. "They shoot at everything that moves." I paused briefly, for I felt as if a large fist had hit me in the chest with all its might. "Even at Dogs."

"Sometimes dogs from the village kill animals. You have dogs too, and I remember that last year there were complaints about you . . ."

I froze. The blow was very painful.

"I don't have my Dogs anymore."

The coffee wasn't good, the instant kind. I felt it in my stomach like a cramp.

I bent double.

"What's wrong? What's happened?" asked the woman.

"It's nothing," I replied, "at my age one has various Ailments. I shouldn't drink instant coffee, and I advise you against it too. It's bad for the stomach."

I put down the mug.

"Well, then? Are you going to write the report?" I asked, in what I considered to be a businesslike tone.

They exchanged glances again, and the man reluctantly drew the form toward him.

"All right, then," he said, and I could almost hear what he was thinking: *I'll write it to shut her up but I won't bother showing it to anyone*, so I added: "And please give me a date-stamped copy with your signature."

As he was writing, I tried to slow down my thoughts, but they must have broken the speed limit by now, and were racing in my head, somehow managing to pervade my body and my bloodstream as well. Yet paradoxically, from the feet, from the ground up, a strange calm was slowly spreading through me. It was a state I recognized—that same state of clarity, divine Wrath, terrible and unstoppable. I could feel my legs itching, and fire pouring into my blood from somewhere, and my blood flowing quickly, carrying this fire to my brain, and now my brain was glowing brightly, my fingertips were filling with fire, and so was my face, and it felt as if my entire body were being flooded by a bright aura, gently raising me upward, tearing me free of the ground.

"Just look at the way those pulpits work. It's evil—you have to call it by its proper name: it's cunning, treacherous, sophisticated evil— they build hay racks, scatter fresh apples and wheat to lure Animals there, and once the Creatures have become habituated, they shoot them in the head from their hiding place, from a pulpit," I began to say in a low tone, with my gaze fixed on the floor. I could sense they were looking at me anxiously while carrying on with their work. "I wish I knew Animal script," I said, "signs in which I could write warnings for them: 'Don't go over there,' 'That food is lethal,' 'Keep away from the pulpits, they won't preach the gospel to you from there, you won't hear any good news over there, they won't promise you salvation after death, they won't take pity on your poor souls, for they say you haven't got souls. They don't see their brethren in you, they won't give you their blessing. The nastiest criminal has a soul, but not you, beautiful Deer, nor you, Boar, nor you, wild Goose, nor you, Pig, nor you, Dog.' Killing has become exempt from punishment. And as it goes unpunished, nobody notices it anymore. And as nobody notices it, it doesn't exist. When you walk past a shop window where large red chunks of butchered bodies are hanging on display, do you stop to wonder what it really is? You never think twice about it, do you? Or when you order a kebab or a chop—what are you actually getting? There's nothing shocking about it. Crime has come to be regarded as a normal, everyday activity. Everyone commits it. That's just how the world would look if concentration camps became the norm. Nobody would see anything wrong with them."

That's what I was saying while he was writing. The woman had left the room, and now I could hear her talking on the phone. No one was listening to me, but I went on with my speech. I couldn't stop, because the words were coming to me from somewhere of their own accord—I simply had to utter them. After each sentence I felt relief. And I was further stimulated by the fact that a client had just come in with a little Poodle; clearly perturbed by my tone, he gently closed the door and at once began whispering to Newman. His Poodle sat down quietly, tilted its head and looked at me. So I carried on:

"In fact Man has a great responsibility toward wild Animals—to help them to live their lives, and it's his duty toward domesticated Animals to return their love and affection, for they give us far more than they receive from us. And they need to be able to live their lives with dignity, to be able to settle their Accounts and register their semester in the karmic index—I was an Animal, I lived and I ate; I grazed in green pastures, I bore Young, I kept them warm with my body; I built nests, I performed my duty. When you kill them, and they die in Fear and Terror—like that Boar whose body lay before me yesterday, and is still lying there, defiled, muddied and smeared with blood, reduced to carrion—you doom them to hell, and the whole world changes into hell. Can't people see that? Are their minds incapable of reaching beyond petty, selfish pleasures? People have a duty toward Animals to lead them—in successive lives—to Liberation. We're all traveling in the same direction, from dependence to freedom, from ritual to free choice."

So I spoke, using wise words.

From a back room a cleaner emerged with a plastic pail and stared at me in curiosity. Stony-faced, the guard was still filling in his form.

"You'll say it's just one Boar," I continued. "But what about the deluge of butchered meat that falls on our cities day by day like never-ending, apocalyptic rain? This rain heralds slaughter, disease, collective madness, the obfuscation and contamination of the Mind. For no human heart is capable of bearing so much pain. The whole, complex human psyche has evolved to prevent Man from understanding what he is really seeing. To stop the truth from reaching him by wrapping it in illusion, in idle chatter. The world is a prison full of suffering, so constructed that in order to survive one must inflict pain on others. Do you hear me?" I said. But now even the cleaner, disappointed by my speech, had set about his work, so I was only talking to the Poodle.

"What sort of a world is this? Someone's body is made into shoes, into meatballs, sausages, a bedside rug, someone's bones are boiled to make broth . . . Shoes, sofas, a shoulder bag made of someone's belly, keeping warm with someone else's fur, eating someone's body, cutting it into bits and frying it in oil . . . Can it really be true? Is this nightmare really happening? This mass killing, cruel, impassive, automatic, without any pangs of conscience, without the slightest pause for thought, though plenty of thought is applied to ingenious philosophies and theologies. What sort of a world is this, where killing and pain are the norm? What on earth is wrong with us?"

Silence fell. My head was spinning, and suddenly I started to cough. Just then the man with the Poodle cleared his throat.

"You're right, madam. You're absolutely right," he said.

This confused me. I glanced at him, angrily at first, but I could see that he was moved. He was a lean, elderly gentleman, neatly dressed, in a suit with a waistcoat, sure to be straight from Good News's shop. His Poodle was clean and well-groomed—I'd say he looked grand. But my declaration had made no impression on the guard. He was one of those ironists who don't like pathos, so they button their lip to avoid being infected by it. They fear pathos more than hell.

"You're exaggerating," was all he said at last, as he calmly laid the sheets of paper on his desk. "I find it truly puzzling. Why is it that old women . . . women of your age are so concerned about animals? Aren't there any people left for them to take care of? Is it because their children have grown up and they don't have anyone to look after anymore, but their instincts prompt them to care for something else? Women have an instinct for caring, don't they?" He glanced at his colleague, but she made no gesture to confirm this Hypothesis. "Take my granny, for example. She has seven cats at home, and she also feeds all the local cats in her area. Would you read this, please?" he said, passing me a sheet of paper with a short text printed on it. "You're approaching this too emotionally. You're more concerned about the fate of animals than people," he repeated himself in conclusion.

I didn't feel like speaking anymore. I thrust a hand into my pocket, pulled out a ball of bloodstained Boar bristles, and put it down on the desk in front of them. Their first impulse was to lean forward, but they instantly recoiled in disgust.

"Christ Almighty, what is that? Yuck," cried Newman the guard. "What the hell! Take it away!"

I leaned back comfortably in my chair and said with satisfaction: "Those are Remains. I pick them up and collect them. I have boxes at home, properly labeled, to store them in. Hair and bones. One day it'll be possible to clone all the murdered Animals. So perhaps there'll be some sort of redress."

"What a nerve," said the female guard into the telephone, leaning over the hairball, her mouth twisted in disgust. "What a nerve you have!"

Caked blood and muck had soiled their papers. The guard leaped to his feet and backed away from the desk.

"Are you repulsed by blood?" I asked mischievously. "But you like black pudding, don't you?"

"Please calm down. That's enough of your nonsense. After all, we're trying to help you."

I signed every copy of the report, and then the female guard took me gently by the arm and led me to the door. Like a madwoman. I didn't resist. Meanwhile she never stopped talking on the phone.

—✖—

Once again I had the same dream. Once again my Mother was in the boiler room. Once again I was angry with her for coming here.

I looked her straight in the face, but her gaze kept veering side-ways, she couldn't look me in the eyes. She was being evasive, as if she knew an embarrassing secret. She kept smiling, and then suddenly becoming serious—the expression on her face was fluid, the image was rippling. I said I didn't want her to keep coming here. This is a place for the living, not the dead. Then she turned to face the door, and I saw that my Grandmother was standing there too, a handsome young woman in a gray dress. She was holding a handbag. They both looked as if they were just on their way to church. I remembered that handbag—a funny one from before the war. What can you have in your handbag when you come to visit from the spirit world? A hand-ful of dust? Ashes? A stone? A moldering handkerchief for your non-existent nose? Now they were both standing in front of me, so close that I thought I could smell their scent—old perfume, bed linen neatly piled in a wooden wardrobe.

"Go on, go home," I said, waving my arms at them as I had at the Deer.

But they didn't move. So I was the first to turn around and get out of there, locking the door behind me.

THE OLD METHOD FOR DEALING WITH BAD DREAMS IS TO TELL them aloud above the toilet bowl, and then flush them away.

VIII.

Uranus in Leo

Every thing possible to be believ'd is an image of truth.

Obviously, the first Horoscope a Person ever calculates is their own, and so it was in my case too. And then a structure emerged, supported by a circle. I examined it in astonishment—is that me? Here before me lay the blueprint for the person I am, my actual self in a basic written record, at once the simplest and the most complicated possible. Like a mirror that changes the sensory image of the face into a simple geometric chart. Everything about my own face that seemed to me familiar and obvious had vanished; what remained was a distinctive scattering of dots that symbolized the planets set against the celestial vault. Nothing ages, nothing is subject to change, their positions in the firmament are unique and permanent. The hour of birth divides the space within the circle into houses, and thus the chart becomes practically unique, like our fingerprints.

I think we all feel great ambivalence at the sight of our own Horoscope. On the one hand we're proud to see that the sky is imprinted on our individual life, like a postmark with a date stamped on a letter—this makes it distinct, one of a kind. But at the same time it's a form of imprisonment in space, like a tattooed prison number. There's no escaping it. I cannot be someone other than I am. How awful. We'd prefer to think we're free, able to reinvent ourselves whenever we choose. This connection with something as great and monumental as the sky makes us feel uncomfortable. We'd rather be small, and then our petty little sins would be forgivable.

Therefore I'm convinced that we should get to know our prison very well.

BY PROFESSION I AM A BRIDGE CONSTRUCTION ENGINEER—HAVE I mentioned that already? I have built bridges in Syria and in Libya, and also in Poland—near Elbląg, and two in Podlasie. The one in Syria was a strange bridge: it spanned the banks of a river that only appeared periodically. Water flowed in its bed for two or three months, then soaked into the sunbaked earth, changing it into something like a bobsled track. Wild desert Dogs would chase each other along it.

I always gained the greatest pleasure from transforming concepts into figures—from these figures a specific image arose, then a drawing, and then a design. The figures came together on my piece of paper and assumed a meaningful shape. My talent for algebra was useful to me for Horoscopes in the days when one had to do all one's calculations on a slide rule. Nowadays that's unnecessary; there are computer programs to do it for us. Who still remembers the slide rule, when the cure for any thirst for knowledge is just a mouse-click away? But it was then, during the best phase in my life, that my Ailments began, and I had to return to Poland. I spent a long time in the hospital, but it still wasn't clear what was really wrong with me.

For a time I slept with a Protestant, who in his turn designed motorways, and he told me, probably quoting Luther, that he who suffers sees the back of God. I wondered if this meant the shoulders, or the buttocks perhaps, and what this divine back looks like, since we're incapable of imagining the front. Maybe it means that he who suffers has special access to God, by a side door, he is blessed, he embraces some sort of truth which without suffering would be hard to comprehend. So in a way, the only person who's healthy is one who suffers, however strange it might sound. I think that would be in harmony with the rest.

For a year I couldn't walk at all, and by the time my Ailments began to ease a little, I knew I would never be able to build bridges across rivers in the desert again, and that I couldn't stray too far from a fridge with glucose in it. So I changed profession and became a teacher. I worked at a school and taught the children various useful things: English, handicrafts and geography. I always did my best to capture their attention fully, to have them remember important things not out of fear of a bad mark but out of genuine passion.

It gave me a lot of pleasure. Children have always attracted me more than adults, for I too am a little infantile. There's nothing wrong with that. The main thing is, I'm aware of it. Children are soft and supple, open-minded and unpretentious. And they don't engage in the sort of small talk in which every adult is able to gabble their life away. Unfortunately, the older they are, the more they succumb to the power of reason; they become citizens of Ulro, as Blake would have put it, and refuse to be led down the right path as easily and naturally anymore. That's why I only liked the smaller children. The older ones, over the age of ten, say, were even more loathsome than adults. At that age the children lost their individuality. I could see them ossifying as they inevitably entered adolescence, which gradually forced them to be hooked on being the same as others. In a few cases there was a bit of an inner struggle as they wrestled with this new state of being, but almost all of them ended up capitulating. I never made the effort to keep in touch with them after that—for it would be like having to witness the Fall, yet again. Usually I taught children up to this limit, at most until the fifth year.

Finally I was pensioned off. Far too early, in my opinion. It's hard to understand why because I was a good teacher, with plenty of experience, and free of troubles, apart from my Ailments, but they only made their presence known from time to time. So I went to the education board, where I submitted the relevant certificates, references and applications to be allowed to go on teaching. Unfortunately, it didn't work. I had run into a bad moment—a time of reforms, overhauling the system, changing the program, and rising unemployment.

Then I looked for work in another school, and then another, half-time and quarter-time, by the hour—I'd have taken a job by the minute if only they'd offered one—but wherever I went I could sense an army of other, younger people standing behind me, breathing down my neck, impatiently treading on my tail, even though it's a thankless, badly paid profession.

Only here did I succeed. Once I'd moved out of the city, bought this house and taken on the job as guardian of my neighbors' properties, a breathless young headmistress came across the hills to see me. "I know you're a teacher," she said—and she used the present tense, which instantly won me over, for I regard my profession as a mental attitude rather than a set of isolated activities. She offered me a few hours teaching English at her school, working with small children, the kind I like. So I agreed, and once a week I started teaching English to seven- and eight-year-olds, who approach learning very enthusiastically but who just as quickly and suddenly get bored. The headmistress wanted me to teach music too—she must have heard us singing "Amazing Grace"—but that would have been beyond my strength. It's quite enough for me to scurry down to the village every Wednesday, to have to dress in clean clothes, brush my hair and put on a little makeup—I paint my eyelids green and powder my face. All this costs me a great deal of time and patience. I could have taken the PE class too, I am tall and strong. I used to go in for sports. Somewhere in the city I still have my medals. Though I had no chance of teaching PE anymore, because of my age.

But I'll admit that now, in winter, it's hard for me to get there. On teaching days I have to get up earlier than usual, when it's still dark, stoke the fire, clear the snow from the Samurai, and if it's parked away from the house on the surfaced road, I must wade through the snow to reach it, which isn't fun at all. Winter mornings are made of steel; they have a metallic taste and sharp edges. On a Wednesday in

January, at seven in the morning, it's plain to see that the world was not made for Man, and definitely not for his comfort or pleasure.

—✕—

Unfortunately, neither Dizzy nor any of my friends shares my passion for Astrology, so I try not to flaunt it. They regard me as a crank already. I only spill the beans when I need to obtain someone's date and place of birth, as in the case of the Commandant. For this purpose I have questioned almost everyone from the Plateau and half the town. In giving me their date of birth, people are actually revealing their real name to me, they're showing me their celestial date-stamp, opening their past and future to me. But there are many people whom I shall never have the opportunity to ask for it.

Obtaining a date of birth is relatively easy. All it takes is an identity card, or just about any other document, and sometimes, by chance it turns up on the Internet. Dizzy has access to all sorts of lists and tables, though I won't elaborate here. But what really matters is the time of birth. That's not recorded in the documents, and yet it's the time that's the real key to a Person. A Horoscope without the exact time is fairly worthless—we know WHAT, but we don't know HOW and WHERE.

I TRIED EXPLAINING TO THE RELUCTANT DIZZY THAT IN THE PAST Astrology was much the same as sociobiology is today. Then at least he seemed a little more interested. There's nothing outrageous about this comparison. The Astrologer believes that the heavenly bodies have an influence on human personality, while the sociobiologist thinks it's the mysterious emanations of molecular bodies that affect us. The difference is in scale. Neither of them knows what's behind this influence or how it is transmitted. They're really talking about the same thing, except that they're using different scales. Sometimes I'm surprised by the similarity, and also by the fact that while I adore Astrology, I have no respect for sociobiology at all.

In a natal Horoscope the date of birth determines the date of death as well. That's obvious—anyone who has been born is going to die. There are many places in the Horoscope that point us toward the time and nature of death—one simply needs to know how to spot and connect them. For example, one has to check the transitory aspects of Saturn to the hyleg, and what's going on in the eighth house. Also to cast an eye on the relative position of the Lights—meaning the Sun and Moon.

It is quite complicated, and it could be boring for anyone who isn't an expert. But when you look carefully, I told Dizzy, when you join up the facts, you'll see that the concurrences of events down here with the position of the planets up there are crystal clear. It always puts me into a state of exhilaration. But the source of my excitement is understanding. That's why Dizzy cannot feel it.

In my defense of Astrology I'm often forced to use statistical arguments, which I hate, but which always appeal to young minds. Without any thought but with religious zeal, young people believe in statistics. It's enough to give them something expressed as a percentage, or as a probability, and they take it in good faith. So then I referred to Gauquelin and his "Mars effect"—a phenomenon that seems bizarre, but the statistics confirm it. What Gauquelin did was to demonstrate that statistically, in the Horoscopes of sportsmen, Mars—the planet of fitness, competition and so on—is more frequently found in one particular location than in the Horoscopes of non-sportsmen. Of course Dizzy made light of this proof, and of all the other evidence that he found uncomfortable. Even when I offered him a whole string of examples of predictions that had come true. For instance concerning Hitler, when Himmler's court Astrologer, Wilhelm Wolf, predicted *"eine grosse Gefahr für Hitler am 20.07.44,"* meaning great danger for Hitler on that day, and as we know, that was the date of the assassination attempt at the Wolf's Lair. And later on, the same sinister Astrologer predicted impassively: *"dass Hitler noch vor dem 7.05.45 eines geheimnisvollen Todes sterben werde,"* meaning that Hitler would die a mysterious death before the seventh of May.

"Incredible," said Dizzy. "How's that possible?" he asked himself, but then instantly forgot it all, and let his incredulity flare up again.

I tried using other methods to convince him, by showing him the perfect harmony between what happens down here and what's going on up there.

"Look at this, for example, look carefully—the summer of 1980, Jupiter in conjunction with Saturn in Libra. A powerful conjunction. Jupiter represents the authorities, and Saturn the workers. What's more, Wałęsa has the Sun in Libra. Do you see?"

Dizzy shook his head dubiously.

"What about the Police? Which celestial body represents the Police?" he asked.

"Pluto. It also represents the secret services and the mafia."

"Well, yes, yes . . ." he repeated, unconvinced, though I could see he had a lot of goodwill and was doing his best.

"Keep looking," I said, and showed him the position of the planets. "Saturn was in Scorpio in 1953—the death of Stalin and the political thaw; 1952 to 1956—repression, the Korean War, the invention of the hydrogen bomb. The year 1953 was the toughest for the Polish economy. Look, that's just when Saturn rose in Scorpio. Isn't that incredible?"

Dizzy fidgeted in his chair.

"Well, all right, look at this: Neptune in Libra—chaos, Uranus in Cancer—the people rebel, the decline of colonialism. Uranus was entering Leo when the French Revolution erupted, when the January Uprising occurred and when Lenin was born. Remember that Uranus in Leo always represents revolutionary power."

I could see he was finding it painful.

No, it was impossible to persuade Dizzy to believe in Astrology. Never mind.

Once I was alone and was laying out my research Tools in the kitchen, I felt pleased that I could keep track of these amazing conformities. First I deciphered Big Foot's Horoscope, and straight after that the Commandant's.

Generally speaking, the tendency of a particular Person to have accidents is shown by the Ascendant, its ruler, and the planets in the Ascendant. The ruler of the eighth house indicates a natural death. If it is in the first house, it means that his death will be the Person's own fault. Maybe he was a careless Person, for instance. If the signifier is connected with the third house, the Person will be aware of the cause of his death. If it is not connected, then the poor fellow will not even realize where he made the fatal error. In the second house death occurs as a result of wealth and money. In this configuration the Person might be attacked and killed for the purposes of robbery. The third house is typical for road and transport accidents. In the fourth we find death because of land ownership, or because of family, especially the father. In the fifth because of children, abuse of pleasure, or because of sport. In the sixth house we bring illness on ourselves through lack of caution or by overworking. When the ruler of the eighth house is in the seventh house, the cause of death is a spouse; that could mean a duel, or despair resulting from infidelity. And so on.

In the Commandant's Horoscope in the eighth house (a threat to life, the house of death) we find the Sun, the body that symbolizes life itself, but also a position of power. It is located in quadrature—a very difficult aspect—to Mars (violence, aggression) in the twelfth house (Murder, assassination) in Scorpio (death, homicide, Crime). The ruler of Scorpio is Pluto, and thus power may be to do with organizations such as the Police, or . . . the mafia. Pluto is in conjunction with the Sun in Leo. In my view, all this means that the Commandant was a very ambiguous and enigmatic person, mixed up in various sinister affairs. That he was capable of being cruel and ruthless, and gained distinct advantages from his position. It's highly possible that as well as his official authority within the Police he had a lot of power somewhere else too, within something secret and ominous.

What's more, the ruler of the Ascendant is in Aries, which governs the head, and thus violence (Mars) is in direct relation to his head. And I also remembered that Saturn in an animal sign—Aries, Taurus, Leo, Sagittarius or Capricorn—portends a threat to life caused by a wild or aggressive Animal.

"In Dante's *Inferno* Virgil says that as their punishment the astrologers had horribly twisted necks," said Dizzy to wrap up my argument.

—✕—

"Come on, my friend, don't let me down," I said to the Samurai, which was growling at me, but then instantly it fired up. It's a form of loyalty. When you've lived together for such a long time and you're reliant on each other, a sort of friendship develops. I know it has reached quite an age by now, and with each year it's finding it harder to move about. Just like me. I also know that I neglect it, and that this winter had made its life a misery. Mine too. In this car I have everything I need in case of an Accident. A rope and shovel, an electric saw, a gas can, some mineral water and a packet of crackers that are sure to be completely damp by now—I've been carrying them about since the autumn. There's also a flashlight (so that's where it is!), a first-aid kit, a spare wheel and an orange camping cooler. I also have a can of pepper spray in case anyone were to attack me on the road, though it's highly unlikely.

We drove across the Plateau toward the village, through meadows and wonderful wilderness. Gently and timidly, everything was starting to go green. Young nettles, still weak and tiny, were poking their tips above the ground. It was hard to imagine that in two months from now they'd be sticking up stiffly, proud and menacing, with fluffy green seed pods. Close to the ground near the road I could see the tiny little faces of daisies—I could never help feeling that they were silently inspecting everyone who came this way, casting their stern judgment on us. An army of flower folk.

I parked outside the school and at once the children from my classes ran up to the car—they were always impressed by the Wolf's head stuck to the Samurai's front door. Then they escorted me to the classroom, twittering away, all chattering at once, and pulling at the sleeves of my sweater.

"Good morning," I said in English.

"Good morning," the children replied.

And as it was Wednesday, we started our Wednesday rituals. Unfortunately, half the class was absent again—the boys had been excused from their lessons to attend rehearsals for first communion. So we'd have to repeat this lesson again next week. I taught the next class some nature vocabulary, and that meant making a lot of mess, which earned me a scolding from the school cleaning lady.

"You always leave a pigsty behind you. This is a school, not a kindergarten. What on earth are these dirty stones and seaweed for?"

At this school she was the only person whom I feared, and her screeching, resentful tone drove me up the wall. The lessons tired me, physically even. I reluctantly trudged off to do my shopping and go to the post office. I bought bread, potatoes and other vegetables, in large quantities. I also went to the expense of buying some Cambozola, to cheer myself up if only with a bit of cheese. There are various magazines and newspapers that I sometimes buy, but reading them usually gives me an unspecified sense of guilt. A feeling that there's something I haven't done, something I've forgotten, that I'm not up to the demands of the task, that in some essential way I'm lagging behind the rest. The newspapers may very well be right. But when one takes a careful look at the people passing in the street, one might assume that many others have the same problem too, and haven't done what they should with their lives either.

The first feeble signs of spring hadn't yet reached the town; it had probably settled in beyond city limits, in allotment gardens and in stream valleys, like enemy troops in the past. The cobblestones were covered in sand left over from the winter, when it was scattered on the slippery pavements, but now, in the Sunshine, it was raising dust, soiling the springtime shoes brought out of the closet. The town flower beds were small and miserable. The lawns were fouled with dog dirt. Along the streets walked ashen people, squinting. They looked stupefied. Some were queuing at the cash machines to withdraw twenty zlotys to pay for today's food. Others were hurrying to the clinic, armed with a ticket for an appointment at one thirty-five, while others were on their way to the cemetery to change the plastic winter flowers for real spring daffodils.

I felt deeply moved by all this human hustle and bustle. Sometimes an emotional mood of this kind assails me—I think it's to do with my Ailments—and my resistance weakens. I stopped in the sloping market square, and gradually I felt flooded by a powerful sense of communion with the people passing by. Each man was my brother and each woman my sister. We were so very much alike. So fragile, impermanent, and easily destroyed. We trustingly went to and fro beneath the sky, which had nothing good in store for us.

Spring is just a short interlude, after which the mighty armies of death advance; they're already besieging the city walls. We live in a state of siege. If one takes a close look at each fragment of a moment, one might choke with terror. Within our bodies disintegration inexorably advances; soon we shall fall sick and die. Our loved ones will leave us, the memory of them will dissolve in the tumult; nothing will remain. Just a few clothes in the wardrobe and someone in a photograph, no longer recognized. The most precious memories will dissipate. Everything will sink into darkness and vanish.

I noticed a pregnant girl sitting on a bench, reading a newspaper, and suddenly it occurred to me what a blessing it is to be ignorant. How could one possibly know all this and not miscarry?

My eyes began to stream again; by now it was becoming truly awkward and problematic. I couldn't hold back the tears. I hoped Ali would know what to do about it.

GOOD NEWS'S SHOP WAS IN A SMALL SIDE STREET OFF THE MARKET square, and one entered it straight from the car park, which wasn't the best incentive for potential buyers of secondhand clothes.

I looked in there for the first time last year in late autumn. I was frozen through and hungry. Damp November darkness was hanging over the town and people were feeling drawn to everything bright and warm.

From the entrance, some clean and colorful rugs led inside, then diverged among the racks, on which the clothes were classified by color, playing a game with the different shades; the place smelled of incense, and it was warm, almost hot, thanks to some large industrial radiators beneath the windows. This had once been home to the Tailors' Cooperative for the Disabled, as indicated by a sign still visible on the wall. There was a large plant in the corner, a huge chestnut vine that must have outgrown its previous owner's apartment long ago; its strong shoots were climbing the walls, aiming for the shop window. The whole thing was a mixture of socialist café, dry cleaner's and fancy-dress costume rental. And in the middle of it all was Good News.

That's what I called her. This name suggested itself irresistibly, at first sight. Irresistibly—that's a beautiful, powerful word; when we use it, we shouldn't really need to provide any further explanation.

"I'd like a warm jacket," I said shyly, and the girl looked at me intelligently, with a gleam in her dark eyes. She nodded encouragingly.

So after a short pause I continued: "To keep me warm and protect me from the rain. I want it to be different from all the other jackets, not gray or black, not the kind that's easily mistaken in the cloakroom. I want it to have pockets, lots of pockets for keys, treats for the Dogs, a cell phone, documents—then I won't have to carry a bag, and can keep my hands free."

As I made my request, I realized that I was placing myself in her hands.

"I think I might have something for you," replied Good News, and led me into the depths of the long, narrow space.

At the far end stood a circular clothes rack with jackets hanging on it. Without having to think, she reached out and extracted a lovely down coat in a crimson shade.

"How about this one?" The large surfaces of the bright windows were reflected in her eyes, which shone with a beautiful, pure light.

Yes, the jacket was a perfect fit. I felt like an Animal that has been given back its stolen fur. In the pocket I found a little shell, and decided it was a small gift from the previous owner. Like a wish: "May it serve you well."

I also bought some gloves at this shop, two pairs. I was just about to rummage in a basket full of hats, when I noticed a large black Cat lying in it. And next to it, among the scarves there was another one, identical, but bigger. Mentally I named the Cats Hat and Scarf, though afterward I always found it very hard to tell them apart. Good News's black Cats.

This sweet little shop assistant with Manchurian beauty (she was also wearing a fake fur hat) made me a cup of tea and pulled a chair up to the gas heater for me to warm myself.

That was how our friendship began.

THERE ARE SOME PEOPLE AT WHOM ONE ONLY HAS TO GLANCE FOR one's throat to tighten and one's eyes to fill with tears of emotion. These people make one feel as if a stronger memory of our former innocence remains in them, as if they were a freak of nature, not entirely battered by the Fall. Perhaps they are messengers, like the servants who find a lost prince who's unaware of his origins, show him the robe that he wore in his native country, and remind him how to return home.

She too suffered from her own special illness—a very rare and bizarre one. She had no hair. No eyebrows, or eyelashes. She'd never had any—she was born like that. Genes, or Astrology. I of course think it's Astrology. Oh yes, I verified it in her Horoscope: Damaged Mars close to the Ascendant, on the side of the twelfth house and in opposition to Saturn in the sixth (this sort of Mars also produces covert activities and unclear motives).

So she drew herself lovely eyebrows with a pencil, and tiny little lines on her eyelids to look like lashes; the illusion was perfect. She always wore a turban, a hat, occasionally a wig, or else she wound a scarf around her head. In summer I gazed in amazement at her forearms, entirely devoid of those little, darker or fairer hairs that we all have.

I often wonder why we find some people attractive and not others.

And I have a Theory about it, which is that there is such a thing as a perfectly harmonious shape to which our bodies instinctively aspire. We choose in others the features that seem to match this ideal. The aim of evolution is purely aesthetic—it's not to do with adaptation at all. Evolution is about beauty, about achieving the most perfect form for each shape.

Only when I saw this girl did I realize how ugly our body hair is—those brows in the middle of the forehead, the eyelashes, the stubble on our heads, armpits and groin. Why on earth do we have this peculiar stigma? I think that in paradise we must have been devoid of hair. Naked and smooth.

She told me she was born in a village outside Kłodzko, into a very large family. Her father drank and died before his time. Her mother was sick, seriously so. She suffered from depression and had ended up in the hospital, drugged into a stupor. Good News coped as best she could. She had passed her final secondary-school exams with flying colors, but hadn't gone to college because she had no money, on top of which she was taking care of her siblings. She decided to earn the money for her studies, but couldn't find a job. Finally the owner of this chain of secondhand shops had taken her on, but the salary was so low she was barely able to survive on it, and from year to year her studies were further and further postponed. When there was nobody in the shop she read. I knew what books she liked, because she put them on a shelf and lent them to her customers—gloomy horror stories, Gothic novels with crumpled covers featuring a drawing of a Bat. Perverted monks, severed hands that murder people, coffins flushed out of graveyards by a flood. Evidently reading this sort of thing confirmed her in the conviction that we are not living in the worst of worlds, and taught her optimism.

When I heard Good News's account of her life, I mentally began to formulate questions that start with the words "Why don't you . . . ," followed by a description of what—in our view—one should do in this sort of situation. My lips were on the point of producing one of these impertinent "why don't yous" when I bit my tongue.

That's just what the color magazines do—just for a moment I'd wanted to be like them: they tell us what we've failed to do, where we've messed up, what we've neglected; ultimately they set us on ourselves, filling us with self-contempt.

So I didn't say a word. Other people's life stories are not a topic for debate. One should hear them out, and reciprocate in the same coin. So I told Good News about my life too, and invited her to my home to meet my Little Girls. And that's what happened.

In an effort to help her I went to the local authority, but I found out there's no support, no grants for people like Good News. The woman behind the desk advised me to arrange a bank loan, the kind you pay back once you finish your studies and start to work. There are also free computer, dress-making and flower-arranging courses. But unfortunately, only for the unemployed. So she would have to quit her job in order to go on one.

I made a trip to the bank as well, where I was given a stack of forms to complete. But there was one vital condition—Good News had to secure a place at college first. And I knew that eventually she would achieve her aim.

It's good to sit in Good News's shop. It's the coziest place in town. Mothers with children meet up here, and old ladies on their way to lunch at the pensioners' canteen. The car park security guard and frozen saleswomen from the vegetable market come here. Everyone is given something hot to drink. One could say that Good News runs a café here.

Today I was to wait for her to lock up this sanctuary, and then we'd be off to the Czech Republic with Dizzy to visit the bookshop that sells Blake. Good News was folding some bandanas. She never said much, and if she did speak, she did it quietly, so you had to listen to her very carefully. The last few customers were still browsing the clothes racks in search of a bargain. I stretched out on a chair and closed my eyes blissfully.

"Have you heard about the foxes that have been seen out on the Plateau, near where you live? Fluffy, white foxes."

I froze. Near where I live? I opened my eyes and saw the Gentleman with the Poodle.

"Apparently that rich fellow with the funny name released some from his farm," he said, standing in front of me with several pairs of trousers slung over his arm. His Poodle was looking at me, a doggy smile on its face—it clearly recognized me.

"Innerd?" I asked.

"That's the one," confirmed the man, and then addressed Good News. "Would you please find me some trousers with an eighty-centimeter waist?" Then at once he went back to his story. "They can't locate the man. He's gone missing. Vanished without trace. Like a needle in a haystack," the old gentleman went on. "He's probably run away with his lover to a warmer country. And as he was rich, he'll find it easy to hide. Apparently he was mixed up in some sort of racket."

A young man with a shaved head who'd been asking about Nike or Puma tracksuits and was now rummaging among the clothes racks responded: "It wasn't a racket, it was the mafia," he said, hardly opening his mouth at all. "They were importing furs illegally from Russia, using his farm as a cover. He hadn't settled up with the Russian mafia, so he got scared and did a runner."

I found this topic alarming. I was starting to feel afraid.

"So is your Poodle a Dog or a Bitch?" I politely asked the old gentleman, in a desperate attempt to divert the conversation onto less sinister tracks.

"My Maxy? He's a boy of course. Still a bachelor," he said, laughing. But he was clearly more interested in the local gossip, because he turned to the skinhead and continued: "He was very wealthy. He had a hotel on the main road out of Kłodzko. A delicatessen. A fox farm. A slaughterhouse and meat-processing plant. A stud farm. But how much more there was in his wife's name!"

"Here's a size eighty for you," I said, handing him a pretty good pair of gray trousers.

He examined them carefully and put on his glasses to read the laundry label.

"Oh yes, I like these, I'll take them. You know what, I like things that are trim, nice and close-fitting. They emphasize the figure."

"Well, sir, how different people can be. I always buy everything too big. It gives me freedom," I said.

DIZZY HAD RECEIVED SOME ENCOURAGING NEWS. THE LOCAL weekly, the *Kłodzko Gazette*, had offered to publish his translations of Blake in its poetry corner. He was excited and intimidated all at once. We drove along the almost deserted highway toward the border.

"First I'd like to translate his *Letters*, and only then go back to the poetry. But if they're asking for poetry . . . My God, what can I give them? What shall we give them first?"

To tell the truth, I couldn't concentrate on Blake anymore. I saw that we were passing the shabby buildings at the border crossing and entering the Czech Republic. The road here was better and Dizzy's car stopped rattling.

"Dizzy, is it true about those foxes?" Good News asked him from the backseat. "That they escaped from Innerd's farm and are going about the forest?"

Dizzy confirmed that it was.

"It happened a few days ago. At first the Police thought he'd sold all the animals to someone before disappearing. But it looks as if he let them go. Strange, isn't it?"

"Are they searching for him?" I asked.

Dizzy replied that no one had reported him missing, so there was no reason to look for him. His wife hadn't come forward, nor had his children. Maybe he'd given himself a holiday. His wife claimed it wasn't the first time it had happened. Once he'd vanished for a week, and then called from the Dominican Republic. Until the banks were after him there was no reason for alarm.

"A man's free to do what he wants with his life, until he falls foul of the banks," Dizzy sermonized with contagious certainty. I think he'd make a superb press spokesman for the Police.

Dizzy also said the Police were trying to establish the source of the money that the Commandant had under his trouser belt. It was a bribe. By now they were sure he'd been on his way back from a meeting with Innerd. It takes the Police a long time to establish things that seem obvious.

"And there's another thing," he said finally. "The weapon that must have been used to kill the Commandant had traces of animal blood on it."

WE CALLED AT THE BOOKSHOP AT THE LAST MOMENT, JUST AS IT was about to close. When silver-haired Honza handed him the two books he had ordered, I saw a blush appear on Dizzy's cheeks. Beaming with joy, he looked at us, then raised his arms, as if to give Honza a hug. They were old editions from the 1970s, properly annotated. Like gold dust. We all went home in a state of elation, and no one mentioned the sinister incidents again.

Dizzy lent me the *Selected Letters* for a few days, and as soon as I got home, I lit the stove, made myself some strong tea and started to read.

One passage particularly appealed to me, so I translated it quickly for myself on a paper bag.

"I believe my Constitution to be a good one," wrote Blake, "but it has many Peculiarities that no one but myself can know. When I was young, many places always laid me up the day after, & sometimes two or three days, with precisely the same Complaint & the same torment of the Stomach. Sir Francis Bacon would say, it is want of Discipline in Mountainous Places. Sir Francis Bacon is a Liar. No discipline will turn one Man into another, even in the least particle, & such discipline I call Presumption & Folly."

I found this captivating. I read and read, unable to stop. And perhaps it was just as the Author would have wished—everything that I read pervaded my dreams—and all Night I saw visions.

IX.

The Largest in the Smallest

A Skylark wounded in the wing,
A Cherubim does cease to sing.

Spring starts in May and is unwittingly heralded by the Dentist, who brings his ancient drilling equipment and his equally antique dental chair outside. He dusts it off with a few flicks of a cloth, one, two, three, and it's free of cobwebs and hay—both pieces of equipment spent the winter in the barn, and were only brought out from time to time when an urgent need arose. The Dentist doesn't really work in winter; it's impossible to do anything here in winter, people lose interest in their health, and besides, it's dark and his sight is poor. He needs the bright light of May or June to shine straight into the mouths of his patients, recruited from among the forest workers and moustachioed men who spend all day standing about on the little bridge in the village, and as a result are known locally as the Bridge Brigade.

Once the April mud had dried, I started to venture more and more boldly into the neighborhood on the pretext of making my rounds. At this time of year I was happy to drop in at Achthozja, the hamlet next to the quarry, where the Dentist lived. And like every year I came upon an astonishing sight—there on the brilliant green grass, under a sheet of blue sky, stood the dilapidated white dental chair, with someone half lying on it, mouth wide open to the Sun, while the Dentist leaned over him, drill in hand. Meanwhile his foot was moving monotonously, steadily pressing on the drill pedal. And a few meters away another two or three fellows were watching this scene in rapt silence as they sipped their beer.

The Dentist's main occupation was pulling out aching teeth, and sometimes, more rarely, treating them. He also made dentures. Before I knew of his existence, I had very often wondered what sort of a race could have settled here, in this area. Many of the local people had quite distinctive teeth, as if they were all a family, with the same genes or the same configuration in their Horoscope. Especially the older ones: their teeth were long and narrow, with a blue tinge. Strange teeth. I came up with an alternative Hypothesis too, for I had heard that under the Plateau there were deep seams of uranium which, as everyone knows, has an effect on various Anomalies.

By now I knew that these were the Dentist's false teeth, his trademark, his brand. Like every artist he was unique.

In my view he could have been a tourist attraction for Kłodzko Valley, if only what he did were legal. Unfortunately, some years ago he was stripped of his license to practice his profession because of alcohol abuse. It's odd that they don't take away a dentist's professional license because of poor sight. This Ailment could be far more dangerous for the patient. And the Dentist wore powerful spectacles, with one of the lenses taped into place.

That day he was drilling a man's tooth. It was hard to recognize the patient's facial features, twisted in pain and mildly numbed by alcohol, with which the Dentist anesthetized his patients. The dreadful noise of the drill bored into my brain, stirring the ghastliest childhood memories.

"How's life?" I said in greeting.

"Bearable," replied the Dentist with a broad smile, which reminded me of the old adage "Physician, heal thyself." "You haven't been here for ages. I think the last time we met was when you were looking for your . . ."

"Yes, yes," I interrupted him. "It was impossible to walk this far in the winter. By the time I'd dug myself out of the snow it would be dark."

He went back to his drilling and I stood with the other onlookers, pensively watching the drill working in the man's mouth.

"Have you seen the white foxes?" one of the men asked me. He had a beautiful face. If his life had turned out differently I'm sure he'd have been a film star. But now his good looks were disappearing beneath a network of furrows and wrinkles.

"They say Innerd let them out before he ran off," said a second man.

"Maybe he had pangs of conscience," I added. "Maybe the Foxes ate him."

The Dentist glanced at me with curiosity. He nodded and sank the drill into the patient's tooth. The poor man jolted in the chair.

"Isn't it possible to fill a tooth without all that drilling?" I asked.

But no one seemed particularly concerned about the patient.

"First Big Foot, then the Commandant, now Innerd . . ." sighed the Beautiful Man. "A man's afraid to leave the house. After dark I tell my old woman to deal with everything outside the house."

"You've found an intelligent solution," I said, and then slowly added: "Animals are taking revenge on them for hunting."

"You must be joking . . . Big Foot didn't hunt," said the Beautiful Man doubtfully.

"But he was a beater," said someone else. "Mrs. Duszejko's right. And he was the biggest poacher around here, wasn't he?"

The Dentist smeared a bit of white paste onto a little plate and put it into the drilled tooth with a spatula.

"Yes, it's possible," he muttered to himself. "It really is possible, there has to be some justice, doesn't there? Yes, yes. Animals."

The patient moaned pitifully.

"Do you believe in divine providence?" the Dentist suddenly asked me, coming to a standstill over the patient. There was a note of provocation in his voice.

The men sniggered, as if they had heard something improper. I had to think about it.

"Because I do," he said, without waiting for an answer. He gave the patient a friendly clap on the shoulder, and the man leaped from the chair, happy. "Next," he said. One of the group of onlookers stepped forward and reluctantly sat in the chair.

"What's up?" asked the Dentist.

In reply the man opened his mouth, and the Dentist peeked into it. He instantly recoiled, saying: "What the fuck!" which must have been the shortest possible assessment of the state of the patient's dentition. For a while he prodded with his fingers to check how secure the man's teeth were, and then reached behind him for a bottle of vodka.

"Here, drink up. We'll pull it out."

The man mumbled something indistinct, utterly disheartened by this unwelcome verdict. He accepted the near-full tumbler of vodka proffered by the Dentist and downed it in one. I was sure he wouldn't feel any pain after that much anesthetic.

While we were waiting for the alcohol to take effect, the men excitedly began to talk about the quarry, which apparently is going to be reopened. Year by year it will swallow the Plateau, until it has devoured the whole thing. We'll have to move away from here. If they do actually reopen it, the Dentist's hamlet will be the first to be relocated.

"No, I don't believe in divine providence," I said. "Form a protest committee," I advised them. "Organize a demonstration."

"*Après nous le déluge*," said the Dentist, sticking his fingers into the mouth of his patient, barely conscious by now. Then with ease, without effort, he extracted a blackened tooth. All we heard was a slight crack. It made me feel faint.

"They should take revenge for all of it," said the Dentist. "Animals should fuck it all to buggery."

"Quite so. Sodding well screw it into oblivion," I followed his lead, and the men glanced at me with surprise and respect.

I went home by a roundabout route; by now it was well into the afternoon. And that was when at the edge of the forest I saw the white Foxes, two of them. They were moving slowly, one behind the other. Their whiteness against the green meadow was like something from another world. They looked like the diplomatic service of the Animal Kingdom, come here to reconnoiter.

————

At the start of May the dandelions flowered. In a good year they were already in bloom on the holiday weekend, when the owners arrived at their houses for the first time after the winter. In a less good year they didn't carpet the meadows in yellow spots until Victory Day, on the eighth. Every year, Dizzy and I admired this miracle of miracles.

Unfortunately, for Dizzy it was a harbinger of tough times; two weeks later his various allergies would hit him—tears streamed from his eyes, he choked and suffocated. In town it was just about bearable, but on Fridays when he came to see me I was obliged to shut all the doors and windows tight to stop the invisible allergens from getting inside his nose. In June, when the grasses were flowering, we had to move our translation sessions to his place in town.

After such a long, tiring, barren winter the Sun was having an exceptionally bad effect on me too. I couldn't sleep in the mornings, I'd get up at dawn and never stop feeling anxious. All winter I'd had to defend myself against the wind eternally blowing on the Plateau, but now I threw the windows and doors wide open to let it come inside and blow away my musty anxieties and every possible Ailment.

Everything was starting to crackle, I could sense a feverish vibration under the grass, under the layer of earth, as if vast, underground nerves, swollen with effort, were just about to burst. I was finding it hard to rid myself of the feeling that under it all lurked a strong, mindless will, as repulsive as the force that made the Frogs climb on top of each other and endlessly copulate in Oddball's pond.

As soon as the Sun came close to the horizon, a family of Bats began to make regular appearances. They'd fly in noiselessly, softly; I always thought of their flight as being fluid. Once I counted twelve of them, as they flew around each house in turn. I'd love to know how a Bat sees the world; just once I'd like to fly across the Plateau in its body. How do we all look down here, as perceived by its senses? Like shadows? Like bundles of shudders, sources of noise?

Toward evening I would sit outside and wait for them to appear, to fly in one by one from over the Professor's house, as they visited each of us in turn. I gently waved to them in greeting. The truth is I had a lot in common with them—I too saw the world in other spheres, upside down. I too preferred the Dusk. I wasn't suited to living in the Sunlight.

My skin reacted badly to the cruel, harsh rays, not yet tempered by any leaves or fluffy clouds. It became red and irritated. As every year, in the first few days of summer small, itchy blisters began to appear on it. I treated them with sour milk and the burn ointment that Dizzy gave me. I had to fetch out last year's wide-brimmed hats, which I secured under my chin with ribbons to stop the wind from tearing them off.

One Wednesday when I was coming home from school in one of these hats I took a roundabout route in order to . . . in fact, I don't really know why I took the detour. There are places we don't choose to visit, and yet something draws us to them. Possibly that something is Dread. Maybe that's why, just like Good News, I like horror stories too.

By some strange chance, that Wednesday I found myself near the Fox farm. I was driving home in the Samurai when suddenly at the crossroads I turned in the opposite direction from my usual route. Soon after, the asphalt came to an end, and at this point I could smell the dreadful stench that scared away anyone out for a walk. The nasty smell was still here, though officially the farm had closed down two weeks ago.

The Samurai was behaving as if it had a sense of smell too—it stalled. I sat in the car, assaulted by the stink, and a hundred meters ahead I saw some buildings surrounded by a high wire fence—some barracks lined up one behind the other. Along the top of the fence ran triple-strand barbed wire. The Sun was dazzlingly bright. Each blade of grass cast a sharp shadow, each branch resembled a skewer. It was as silent as the grave. I pricked up my ears, as if expecting to hear horrifying sounds coming from behind this barricade, the echoes of what had happened here in the past. But it was plain to see there wasn't a living soul inside, neither human nor animal. In the course of the summer the farm would be overgrown with burdock and nettles. In a year or two it would vanish among the greenery, at best becoming a house of horror. It crossed my mind that one could set up a museum here. As a warning.

A little later I started the car and drove back to the main road.

Oh yes, I knew what the missing owner looked like. Not long after I moved here I met him on our little bridge. It was a strange encounter. I didn't yet know who he was.

That afternoon I was on my way home in the Samurai from shopping in town. Ahead of the bridge across our stream I saw a four-by-four; it had driven onto the shoulder, as if it had suddenly felt the urge to stretch its bones: all its doors were open. I slowed down. I don't like those high, powerful cars, made with war in mind, rather than walks in the lap of nature. Their large wheels churn up the ruts in the dirt roads and damage the footpaths. Their mighty engines make a lot of noise and produce exhaust fumes. I am convinced that their owners have small dicks and compensate for this deficiency by having large cars. Every year I protest to the village representative against the rallies held in these dreadful vehicles, and I issue a petition. I get a perfunctory reply, saying that the representative will consider my comments in due course, and that's the end of it. But now one of them was parked here, right by the stream, at the way into the valley, almost on my doorstep. Driving very slowly indeed, I scrutinized this undesirable guest.

There was a pretty young woman sitting in the front seat, smoking a cigarette. She had peroxide-blond shoulder-length hair and carefully applied makeup, a notable feature of which were lips outlined with a dark pencil. She had such a deep tan that she looked as if she'd just been removed from the barbecue. Her toenails were painted red. She was dangling her legs outside the car, and a sandal had slipped off one of her feet and fallen into the grass. I stopped and leaned out of the window.

"Need any help?" I asked amicably.

She shook her head to say no, then raised her eyes skyward and pointed her thumb somewhere behind her; at the same time she smiled knowingly. She seemed perfectly nice, though I couldn't understand her gesture. So I got out of the car. The fact that she had answered with a gesture, rather than words, prompted me to act quietly; I approached her almost on tiptoes. I raised my brows inquiringly. I liked this air of mystery.

"No worries," she said in a whisper. "I'm waiting for my . . . husband."

For her husband? Here? I simply couldn't understand the scene in which I too was accidentally taking part. I looked around suspiciously and then I saw him, this husband. He was coming out of the bushes. He looked rather weird and comical. He was dressed in something like a uniform, in green-and-brown camouflage. From head to toe he had spruce twigs stuck all over him. His helmet was covered with the same fabric as the uniform.

His face was smeared in black paint, with a white, neatly trimmed moustache standing out against it. I couldn't see his eyes—they were hidden behind an unusual optical device, a bit like an optician's instrument for testing sight defects, with lots of screws and joints. Whereas his broad chest and ample belly were festooned in mess tins, map cases, compass sets and a bullet belt. He was holding a shotgun with a scope; it looked like a weapon out of *Star Wars*.

"Holy Mother of God," I gasped in spite of myself.

For a few seconds I couldn't produce any human sound. I gazed at this freak, feeling frightened and amazed, until the woman flicked her cigarette into the road and said in a rather ironic tone: "And here he is."

The man came up to us and took off his helmet.

I don't think I had ever seen a Person with such a saturnine look before. He was of average build, with a wide forehead and bushy eyebrows. He stooped slightly and stood with his feet pointing inward. I couldn't help thinking he was inured to debauchery and that throughout his life he had been led by one thing—the consistent gratification of his own desires, at any cost. This was the richest man in the neighborhood.

I sensed that he was pleased to be seen by someone other than his wife. He was proud of himself. He greeted me with a wave of the hand, but instantly ignored my existence. He put the helmet and the bizarre spectacles on again and gazed in the direction of the border. At once I understood everything and felt a surge of Anger.

"Let's get going," said his wife impatiently, as if to a child. Perhaps she could sense the waves of Anger emanating from me.

For a while he pretended not to hear, but then he went up to the car, removed all the tackle from his head, and set aside the shotgun.

"What are you doing here?" I asked him, for nothing else occurred to me.

"What about you?" he said, without looking at me.

His wife was putting on her sandal and settling in the driver's seat.

"I live here," I replied coldly.

"Ah, you're the lady with those two dogs . . . We've told you before to keep them close to the house."

"They're on private land . . ." I began, but he interrupted me. The whites of his eyes gleamed ominously in his blackened face.

"For us there's no such thing as private land, madam."

THAT WAS TWO YEARS AGO, WHEN I WAS STILL FINDING THINGS easier. I had forgotten about this encounter with Innerd. What did he matter? But later on, a fast-moving planet had suddenly crossed an invisible point and a change had occurred, one of the kind we're not aware of down here. Perhaps tiny signs reveal this sort of cosmic event to us, but we don't notice them either—someone has stepped on a twig lying on the path, a bottle of beer has cracked in the freezer when someone forgot to remove it in time, or two red fruits have fallen from a wild rose bush. How could we possibly understand it all?

It's clear that the largest things are contained in the smallest.

There can be no doubt about it. At this very moment, as I write, there's a planetary configuration on this table, the entire Cosmos if you like: a thermometer, a coin, an aluminum spoon and a porcelain cup. A key, a cell phone, a piece of paper and a pen. And one of my gray hairs, whose atoms preserve the memory of the origins of life, of the cosmic Catastrophe that gave the world its beginning.

X.

Cucujus Haematodes

Kill not the Moth nor Butterfly
For the Last Judgment draweth nigh.

By early June the houses were inhabited, at the weekends at least, but I was still taking my duties quite seriously. For instance, at least once a day I'd go up the hill and conduct my usual surveillance through binoculars. First I'd monitor the houses, of course. In a sense, houses are living creatures that coexist with Man in exemplary symbiosis. My heart swelled with joy, for now it was plain to see that their symbionts had returned. They had filled the empty interiors with their comings and goings, the warmth of their own bodies, their thoughts. Their dainty hands were mending all the little cuts and bruises left by the winter, drying out the damp walls, washing the windows and fixing the ballcocks. Now the houses looked as if they had awoken from the deep sleep into which material sinks when it's not disturbed. Plastic tables and chairs had already been carried into the front yards, the wooden shutters had been opened, and finally the

Sunlight could get inside. At the weekends smoke rose from the chimneys. The Professor and his wife appeared more and more often, always in the company of friends. They'd walk along the road—they never ventured onto the field boundaries. They went on a daily postprandial walk to the chapel and back, stopping on the road, deep in conversation. Occasionally, when the wind was blowing from their direction, the odd word would reach me: Canaletto, chiaroscuro, tenebrism.

Every Friday the Wellers started to show up too. In unison, they set about tearing up the plants that had been growing around their house until now, in order to plant others that they'd bought at a shop. It was hard to tell what logic was driving them, why they didn't like elderberry, but preferred wisteria in its place. One time, standing on tiptoes to look at them over their enormous fence, I told them the wisteria probably wouldn't survive the February frosts here, but they just smiled, nodded and went on doing their thing. They cut down a beautiful wild rose and ripped up some clumps of thyme. They arranged some stones to build a fanciful mound in front of the house, and planted it with conifers, as they put it: ornamental cedars, creeping pine, dwarf cypresses and firs. Utterly pointless, to my mind.

The Gray Lady was coming for longer stays by now, and I'd see her walking along the field boundaries at a slow pace, stiff as a post. One evening I went to her house with the keys and the repair bills. She offered me some herbal tea. To be polite, I drank it. Once we had finished settling the accounts, I dared to ask a question.

"If I wanted to write my memoirs, how would I go about it?" I said, sounding confused.

"You must sit at the table and force yourself to write. It'll come of its own accord. You mustn't censor yourself. You must write down everything that comes into your head."

Strange advice. I wouldn't want to write down "everything." I'd only like to write down the things that I find good and positive. I thought she was going to say more, but she didn't. I felt disappointed.

"Disappointed?" she asked, as if she could read my thoughts.

"Yes."

"When one can't speak, one should write," she said. "It helps a lot," she added, and fell silent. The wind grew stronger, and now we could see the trees outside swaying steadily to the rhythm of inaudible music, like the audience at a concert in an amphitheater. Upstairs a draft slammed a door shut. As if someone had fired a shot. The Gray Lady shuddered.

"Those noises upset me—it's as if everything here were alive!"

"The wind always makes that noise. I've grown used to it," I said.

I asked her what sort of books she wrote, and she replied horror stories. That pleased me. I must definitely introduce her to Good News, they're sure to find plenty to talk about. They're links in the same chain. Anyone who's capable of writing things like that must be a courageous Person.

"And does evil always have to be punished at the end?" I asked.

"I don't care about that. I'm not concerned with punishment. I just like to write about frightening things. Maybe because I'm so fearful myself. It does me good."

"What happened to you?" I asked, emboldened by the falling Dusk, and pointed at the orthopedic collar around her neck.

"Degeneration of the cervical vertebrae," she said impassively, as if telling me about a broken domestic appliance. "Evidently my head is too heavy. That's how it seems to me. My head's too heavy. My vertebrae can't hold up the weight of it, so crunch, crunch, they degenerate."

She smiled and poured me some more of the awful tea.

"Don't you feel lonely here?" she asked.

"Sometimes."

"I admire you. I wish I were like you. You're brave."

"Oh no, I'm not in the least brave. It's a good thing I have something to do here."

"I feel uneasy without Agata too. The world here is so large, so impossible to take in," she said, fixing her gaze on me for a few seconds, testing me. "Agata is my wife."

I blinked. I had never heard one woman referring to another as "my wife" before. But I liked it.

"You're surprised, aren't you?"

I thought for a while.

"I could have a wife too," I said with conviction. "It's better to live with someone than alone. It's easier to go through life together than on one's own."

She didn't respond. It was difficult to talk to her. Finally I asked her to lend me her book. The most frightening one. She promised she'd ask Agata to bring it. Dusk was falling, but she didn't put on the light. Once we were both plunged in darkness, I said good-bye and went home.

— ✖ —

Now, confident that the houses were back in the care of their owners, I enjoyed going on longer and longer walks, though I still called these expeditions my rounds. I was widening my estates, like a solitary

She-Wolf. I was thankful to leave behind the views of the houses and the road. I would go into the forest—I could wander around it endlessly. Here things were quieter, the forest was like a vast, deep, welcoming refuge in which one could hide. It lulled my mind. Here I didn't have to conceal the most troublesome of my Ailments—the fact that I weep. Here my tears could flow, bathing my eyes and improving my sight. Maybe that's why I could see more than people with dry eyes.

First I noticed the lack of Deer—they had vanished. Or perhaps the grass was so high that it hid their perfect red backs? What it actually meant was that the Deer had already started to calve.

On the same day when I first came upon a Young Lady with a beautiful spotted Fawn, I saw a man in the forest. At quite close range, though he did not see me. He had a backpack with him, green with an external frame, like the ones they used to make in the 1970s, so it occurred to me that the man must be of a similar age to me. And to tell the truth he looked it too—old. He was bald, and his face was covered in gray stubble, trimmed short, probably with one of those cheap Chinese clippers bought at the street market. His oversized, faded jeans bulged unattractively on the buttocks.

This man was moving down the road that ran along the forest, cautiously, gazing underfoot. That was probably why he let me come so close. When he reached the intersection, where felled pine trunks were stacked, he took off his pack, leaned it against a tree, and went into the forest. My binoculars showed me a wobbly, out-of-focus image, so I could only guess what he was doing there. I did see him leaning down to the forest floor and rummaging in the pine needles. One might have thought he was a mushroom picker, but it was too early for mushrooms. I watched him for about an hour. He sat on the grass, ate sandwiches and wrote something in a notebook. For thirty minutes or so he lay on his back with his arms folded behind his head and stared into the sky. Then he took the backpack and disappeared into the greenery.

FROM THE SCHOOL I CALLED DIZZY TO TELL HIM THIS NEWS— that I'd seen a stranger roaming about in the forest. I also told him what people were saying at Good News's shop, which was that the Commandant was mixed up in the illegal transportation of terrorists across the border. Some suspicious types had been caught not far from here. But Dizzy reacted rather skeptically to these revelations. And refused to be persuaded that the stranger could be wandering about the forest in order to erase potential evidence. Maybe a weapon was hidden there?

"I don't want to worry you, but the investigation is probably going to be shelved, because nothing has been found that could cast new light."

"What do you mean? What about the Animal prints around the site? It was the Deer that pushed him down the well."

There was silence, and then Dizzy asked: "Why do you keep telling everyone about those Animals? No one believes you anyway, and they take you for a bit of a . . . a . . ." he faltered.

"A nutter, right?" I said to help him.

"Well, yes. Why do you keep going on about it? You know perfectly well it's impossible," said Dizzy, and it occurred to me that I really would have to explain it to them clearly.

I was outraged. But when the bell rang for lessons, I quickly said:

"One has to tell people what to think. There's no alternative. Otherwise someone else will do it."

I didn't sleep too well that Night, knowing that a stranger was lurking so close to the house. But the news of the potential closure of the investigation prompted stressful, disagreeable anxiety too. How could it be "shelved"? Just like that? Without checking all the possibilities? And what about those prints? Had they taken them into consideration? After all, a Person had died. How could they "shelve" it, for goodness' sake?

For the first time since moving here I locked the door and windows. At once the house felt stuffy. I couldn't get to sleep. It was early June, so the Nights were already warm and scented. I felt as if I had been locked for life in the boiler room. I listened out for footsteps around the house, analyzed every rustle, and jumped at every snap of a twig. The Night magnified the subtlest sounds, changed them into grunts, groans, voices. I think I was terrified. For the first time since coming to live here.

The next morning I saw the same man with the backpack standing outside my house. At first I was paralyzed by fear and started reaching a hand into the secret closet for the pepper spray.

"Good morning. Excuse me for disturbing you," he said in a low baritone, which set the air quivering. "I'd like to buy some milk from the cow."

"From the Cow?" I said in amazement. "I don't have milk from a

Cow, only from the Froggy, will that do?" The Froggy was the name of the village grocery store.

He was disappointed.

Now, in the daylight, he looked perfectly agreeable. I wouldn't have to use my spray. He had a white linen shirt with a mandarin collar, the sort people wore in the good old days. Close up it was also plain to see that he wasn't bald after all. He still had some hair left at the back of his head, and he'd plaited it into a skinny little pigtail, which looked like a grubby shoelace.

"Do you bake your own bread?"

"No," I replied in surprise. "I buy that in the shop down the hill too."

"Aha. Good, all right."

I was already on my way to the kitchen, but I turned round to inform him: "I saw you yesterday. Did you sleep in the forest?"

"Yes, I did. May I sit here a while? My bones are rather stiff."

He seemed distracted. The back of his shirt was green with grass stains. He must have slipped out of his sleeping bag. I giggled to myself.

"Would you like a cup of coffee?"

He flapped his hands.

"I don't drink coffee."

Plainly he wasn't very bright. If he were, he'd have known that I wasn't interested in his culinary likes and dislikes.

"Then maybe you'd like a piece of cake," I said, pointing to the table, which Dizzy and I had recently brought outside. There was a rhubarb tart on it, which I had baked the day before yesterday and had almost entirely eaten.

"May I please use the bathroom?" he asked as if we were bargaining.

"Of course," I said, letting him into the house ahead of me.

He drank some tea and ate a slice of tart. He was called Borys Sznajder, but he pronounced his first name funnily, stretching the vowels: "Boorooos." And for me, that name stuck. He had a soft, eastern accent, and his next few remarks explained its origin—he was from Białystok.

"I'm an entomologist," he said with his mouth full of cake. "I'm studying a particular species of flat bark beetle, endangered, rare and beautiful. Do you know that you live at the southernmost site in Europe where *Cucujus haematodes* is found?"

I was not aware of this. Frankly, I was pleased—it was as if a new family member had come to join us here.

"What does it look like?" I asked.

Boros reached into a tatty canvas knapsack and carefully extracted a small plastic box. He shoved it under my nose.

"Like this."

Inside the transparent box lay a dead Bug, that's what I'd have called it—a Bug. Small, brown, quite average-looking. I had sometimes seen very beautiful Bugs. This one was not exceptional in any way.

"Why is it dead?" I asked.

"Please don't think I'm one of those amateurs who kill insects just to make them into specimens. It was dead when I found it."

I cast a glance at Boros and tried to guess what his particular illness was.

He searched dead tree stumps and logs, whether they'd been felled or were rotting naturally, looking for *Cucujus* larvae. He counted and cataloged the larvae, and wrote down the results in a notebook entitled: "Distribution in the Kłodzko County Forests of selected species of saproxylic beetle, as featured on the lists of annexes II and IV of the European Union Habitat Directive, and proposals for their protection. A project." I read the title very carefully, which saved me from having to look inside.

Just imagine, he told me, the State Forests are totally unaware of the fact that article 12 of the Directive obliges member states to establish a rigorous system to protect reproduction habitats and prevent their destruction. But they were allowing the removal from the forest of timber in which the Insects were laying their eggs, from which the larvae would later hatch. The larvae were ending up at sawmills and wood-processing plants. There was nothing left of them. They were dying, but no one was taking any notice. So it was as if no one were to blame.

"Here, in this forest, every log is full of *Cucujus* larvae," he said. "When the forest is cleared some of the branches are burned. So they're throwing branches full of larvae onto the fire."

It occurred to me that every unjustly inflicted death deserved public exposure. Even an Insect's. A death that nobody noticed was twice as scandalous. And I liked what Boros was doing. Oh yes, he convinced me, I was entirely on his side.

As I had to go on my daily round anyway, I decided to combine the useful with the interesting, and went into the forest with Boros. With his help, the tree trunks revealed their secrets to me. The most ordinary stumps turned out to be entire kingdoms of Creatures that bored corridors, chambers and passages, and laid their precious eggs there. The larvae may not have been beautiful, but I was moved by their sense of trust—they entrusted their lives to the trees, without imagining that these huge, immobile Creatures are essentially very fragile, and wholly dependent on the will of people too. It was hard to think of the larvae perishing in fires. Boros scooped up the forest litter to show me other rare and less rare species: the Hermit Beetle, the Deathwatch Beetle—who'd have thought it was sitting here, under a flake of bark? The Golden Ground Beetle—ah, so that's what it's called; I had seen it so many times before, and always thought of it as shiny but nameless. The Clown Beetle, like a lovely drop of mercury. The Lesser Stag Beetle. A curious name. The names of Insects should be given to children. So should the names of Birds and other Animals. Cockchafer Kowalski. Drosophila Nowak. Corvus Duszejko. Those are just a few of the names I could remember. Boros's hands did conjuring tricks, drew mysterious signs, and lo and behold, an Insect appeared, a larva, or some tiny eggs laid in a cluster. When I asked which of them are useful, Boros was outraged.

"From nature's point of view no creatures are useful or not useful. That's just a foolish distinction applied by people."

He came by that evening, after Dusk, because I had invited him to stay the night. As he had nowhere to sleep . . . I made up a bed for him in the dayroom, but we sat and talked a while longer. I fetched out half a bottle of liqueur left over from Oddball's visit. Once Boros had told me about all the abuses and vile acts committed by the State Forests, he finally relaxed a bit. I found it hard to understand him, for how can one have such a very emotional attitude to something called the State Forests? The only person whom I associated with this institution was the forester, Wolf Eye. That's what I called him because he seemed to have oblong pupils. He was a decent Person, too.

———————

AND SO BOROS SETTLED IN AT MY HOUSE FOR A GOOD FEW DAYS. Each night he announced that his students or volunteers from Action against the SF were coming to fetch him in the morning, but every day there was a new problem: either their car had broken down, or they'd had to go somewhere on urgent business, or they'd stopped off in Warsaw on the way, and once they'd even lost a bag full of documents. And so on. I was starting to worry that Boros was going to infest my house, like a *Cucujus* larva in a spruce log, and only the State Forests would be capable of smoking him out. Though I could tell he was trying hard not to be a nuisance, and was actually being helpful. For instance, he cleaned the bathroom from top to bottom with great care.

In his backpack he had a miniature laboratory, including a box full of small flasks and bottles, apparently containing some chemical Substances which, though synthetic, were deceptively similar to natural insect pheromones. He and his students had been doing experiments with these potent chemical agents, to be able in case of need to induce the Insects to reproduce in a different place.

"If you smear this substance on a piece of wood, the female beetles will rush there to lay their eggs. They'll come running to this particular log from all over the area—they can smell it from several kilometers away. All it takes is a few drops."

"Why don't people smell like that?" I asked.

"Who told you that they don't?"

"I can't smell anything."

"Maybe you don't know you can, my dear, and in your human pride you persist in believing in your free will."

Boros's presence reminded me what it's like to live with someone. And how very awkward it is. How much it diverts you from your own thoughts and distracts you. How another Person starts to irritate you without actually doing anything annoying, but simply by being there. Each morning when he went off to the forest, I blessed my glorious solitude. How do people manage to spend decades living together in a small space? I wondered. How can they possibly sleep in the same bed together, breathing on and jostling each other accidentally in their sleep? I'm not saying it hasn't happened to me too. For some time I shared my bed with a Catholic, and nothing good came of it.

XI.

The Singing of Bats

A Robin Red breast in a Cage
Puts all Heaven in a Rage.

To the Police,

I feel obliged to write this letter, in view of my concern at
the lack of progress by the local Police in their inquiry into
the death of my neighbor in January of this year, and the
subsequent death of the Commandant six weeks later.

As both of these grievous incidents happened in my
immediate neighborhood, you will find it no surprise that
I feel personally Saddened and Disturbed by them.

It is my belief that there are many obvious pieces of
evidence to imply that they were Murdered.

I would never venture to make such an extreme claim if
not for the fact (and I realize that for the Police facts are

what bricks are for a house, or cells for an organism—they build the entire system) that together with my Friends I was a witness, not to the actual death, but to the situation immediately after the death, before the Police arrived. In the first case my fellow witness was my neighbor, Świerszczyński, and in the second it was my former pupil, Dionizy.

My conviction that the Deceased were the victims of Murder is based on two kinds of observation.

Firstly: in both instances Animals were present at the scene of the Crime. In the first case, both the witness Świerszczyński and I saw a group of Deer near Big Foot's house (while their companion lay butchered in the victim's kitchen). As for the case of the Commandant, the witnesses, including the undersigned, saw numerous deer hoofprints on the snow around the well where his body was found. Unfortunately, weather unfavorable to the Police caused the rapid obliteration of this most important and unusual piece of evidence that points us straight toward the perpetrators of both crimes.

Secondly: I decided to examine certain highly distinctive pieces of information to be gained from the victims' cosmograms (commonly known as Horoscopes), and in both cases it appears obvious that they may have been fatally attacked by Animals. This is a very rare configuration of the planets, and thus I have great confidence in commending it to the attention of the Police. I am taking the liberty of enclosing both Horoscopes, in the expectation

that the police Astrologer will consult them, and then
support my Hypothesis.

Yours sincerely,
Duszejko

—✕—

Boros had been staying with me for three or four days when I saw
Oddball trudging over to my house, yet another special event considering he never came to see me. I thought he may have been slightly
put out by the presence of a strange man in my house and had come
to investigate. He shuffled along bent double, resting a hand on the
small of his back and wearing a pained look on his face. He sat down
with a sigh.

"Lumbago," he said by way of greeting.

It turned out that while building a new, dry path to his house
from the courtyard he had mixed the concrete in buckets and had
been on the point of pouring it, but when he'd leaned to pick up
the bucket something had cracked in his spine. So he'd been stuck
in the most uncomfortable position with a hand stretched out toward the bucket, for the pain wouldn't let him straighten up at all.
Now that it had eased a bit, he'd come to ask for my help as he was
aware that I knew all about construction—last year he'd seen me
pouring concrete in a similar way. He cast a very critical glance at

Boros, especially at his pigtail, which he must have found highly pretentious.

I introduced them to each other. Oddball offered his hand with noticeable hesitation.

"It's dangerous to wander the neighborhood—there are strange things going on around here," he said ominously, but Boros ignored this warning.

So we went to save the concrete from solidifying in the buckets. Boros and I worked while Oddball sat on a chair and gave us orders disguised as advice, starting each remark with the words "I'd advise you to . . ."

"I'd advise you to pour a little at a time, now here, now there, topping it up once it evens out. I'd advise you to wait a while until it settles. I'd advise you not to get in each other's way or you'll have confusion."

It was rather annoying. But once the work was done, we sat down in a warm patch of Sunlight outside his house where the peonies were slowly coming into bloom, and the whole world seemed covered in a fine layer of gold leaf.

"What have you done in life?" Boros suddenly asked.

This question was so unexpected that I instantly let myself be carried away by memories. They began to sail past my eyes, and typically for memories, everything in them seemed better, finer, and happier than in reality. It's strange, but we didn't say a word.

For people of my age, the places that they truly loved and to which they once belonged are no longer there. The places of their childhood and youth have ceased to exist, the villages where they went on holiday, the parks with uncomfortable benches where their first loves blossomed, the cities, cafés and houses of their past. And if their outer form has been preserved, it's all the more painful, like a shell with nothing inside it anymore. I have nowhere to return to. It's like a state of imprisonment. The walls of the cell are the horizon of what I can see. Beyond them exists a world that's alien to me and doesn't belong to me. So for people like me the only thing possible is here and now, for every future is doubtful, everything yet to come is barely sketched and uncertain, like a mirage that can be destroyed by the slightest twitch of the air. That's what was going through my mind as we sat there in silence. It was better than a conversation. I have no idea what either of the men was thinking about. Perhaps about the same thing.

But we did agree to meet that evening, when we drank a little wine together. We even managed to have a singsong. We started with "Today I cannot come to see you . . . ," but softly and shyly, as if beyond the windows opening onto the orchard the large ears of the Night were lurking, ready to eavesdrop on our every thought, our every word, even the words of the song, and then submit them to the scrutiny of the highest court.

Only Boros wasn't bothered. It's understandable—he wasn't at home, and guest performances are always among the craziest. He leaned back in his chair, pretending to be playing a guitar, and started to sing with his eyes closed:

"*Dere eeez a hooouse in Noo Orleeenz, dey caaal de Riiisin' Sun . . .*"

As if under a magic spell, Oddball and I picked up the words and tune, and exchanging glances, surprised by this sudden mutual agreement, sang along with him.

It turned out we all knew the words more or less up to the line "*Oh mother, tell your children,*" which says a lot for our memories. At that point we started to mumble, pretending to know what we were singing. But we didn't. We burst out laughing. Oh, it was lovely, touching. Then we sat in silence, doing our best to remember other songs. I don't know about the other singers, but my entire songbook flew straight out of my head. Then Boros went indoors to fetch a little plastic bag from which he took a pinch of dried herbs, and started to roll a cigarette with them.

"Good heavens, I haven't smoked for twenty years," said Oddball suddenly, and his eyes lit up; I looked at him in amazement.

It was a very bright Night. The full moon in June is called the Blue Moon, because it takes on a very beautiful sapphire shade at this time of year. According to my Ephemerides, this Night only lasts for five hours.

We were sitting in the orchard under an old apple tree on which the apples were already fruiting. The orchard was fragrant and soughed in the wind. I had lost my sense of time, and each break between utterances seemed endless. A great gulf of time opened before us. We chattered for whole centuries, talking nonstop about the same thing over and over, now with one pair of lips, now with another, all of us failing to remember that the view we were now contesting was the one we had defended earlier on. But in fact we weren't arguing at all; we were holding a dialogue, a trialogue, like three fauns, another species, half human and half animal. And I realized there were lots of us in the garden and the forest, our faces covered in hair. Strange beasts. And our Bats had settled in the tree and were singing. Their shrill, vibrating voices were jostling microscopic particles of mist, so the Night around us was softly starting to jingle, summoning all the Creatures to nocturnal worship.

Boros disappeared into the house for an eternity, while Oddball and I sat without a word. His eyes were wide open and he was staring at me so intensely that I had to slip into the shadow of the tree to escape his gaze. And there I hid.

"Forgive me," was all he said, and my mind moved like a great locomotive trying to understand it. What on earth would I have to forgive him for? I thought about the times when he hadn't responded to my greeting. Or the day he'd talked to me across the threshold when I'd brought him his post, but refused to let me inside, into his lovely, spick-and-span kitchen. Another thought was that he'd never taken any interest in me when I was laid up in bed by my Ailments, breathing my last.

But why would I have to forgive him for any of these things? Maybe he was thinking of his cold, ironic son in the black coat. But we're not answerable for our children, are we?

Finally Boros appeared in the doorway with my laptop, which he'd been using before now anyway, and plugged in his pendant, shaped like a wolf's fang. For a very long time there was total silence, while we waited for a sign. Finally we heard a storm, but it didn't frighten or surprise us. It dominated the sound of bells ringing in the mist. No other music could have suited the mood better—it must have been composed specially for this evening.

"*Riders on the storm,*" the words echoed out of nowhere.

Boros hummed and rocked in his chair, while the first five lines of the song repeated over and over again, the same ones every time, never any others.

"Why are some people evil and nasty?" asked Boros rhetorically.

"Saturn," I said. "The traditional ancient Astrology of Ptolemy tells us it's down to Saturn. In its discordant aspects Saturn has the power to make people mean-spirited, spiteful, solitary and plaintive. They're malicious, cowardly, shameless and sullen, they never stop scheming, they speak evil, and they don't take care of their bodies. They endlessly want more than they have, and nothing ever pleases them. Is that the sort of people you mean?"

"It could be the result of mistakes in their upbringing," added Oddball, enunciating each word slowly and carefully, as if afraid his tongue was about to play tricks on him and say something else entirely. Once he had managed to utter this one sentence, he dared to add another: "Or class war."

"Or poor potty training," added Boros, and I said: "A toxic mother."

"An authoritarian father."

"Sexual abuse in childhood."

"Not being breastfed."

"Television."

"A lack of lithium and magnesium in the diet."

"The stock exchange," shouted Oddball, with incredible enthusiasm, but to my mind he was exaggerating.

"No, don't be silly," I said. "In what way?"

So he corrected himself: "Post-traumatic shock."

"Psychophysical structure."

We tossed around ideas until we ran out of them, a game we found highly amusing.

"But it is Saturn," I said, dying of laughter.

WE WALKED ODDBALL BACK TO HIS COTTAGE, TRYING HARD TO keep extremely quiet, for fear of waking the Writer. But we weren't very good at it—every few seconds we snorted with laughter.

As we were off to bed, emboldened by the wine, Boros and I embraced, to say thank you for this evening. A little later I saw him in the kitchen, taking his pills and swallowing them with water from the tap.

It occurred to me that he was a very good Person, this Boros. And it was a good thing he had his Ailments. Being healthy is an insecure state and does not bode well. It's better to be ill in a quiet way, then at least we know what we're going to die of.

He came to me in the Night and squatted by my bed. I wasn't asleep.

"Are you asleep?" he asked.

"Are you religious?" I had to put the question.

"Yes," he replied proudly. "I'm an atheist."

I found that curious.

I raised the quilt and invited him to join me, but as I am neither Maudlin nor Sentimental, I shall not dwell on it any further.

—✕—

The next day was Saturday, and early in the morning Dizzy appeared.

I was working in my garden patch, testing one of my Theories. I think I can find proof for the fact that we inherit phenotypes, which flies in the face of modern genetics. I had noticed that certain acquired features make irregular appearances in subsequent generations. So three years ago I set about repeating Mendel's experiment with sweet peas; I am now in the middle of it. I notched the petals of the flowers, through five generations in a row (two a year), and then checked to see if the seeds would produce flowers with damaged petals. I must say that the results of this experiment were looking very encouraging.

Dizzy's rickety old car emerged from round the bend in such a hurry that one could describe it as breathless and overexcited. Dizzy hopped out, just as agitated.

"They've found Innerd's body. Dead as a doornail. For weeks and weeks."

I felt extremely faint. I had to sit down. I wasn't prepared for this.

"So he hadn't run away with his lover," said Boros, emerging from the kitchen with a mug of tea. He didn't hide his disappointment.

Dizzy looked at him and at me hesitantly, and was too surprised to say anything. I had to do a quick presentation. They shook hands.

"Oh, they knew that ages ago," said Dizzy, his excitement waning. "He left his credit cards behind and his bank accounts haven't been touched. Though actually his passport has never turned up."

We sat down outside the house. Dizzy said he'd been found by timber thieves. Yesterday afternoon they had driven into the forest from the direction of the Fox farm, and there, just before Dusk, they had come upon the remains—that's what they'd said. They were lying among the ferns, in a pit where clay was once mined. And apparently these remains were quite appalling, so twisted and deformed that it took them a while to realize they were looking at a man's body. At first they had fled in horror, but their consciences had nagged them. Naturally, they were afraid to go to the Police for one simple reason—as soon as they did, their criminal activity would instantly be exposed. Oh well, they could always claim they'd just been driving through that way . . . Late that evening they'd called the Police, and during the Night the forensic team had arrived. From what was left of the clothing they had provisionally managed to identify Innerd because he wore a distinctive leather jacket. But we'd be sure to know everything on Monday.

ODDBALL'S SON LATER DEFINED OUR BEHAVIOR AS "CHILDISH," BUT to me it seemed as coherent as can be—namely, we all got in the Samurai and drove to the forest beyond the Fox farm to the site where the body was found. And we were by no means the only ones to behave childishly—about twenty people had come, men and women from Transylvania, and also forest workers, those men with moustaches were there too. Plastic orange tape had been stretched between the trees, and from the distance stipulated for spectators it was hard to make out anything at all.

A middle-aged woman came up to me and said: "Apparently he was lying here for months on end and had already been well gnawed by foxes."

I nodded. I recognized her. We had often met at Good News's shop. Her name was Innocenta, which impressed me greatly. Beyond that I did not envy her—she had several ne'er-do-well sons who were no use at all.

"The boys said he was all white with mold. They said he'd gone all moldy."

"Is that possible?" I asked in dismay.

"Oh yes, madam," she said very confidently. "And they said he had a wire around his leg, as if grown into the flesh, it was drawn so tight, it was."

"A snare," I said, "he must have been caught in a snare. They were always setting them around here."

We moved along the tape, trying to make out something in

particular. A crime scene always prompts horror, so the onlookers were hardly speaking to one another, and if they were, they were talking softly, as if at a cemetery. Innocenta shuffled after us, speaking for all those who were shocked into silence:

"But no one dies because of a snare. The Dentist keeps insisting it's the animals' revenge. Because they hunted, did you know that? He and the Commandant."

"Yes, I know," I replied, surprised that the news had spread so quickly. "I agree with him."

"Really? You think it's possible that animals . . ."

I shrugged.

"I know it is. I think they were taking revenge. There are some things we may not understand, but we can sense them perfectly well."

She thought for a while, and finally agreed that I was right. We walked around the tape and stopped at a spot where we had a good view of the police cars and men in rubber gloves squatting close to the forest floor. Evidently the Police were now trying to collect all the potential evidence, to avoid making the same mistakes as they had in the case of the Commandant. Because they really had made mistakes. We couldn't go any nearer, two policemen in uniform kept herding us back onto the road like a flock of Hens. But we could see that they were diligently searching for clues, and several officers were trudging about the forest, paying attention to every detail. Dizzy was frightened of them. He preferred not to be recognized in these circumstances; come what may, he did work for the Police.

DURING AN AFTERNOON SNACK, WHICH WE ATE OUTSIDE—THE weather was so lovely—Dizzy elaborated his thoughts:

"This means my entire hypothesis is in ruins. I'll admit that I was pretty sure Innerd had helped the Commandant to fall into the well. They had mutual interests, and they'd quarreled, or maybe the Commandant was blackmailing him. I thought they'd met by the well and started squabbling. Then Innerd had pushed the Commandant, and the accident had occurred."

"But now it turns out to be even worse than everyone thought. The murderer is still at large," said Oddball.

"And to think he's lurking somewhere near here," said Dizzy, tucking into the strawberry dessert.

I found the strawberries completely tasteless. I wondered whether it was because they fertilize them with some muck, or maybe because our taste buds have grown old, along with the rest of our bodies. And we shall never again taste the flavors of the past. Yet another thing that's irreversible.

Over a cup of tea Boros gave us a professional description of how Insects contribute to the decomposition of flesh. I let myself be persuaded to go back to the forest again after Dark, once the Police had left, so that Boros could conduct his research. Disgusted by what they regarded as ghoulish eccentricity, Dizzy and Oddball stayed behind on the terrace.

—✕—

The gleaming orange tape phosphoresced amid the soft darkness of the forest. At first I refused to go any closer, but Boros was very sure of himself and unceremoniously dragged me after him. I stood over him, as he shone his headlamp into the undergrowth, searching among the ferns and poking a finger into the leaf litter for traces of Insects. It's strange how the Night erases all colors, as if it didn't give a damn about such worldly extravagance. Boros muttered away to himself, while with my heart in my mouth, I let myself be carried away by a vision:

WHEN HE ARRIVED AT THE FARM AND LOOKED THROUGH THE window, Innerd usually saw the forest, the wall of forest full of ferns, but that day he'd seen some beautiful, fluffy, wild red Foxes. They weren't in the least afraid; they were just sitting there like Dogs, steadily watching him in a challenging way. Maybe in his small, avaricious heart a hope was born—that here he had chanced upon an easy profit, for such tame, beautiful Foxes could be lured and caught. But how come they're so trusting and tame? he thought. Perhaps they're a cross with the ones that live in cages and spend the whole of their short lives turning circles, in a space so small that their noses touch their precious tails. No, it's not possible. And yet these Foxes were large and beautiful. So that evening, when he saw them again, he thought he'd go after them, to see for himself what exactly was tempting him, what sort of a devil it was. He threw on his leather jacket and off he went. Then he realized that they were expecting him— beautiful, noble Animals with wise faces. "Here boy, here boy," he called to them as if to puppies, but the closer he came, the further they retreated into the forest, still bare and damp at this time of year. He figured it wouldn't be hard to grab hold of one—they were almost rubbing against his legs. It also crossed his mind that they could be rabid, but in fact it was all the same to him by now. He'd already been inoculated against rabies, when a Dog he'd shot had bit him. He'd had to finish it off with his rifle butt. So even if they were, it didn't matter. The Foxes were playing a strange game with him, vanishing from sight and then reappearing, two, three of them, and then he thought he could see some beautiful, fluffy Fox Cubs too. And finally, when one of them, the biggest, most handsome Dog Fox calmly sat down in front of him, Innerd crouched in amazement and began to advance very slowly, legs bent, leaning forward, with a hand stretched out ahead of him; his fingers pretended to be holding a tasty morsel, which might tempt the Fox, and then he could be made into a fine fur collar. But then suddenly he realized he was tangled in something, his legs were stuck and he couldn't move after the Fox. As his trouser leg rode up, he felt something cold and metallic on his ankle. His foot was caught. And when it dawned on him that he'd stepped in a snare, he instinctively yanked his leg backward, but it was too late. By making this movement he passed his own death sentence. The wire tightened and released a primitive hook—a young birch tree, bent and pinned to the ground, suddenly sprang straight, pulling Innerd's Body upward with such force that briefly it hung in the air, waving its legs about, but only briefly, for at once it became still. Seconds later, the overburdened birch tree snapped, and that was how Innerd came to rest on the ground, in a dug-out clay pit, where fern shoots were budding beneath the forest litter.

Now Boros was kneeling in that spot.

"Give me some light, please," he said, "I think we have some *Cleridae* larvae here."

"Do you believe that wild Animals could kill a Person?" I asked him, preoccupied with what I had seen in my vision.

"Oh yes, of course they can. Lions, leopards, bulls, snakes, insects, bacteria, viruses . . ."

"What about Animals like Deer?"

"I'm sure they could find a way." So he was on my side.

Unfortunately, my vision did not explain how the Foxes from the farm had got out. Nor how the snare on his leg had been the cause of his death.

"I FOUND ACARINA, CLERIDAE, WASP LARVAE AND DERMAPTERA, that's to say earwigs," said Boros over supper, which Oddball had made in my kitchen. "And ants of course. Yes, and lots of mold, but they damaged it very badly while removing the corpse. In my view it all proves that the body was found at the stage of butyric fermentation."

We were eating pasta with blue cheese sauce.

"You can't tell," said Boros, "if it was mold or adipocere, in other words corpse wax."

"What did you say? What on earth is corpse wax? How do you know all this?" asked Oddball with his mouth full of noodles; he had Marysia on his lap.

Boros explained that he used to be a consultant for the Police. And had done some training in taphonomy.

"Taphonomy?" I asked. "What on earth is that?"

"It's the science of how corpses decompose. *Taphos* is the Greek for 'a grave.'"

"Oh my God," sighed Dizzy, as if asking for divine intervention. But of course nothing happened.

"That would indicate that the body was lying there for some forty to fifty days."

We quickly did some mental arithmetic. Dizzy was the fastest.

"So it could have been early March," he said thoughtfully. "That's only a month after the Commandant's death."

FOR THREE WEEKS NO ONE TALKED OF ANYTHING ELSE, UNTIL THE next incident occurred. But now the number of versions of Innerd's death going around the neighborhood was vast. Dizzy said that the Police hadn't looked for him at all after he went missing in March, because his lover had disappeared too. Everyone knew about her, even his wife. And although various acquaintances had thought it odd that they'd gone away so suddenly, they were all convinced that Innerd had his own shady business going on. Nobody wanted to stick their noses into someone else's affairs. And his wife was reconciled to his disappearance too—what's more, it probably suited her fine. She had already filed for divorce, but obviously that was no longer necessary. Now she was a widow, and it was better for her that way. Meanwhile the lover had been found; it turned out they'd broken up in December, and she'd been living with her sister in the United States since Christmas. Boros thought the Police should have issued a wanted notice for Innerd, seeing they had all sorts of suspicions. But maybe the Police knew something that we didn't.

The next Wednesday I found out at Good News's shop that apparently a Beast was stalking the neighborhood, and that it was particularly fond of killing people. And that last year this same Beast had been on the prowl in the Opole region, the only difference being that there it had attacked domestic Animals. Now people in the country-side were scared out of their wits, and everyone was bolting their houses and barns at night.

"Yes, I've nailed up all the holes in my fence," said the Gentleman with the Poodle, who this time was buying an elegant waistcoat.

I was pleased to see him. And his Poodle. It sat politely, gazing at me with a wise expression in its eyes. Poodles are more intelligent than people think, though they certainly don't look it. The same thing applies to many other brave Creatures—we don't appreciate their intelligence.

We left Good News's shop together, and stood a while by the Samurai.

"I remember what you said that time, at the City Guard post. I found it very convincing. I don't think this is to do with a single killer animal, but animals in general. Perhaps thanks to climatic changes they've become aggressive, even deer and hares. And now they're taking vengeance for everything."

So said the old gentleman.

BOROS LEFT. I DROVE HIM TO THE STATION IN TOWN. HIS ECOLOGY students had never arrived—eventually their vehicle had broken down beyond repair. Maybe there weren't any students at all. Maybe Boros had other matters to see to here, not just to do with *Cucujus haematodes*.

For several days I missed him very much—his toiletries in the bathroom and even the empty teacups he left all over the house. He called every day. Then less often, every other day or so. He sounded as if he were living in another dimension, in a spirit world in the north of the country, where the trees are thousands of years old, and large Animals move among them at a slowed-down pace, outside time. I calmly watched as the image of Boros Sznajder, entomologist and taphonomist, faded and evaporated, until all that was left of him was a little gray pigtail hanging in midair, ridiculous. Everything will pass.

The wise Man knows this from the start, and has no regrets.

XII.

The Vengeful Beast

The Beggar's Dog & Widow's Cat
Feed them & thou wilt grow fat.

Toward the end of June the rain began to come down in torrents. That often happens here in summer. Then in the omnipresent damp one can hear the rustle of the grasses growing, the ivy climbing up the walls, and the mushroom spore expanding underground. After the rain, when the Sun breaks through the clouds for a while, everything takes on such depth that one's eyes are filled with tears.

Several times a day I went to examine the state of the little bridge across the stream, to make sure the agitated waters hadn't washed it away.

One warm, stormy day Oddball appeared at my house with a timid request. He wanted me to help him make a costume for the mushroom pickers' ball, taking place on Midsummer's Eve, organized by the Penny Buns Mushroom Pickers' Society, of which, as I learned to my surprise, he was the treasurer.

"But the season hasn't started yet," I said hesitantly, unsure what to think.

"You're wrong. The season starts when the first ceps and field mushrooms appear, and that's usually in mid-June. After that there won't be any time for balls, because we'll be out picking mushrooms." As proof he stretched out a hand, in which he was holding two lovely birch boletes.

I happened to be sitting under my terrace roof, doing my astrological research. Since mid-May, Neptune had been well-aspected to my Ascendant which, as I had noticed, was having an inspirational effect on me.

Oddball tried to persuade me to go to a Society meeting with him. I think he even wanted me to enroll and instantly pay my member's fee. But I don't like belonging to any sort of society. I took a quick glance at his Horoscope too, and discovered that Neptune was well-aspected to Venus for him as well. Maybe it would be a good idea for me to go to the mushroom pickers' ball? I glanced at him. He was sitting opposite me in a gray, faded shirt, with a small basket of strawberries on his knees. I went into the kitchen and fetched a bowl. We started to remove the strawberry stalks; they were slightly overripe, so we needed to hurry up. He used a special pair of tweezers of course. I tried removing the stalks with them too, but found it more convenient to do it with my fingers.

"What is your first name, by the way?" I asked. "What does the Ś before your surname stand for?"

"Świętopełk," he replied after a brief pause, without looking at me.

"No!" I exclaimed as a first reaction, but then I thought that whoever had given him that strange, traditional name had hit the bull's-eye. Świętopełk. It looked as if this confession brought him relief. He put a strawberry in his mouth and said: "My father called me that to spite my mother."

His father was a mining engineer. After the war he'd been given the task of revitalizing a formerly German coal mine in Waldenburg, which—now that this region was part of Poland—had been renamed Wałbrzych. He was to work alongside an older man, the German technical manager of the mine, who wasn't allowed to leave the country until the machines started working. At the time, the city was deserted; the Germans had left, and every day the trains brought new workers transferred from what had been eastern Poland, but they all settled in the same place, in one district only, as if the enormity of the empty city frightened them. The German manager did his best to perform his duty as quickly as possible, so he could finally leave for Swabia or Hesse or wherever. So he would invite Oddball's father home for dinner, and soon the engineer had taken a fancy to the manager's attractive daughter. In fact it was the best possible solution—for the young people to marry. Both for the mine and for the manager, as well as for the so-called people's power, which now had the daughter of a German as a sort of hostage. But their marriage was troubled from the start. Oddball's father spent a lot of time at work, often going to the bottom of the pit, because it was a difficult and demanding mine, where the anthracite was extracted from immense depths. Finally he came to feel better under the ground than above it, hard as that is to imagine. Once everything had gone to plan and the mine was up and running, their first child was born. The little girl was given the name Żywia, a traditional Slavic name, as a way of celebrating the return of the Western Territories to the Motherland. But gradually it became clear that the husband and wife simply disliked each other intensely. Świerszczyński began to use a separate entrance to the house and converted the basement area to provide himself with his own study and bedroom. At this point their son was born, in other words Oddball, perhaps the fruit of their final, farewell sexual intercourse. And then, knowing that his German wife had trouble pronouncing her own new surname, driven by some vengeful emotion that's quite incomprehensible nowadays, the engineer gave his son the old-fashioned Slavic name Świętopełk. The mother, who couldn't pronounce her own children's names, died as soon as she had seen them through secondary school. Meanwhile the father lost his mind completely and spent the rest of his life underground, in the basement, continually extending his network of rooms and corridors underneath the villa.

"I must have inherited my eccentricities from my father," Oddball concluded.

I was truly moved by his story, but also by the fact that never before (or since) had I heard him make such a long speech. I'd love to have known about further episodes in his life—for instance I was curious to learn who Black Coat's mother was—but now he seemed sad and exhausted. And we also found we had quite unconsciously eaten all the strawberries.

Now that he had revealed his real name to me, I couldn't refuse to go to the meeting with him, so that afternoon we went. The Tools that I kept in the back of the Samurai rattled as we drove along.

"What are you carrying about in this car?" asked Świętopełk. "What on earth do you need all those things for? A camping cooler? A gas can? Shovels?"

Surely he knew that if you live on your own in the mountains you have to be self-sufficient?

By the time we arrived everyone was seated at the table, drinking strong coffee brewed in the glass. To my surprise I noticed that the Penny Buns Mushroom Pickers' Society had a large membership, including people whom I knew well from the shops and kiosks, and from the street, and some whom I hardly recognized. So this was the one thing capable of bringing people together—mushroom picking. The conversation was dominated from the start by two men of the genus Woodcock who, like those noisy birds, outshouted each other in an effort to recount their rather unexciting adventures, which they both called "anecdotes." Several other people endeavored to silence them, but to no effect. As I learned from the woman sitting to my left, the ball was to be held at the firehouse, which was situated near the Fox farm, not far from Ox Heart Corner, but some of the members were protesting against that plan.

"It won't be much fun having a party near the spot where a friend of ours died," said the man chairing the meeting, in whom I was pleased to recognize the school's history teacher. I would never have guessed he was keen on mushrooms too.

"That's one thing," said the woman sitting opposite me, who ran a newspaper kiosk and often kept magazines for me. "Apart from that, it could still be dangerous around there. Some of the ladies and gentlemen smoke, for instance, and will want to go outside into the fresh air . . ."

"I should mention that smoking is not allowed inside the firehouse, whereas we can only drink alcohol indoors, according to the permission we've obtained. Otherwise it'll be classed as public consumption and it'll be illegal."

A murmur ran through the assembled company.

"What's that?" called a man in a khaki waistcoat. "I, for one, like to smoke when I drink. And vice versa. So what am I to do?"

The history teacher chairing the meeting was perplexed, and in the confusion that followed, everyone started giving advice on how to resolve the situation.

"You can stand in the doorway, with one hand holding your glass inside, and the other holding your cigarette outside," someone shouted from the back of the room.

"The smoke will get inside anyway . . ."

"There's a roofed terrace there. Does the porch count as inside, or outside?" someone else asked sensibly.

The chairman rapped on the table, and at that very moment a late arrival entered the room—it was "the President," apparently an honorary member of the Society. Everyone fell silent. The President was one of those people who are used to being the center of attention. From his early youth he had been on the board of something or other: the school student union, the Boy Scouts Service for People's Poland, the local council, the quarry company—supervisory bodies of every possible kind. Even though he had served as a member of parliament for one term, everyone called him the President. In the habit of running the show, he solved the problem immediately.

"In truth, we can have a buffet on the porch, and we'll declare the terrace the buffet zone," he joked genially, though few people laughed at his pun.

Admittedly, he was a good-looking man, though disfigured by an ample belly. He was self-confident, charming, and his Jovian physique inspired confidence. Oh yes, this man was born to rule. And he didn't know how to do anything else.

The smug President delivered a short speech about how life must go on, even after the greatest tragedies. He larded it with little jokes, and kept appealing to "our lovely ladies." He had the rather common habit of repeating a favorite phrase every now and then. In his case it was "in truth."

I had my Theory about interjections of this kind: every single Person has their own expression which he or she overuses. Or uses incorrectly. These words or phrases are the key to their intellect. Mr. "Apparently," Mr. "Generally," Mrs. "Probably," Mr. "Fucking," Mrs. "Don't You Think?," Mr. "As If." The President was Mr. "In Truth." Of course there are entire fashions for some words, just like the ones that for some crazy reason suddenly make everyone start going about in identical shoes or clothes—people just as suddenly start using one particular word or phrase. Recently the word "generally" was fashionable, but now "actually" is out in front.

"In truth, the dearly departed"—at this point he made a gesture, as if trying to cross himself—"was a good friend of mine—we had many shared interests. He was also a keen mushroom picker, and I'm sure he would have joined us this year. In truth, he was a very decent man, of broad horizons. He gave people jobs, and in truth, for that alone we should respect his memory. Jobs don't grow on trees. He died in mysterious circumstances, but in truth, the Police will soon get to the bottom of the case. In truth, we shouldn't let ourselves be terrorized, or give in to fear. Life has its rules, and we cannot ignore them. Courage, dear friends, my lovely ladies, in truth, I'm all for putting an end to the gossip and groundless hysteria. In truth, we must trust the authorities and live according to our common values." He spoke as if he were a candidate in a forthcoming election.

I couldn't help thinking that someone who overuses the phrase "in truth" is sure to be a liar.

The people at the meeting went back to their chaotic debate. Once again someone brought up the topic of the beast lurking in the countryside near Kraków last year. Was it really safe to hold the ball in the firehouse, right at the edge of the biggest forest in the area?

"Do you remember how the television followed the operation run by the Police in September to catch the mysterious animal in a village near Kraków? One of the locals happened to have filmed a predator on the run, probably a young lion," said an excited young man. I thought I recognized him from Big Foot's house.

"Naah, you must have got something mixed up. A lion? Here?" said the man in khaki.

"It wasn't a lion, it was a young tiger," said Mrs. Merrilegs; that was what I called her, because she was tall and nervous and sewed very elaborate costumes for the local ladies, so this name suited her best. "I saw the pictures on TV."

"He's right, let him finish, that's how it was," the women said indignantly.

"The Police spent two days searching for that lion or tiger, that animal, they used helicopters and an antiterrorist brigade, remember? It all cost half a million but they never found it."

"Perhaps it has moved here?"

"Apparently it could kill with a stroke of its paw."

"It bit off heads."

"The Chupacabra," I said.

There was a silence. Even the two Woodcocks fixed their gaze on me.

"What is a chupacabra?" asked Merrilegs, sounding alarmed.

"It's a mysterious Animal that can't be caught. A vengeful Beast."

Now everyone was talking at once. I could see that Oddball was getting flustered. He was rubbing his hands, as if about to leap to his feet and strangle the first person to come along. Plainly the meeting was at an end and nobody could possibly restore order now. I felt rather guilty about bringing up the Chupacabra, but so what? I was conducting my own sort of campaign too.

No, no, people in our country don't have the ability to club together to form a community, not even under the banner of the penny bun. This is a land of neurotic egotists, each of whom, as soon as he finds himself among others, starts to instruct, criticize, offend, and show off his undoubted superiority.

I think in the Czech Republic it's totally different. The people there are capable of discussing things calmly and nobody quarrels with anyone else. Even if they wanted to, they couldn't, because their language isn't suited to quarreling.

—— ✖ ——

We got home late, and in a stew. Oddball didn't say a word on the return journey. I drove the Samurai via shortcuts, down tracks full of potholes, and I enjoyed the way it kept throwing us from door to door as it jumped one puddle after another. We said good-bye with a curt "See you."

I stood in the dark, empty kitchen and sensed that I was just about to be seized by the same thing as usual—weeping. So I thought it would be best if I stopped thinking and did something. To this end I sat at the table and wrote the following letter:

To the Police,

As I have not received an answer to my previous letter, although according to law every public office in the country is obliged to respond within a period of fourteen days, I am forced to repeat my explanations concerning the recent, highly tragic incidents in our district, and in so doing to present certain observations that cast light on the mysterious deaths of the Commandant and of Innerd, owner of the fox farm.

Although it looks like an accident while performing the dangerous job of a policeman, or perhaps an unfortunate coincidence, one does have to ask if the Police have established WHAT WAS THE VICTIM DOING AT THAT TIME IN THAT PLACE? Are there any known motives, for to many people, including the undersigned, it seems extremely odd. Moreover, the undersigned was there on the spot, and found (which could be important to the Police) a vast number of Animal prints, especially the marks of deer hooves. It looked as if the deceased had been lured out of his car and led into the undergrowth, under which the fatal well was hidden. It is highly possible that the Deer he persecuted inflicted summary justice.

The situation of the next victim looks similar, although it won't be possible to confirm the presence of any footprints after such a long time. However, the dramatic course of events can be explained by the form of death. Here we have a situation that is easy to imagine, where the victim is enticed into the bushes, into a spot where snares are usually set. There he falls into the trap and is deprived of his life (as to how, that would have to be investigated).

At the same time I wish to appeal to the gentlemen of the Police not to shy away from the idea that the perpetrators of the above-mentioned tragic incidents could be Animals. I have prepared some information that casts a little light on these matters, for it is a long time since we have had cases of crimes committed by these creatures.

I must start with the Bible, in which it is clearly stated that if an Ox kills a woman or a man, it should be stoned to death. Saint Bernard excommunicated a swarm of Bees, whose buzzing prevented him from working. Bees also had to answer for the death of a Man from the city of Worms in the year 846. The local parliament condemned them to death by suffocation. In 1394 in France some Pigs killed and ate a child. The Sow was sentenced to hang, but her six children were spared, taking their young age into consideration. In 1639 in France, a court in Dijon sentenced a Horse for killing a Man. There have been cases not only of Murder, but also of crimes against nature. Thus in Basel in 1471 there was a lawsuit against a Hen, which laid strangely colored eggs. It was condemned to death by burning, for being in cahoots with the devil. Here I must add my own comment, that intellectual limitation and human cruelty know no bounds.

The most famous trial took place in France, in 1521. It was the trial of some Rats, which had been causing a lot of destruction. They were summoned to court by the townsfolk and were appointed a public defense counsel, a quick-witted lawyer named Bartolomeo Chassenée. When his clients failed to appear at the first hearing, Chassenée petitioned for a deferment, testifying that they lived in wide dispersal, on top of which many dangers lay in wait for them on the way to the court. He even appealed to the court to provide a guarantee that Cats belonging to the plaintiffs would not do the defendants any harm on their way to the hearing. Unfortunately, the court could not provide any such guarantee, so the case was postponed several times more. Finally, after an ardent speech by their defense counsel, the Rats were acquitted.

In 1659 in Italy the owners of vineyards destroyed by Caterpillars submitted to them a written summons to court. Pieces of paper with the wording of the summons were nailed to trees in the area, so the Caterpillars might become acquainted with the indictment.

In citing these recognized historical facts, I demand that my Suppositions and Conjectures be given serious consideration. They demonstrate that similar thinking has occurred in European jurisdiction before, and that they can be taken as a precedent.

At the same time I petition for the Deer and other eventual Animal Culprits to go unpunished, because their alleged deed was a reaction to the soulless and cruel conduct

of the victims, who were, as I have thoroughly investigated,
active hunters.

Yours faithfully,
Duszejko

First thing next morning I drove to the post office. I wanted the letter to be sent registered, as then I would have proof of posting. However, it all seemed a little pointless, for the Police station is bang opposite the post office, on the other side of the street.

As I emerged, a taxi stopped in front of me and the Dentist leaned out of it. When he drinks, he has himself carried about by taxi, and that's how he spends the money he earns from pulling teeth.

"Hey, Mrs. Duszeńko," he called. He had a red face and a foggy look in his eyes.

"Duszejko," I corrected him.

"The day of vengeance is nigh. The regiments of hell are closing in," he shouted, and waved at me through the window. Then with a squeal of tires the taxi set off in the direction of Kudowa.

XIII.

The Night Archer

He who torments the Chafers Sprite
Weaves a Bower in endless Night.

Two weeks before the mushroom pickers' planned festivity I went to see Good News, and in the back room we searched through tons of clothes looking for costumes. Unfortunately there wasn't a very large choice of things for adults. Most of the fancy dress was for children, and here there was plenty to raise a smile—the children could be whomever they wished—a Frog, Zorro, Batman or a Tiger. But we did manage to find a pretty good wolf mask. So I decided to be a Wolf; we fashioned the rest of the outfit ourselves by finishing off a furry jumpsuit with paws made out of stuffed gloves. The costume fitted me perfectly. Dressed in the mask, I could freely look out at the world from inside the jaws of a Wolf.

It was worse for Oddball, unfortunately. We failed to dig out anything for such an imposing physique. Everything was too small for him. But finally Good News hit upon a simple, but brilliant idea. Since we already had a Wolf . . . All that remained was to bring Oddball round to this idea.

Early on the day of the party, after a nocturnal storm, I was studying the damage the downpour had caused to my experimental pea plants when I saw the forester's car on the road and waved at him to stop. He was a nice young man for whom my private name was Wolf Eye, for I'd swear blind there was something odd about his pupils—they seemed to be an uncanny shape, oblong. He was here because of the storm too—he was counting how many large old spruces had been damaged in the entire area.

"Are you familiar with *Cucujus haematodes?*" I asked him, passing from initial courtesies to the heart of the Matter.

"Yes," he replied. "More or less."

"And did you know that they lay their eggs in tree trunks?"

"Yes, unfortunately." I could see that he was trying hard to foretell where this interrogation was leading. "In the process they destroy healthy, valuable wood. But what are you driving at?"

I briefly presented the issue. I repeated almost exactly what Boros had told me. But from Wolf Eye's expression I could tell that he took me for a madwoman. His eyes narrowed in a nice, patronizing smile and he spoke to me as if to a child.

"Mrs. Duszeńko . . ."

"Duszejko," I corrected him.

"You're such a good woman. You care about everything in a very personal way. But surely you don't imagine we're going to stop harvesting timber because of some beetles in the logs? Have you anything cold to drink?"

Suddenly all the energy drained out of me. He wasn't taking me seriously. If I were Boros, or Black Coat, perhaps he'd have heard me out, considered his arguments and debated the matter. But to him I was just an old woman, gone off her rocker living in this wilderness. Useless and unimportant. Though I wouldn't say he disliked me. I could sense that he was even quite fond of me.

I trudged into the house, and he followed me. He made himself comfortable on the terrace and lapped up half a liter of compote. As I watched him drink, it occurred to me that I could have mixed extract of lily-of-the-valley into his compote, or powdered some of the sleeping pills that Ali had prescribed for me and added those. And once he'd fallen asleep, I could have locked him in the boiler room and kept him prisoner for some time on bread and water. Or vice versa—I could have fattened him up and checked each day by the thickness of a finger whether he was fit to be roasted yet. He'd have learned respect.

"There's nothing natural about nature anymore," he said, and at that point I saw who this forester really was: just another official. "It's too late. The natural processes have gone wrong, and now we must keep it all in control to make sure there's no catastrophe."

"Are we in danger of a Catastrophe because of the *Cucujus* beetle?"

"Of course not. We need timber for stairs and floors, furniture and paper. What do you imagine? Do you think we're going to tiptoe about the forest because *Cucujus haematodes* is reproducing there? We have to shoot the foxes, or else their population will grow so large that they'll be a threat to other species. A few years ago there were so many hares that they were destroying the crops . . ."

"We could scatter contraceptives to stop them from multiplying instead of killing them."

"Do you realize how much that costs? And it's not effective. One gets too little, another gets too much. We have to keep some sort of order, seeing the natural one no longer exists."

"Foxes . . ." I began, with the noble Consul in mind, going to the Czech Republic and back again.

"Well, quite," he interrupted me. "Can you imagine what a hazard those foxes released from the farm present, for example? Luckily some of them have been caught now and taken to another farm."

"No," I said with a groan. I found this thought unbearable, but at once consoled myself with the idea that at least they'd known a little freedom.

"They weren't suited to life at liberty, Mrs. Duszejko. They would have perished. They didn't know how to hunt, their digestive systems were altered, their muscles were weak. What use would their beautiful fur be to them at liberty?"

He cast me a look, and I saw that the pigment in his irises was very unevenly distributed. His pupils were completely normal, round, just like yours and mine.

"Don't get so upset about things. Don't take the whole world on your shoulders. It'll all be fine," he said, getting up from his chair. "All right, off to work. We're going to take down those spruce trees. Would you like to buy some wood for the winter? It'd be a bargain."

I refused. Once he was gone, I felt the weight of my own body acutely, and had no desire at all to go to a party, least of all the boring mushroom pickers' ball. People who spend all day tramping about the forest in search of mushrooms are bound to be deadly boring.

—✖—

I felt pretty hot and uncomfortable in my costume; my tail trailed on the ground and I had to be careful not to tread on it. I drove the Samurai up to Oddball's house and admired his peonies while I waited for him. He soon appeared in the doorway. I was speechless with wonder. He was wearing black lace-up boots, white stockings and a sweet flowery dress with a little apron. On his head, tied under his chin with a bow, was a little red hood.

He was in a bad mood. He settled in the passenger seat and didn't say a single word the whole way to the firehouse. He held his red headgear on his knees and only put it back on once we had stopped outside the firehouse.

"As you can see, I have absolutely no sense of humor," he said.

Everyone had come here straight from a special mass for the mushroom pickers and the toasts were just starting. The President was eagerly joining in with these toasts, so very sure of his own splendid appearance that he had simply come in a suit, and thus was dressed up as himself. Most of the partygoers were only now getting changed in the toilet; they wouldn't have dared go to church in their costumes. But the priest, Father Rustle, was here as well, with his unhealthy complexion, and in his black cassock he too looked as if he were only disguised as a priest. Invited as guests, the Village

Housewives' Circle sang some folk songs, and then came the turn of the band, consisting of one man who artfully handled a device with a keyboard, managing to simulate all the best-known hits quite well.

That's what it was like. The music was loud and intrusive. It was hard to talk over it, so everyone set to work on the salads, hunter's stew and slices of cold meat. There were bottles of vodka standing in small crocheted baskets made to look like various species of mushroom. After some food and several glasses of vodka Father Rustle got up from the table and crossed himself. Only then did people start to dance, as if the priest's presence had made them feel awkward until now. The sounds echoed off the high ceiling of the old firehouse and came hammering down on the dancers.

Near me sat a petite woman in a white blouse, straight-backed and tense. She reminded me of Oddball's Dog, Marysia—she was just as nervous and tremulous. Earlier I had seen her go up to the tipsy President and talk to him a while. He leaned over her, and then scowled, losing patience. He grabbed her by the arm and must have squeezed it tight, because she flinched. Then he waved a hand, as if shooing away an annoying Insect, and disappeared among the dancing couples. So I guessed she must be his wife. She went back to the table and poked at the stew with a fork. And since Oddball was having immense success as Little Red Riding Hood, I moved over to her and introduced myself. "Oh, it's you," she said, and the shadow of a smile appeared on her sad face. We tried to have a conversation, but the noise of the music was now augmented by the thunder of dance steps on the wooden floor. Thud, thud, thud. To understand what she was saying I had to stare closely at her lips. I understood that she was anxious to drag her husband home as soon as possible. Everyone knew the President was pretty good at carousing, and had a wild, typically Slavic streak, dangerous for himself and others. Afterward it was necessary to hush up his antics. It turned out I was teaching their youngest daughter English, and that made the conversation easier, especially as the daughter regarded me as "cool." It was a very nice compliment.

"Is it true that you found our Commandant's body?" the woman asked me, while trying to spot the tall figure of her husband.

I confirmed that I had.

"Weren't you afraid?"

"Of course I was."

"Do you know, all those things have happened to my husband's friends. He was closely bound up with them. I think he's afraid too, though I'm not entirely sure what sort of business they had in common. Just one thing bothers me . . ." She hesitated, and fell silent. I looked at her, waiting for the end of the sentence, but she just nodded and I saw tears in her eyes.

The music became even brisker and noisier, for now they were playing "Hey Falcons." Everyone who hadn't yet danced leaped to their feet as if scalded and headed for the dance floor. I wasn't going to try making myself heard over the one-man band.

When her husband came into view for a while with an attractive Gypsy, she tugged at my paw and said: "Let's go outside for a cigarette."

The way she said it implied that whether I smoked or not was neither here nor there. So I didn't protest, though I'd given up smoking a decade ago.

As we pushed our way through the now delirious crowd, we were jostled and impulsively invited to dance. The merry mushroom pickers' ball had changed into a bacchanal. We found it a relief to stand outside, in a pool of light streaming from the firehouse windows. It was a wet, jasmine-scented June evening. Warm rain had just stopped falling but the sky hadn't brightened at all. It looked as if it were just about to start pouring again. I remembered evenings like this one from childhood, and suddenly I felt sad. I wasn't sure I wanted to go on talking to this anxious, disoriented woman.

She nervously lit a cigarette, took a deep drag and said: "I can't stop thinking about it. Dead bodies. You know what, whenever he comes home from hunting he tosses a quarter of a deer on the kitchen table. They usually divide it into four parts. Dark blood spills across the tabletop. Then he cuts it into pieces and puts it in the freezer. Whenever I walk past the fridge I think about the fact that there's a butchered body in there." She took another deep drag on her cigarette. "Or he hangs dead hares on the balcony in winter to season, and they dangle there with their eyes open and caked blood on their noses. I know, I know I'm neurotic and oversensitive, and I should go and get treatment."

She glanced at me with sudden hope, as if expecting me to contradict her, but meanwhile I was noting mentally that there are still normal people in this world.

But I hadn't time to react before she spoke again.

"I remember when I was little they used to tell the tale of the Night Archer. Do you know it?"

I shook my head.

"It's from around here, it's a local legend, they say it dates back to the Germans. It tells of the Night Archer, who prowled after dark, hunting down bad people. He flew on a black stork, accompanied by dogs. Everyone was afraid of him, and at night they locked and bolted their doors. One day a boy who came from here, or maybe from Nowa Ruda, or Kłodzko, shouted up the chimney, wishing the Night Archer would do some hunting for him. A few days later a quarter of a human body fell down the chimney into the boy and his family's house, and then the same thing happened three times more, until they were able to put an entire body back together and bury it. The archer never appeared again, and his dogs changed into moss."

A chill suddenly sailed in from the forest, making me shiver. The image of the Dogs changing into moss refused to vanish from my sight. I blinked.

"It's a strange story, like a bad dream, isn't it?" She lit another cigarette, and now I could see that her hands were shaking.

I tried to think of a way to calm her down, but I had no idea what to do. I had never seen a person on the edge of a nervous breakdown before. I laid a paw on her forearm and stroked it gently.

"You are a good Person," I said. She gazed at me with the eyes of Marysia, and suddenly began to cry. She cried very softly, like a little girl, except that her shoulders were quivering. It lasted a long time; evidently she had a great deal to cry about. I had to bear witness, stand by her and watch. It seems that was all she expected. I put my arms around her, and there we stood together—a fake Wolf and a small woman in a pool of light from the firehouse window. The shadows of the dancers flew across us.

"I'm going home. I've run out of strength," she said pitifully.

Loud stamping noises came from inside. They were dancing to the disco version of "Hey Falcons" again—it must have been more popular than any other song, and over and over we heard them shouting: "Hey! Hey!" Like shells exploding.

"You go, my dear," I said, after a pause for thought. I found it a relief to speak to her so personally and directly. "I'll wait for your husband and give him a lift home. I'm quite prepared for that. I have to wait for my neighbor anyway. Where exactly do you live?"

She mentioned one of those turnings beyond Ox Heart Corner. I knew where it was.

"Don't worry about a thing," I said. "Run yourself a bath and get some rest."

She took the car keys from her handbag and hesitated.

"Sometimes I think you can entirely fail to know the person you've lived with for years on end," she said, looking me in the eyes with such horror that I stiffened. I realized what she had in mind.

"No, it's not him. It's definitely not him. I'm sure of it," I said.

Now she was looking at me inquiringly. I was uncertain whether to tell her this at all.

"I used to have two Dogs. They kept close watch to make sure everything was divided fairly—food, petting, privileges. Animals have a very strong sense of justice. I remember the look in their eyes whenever I did something wrong, whenever I scolded them unfairly or failed to keep my word. They'd gaze at me with such awful grief, as if they simply couldn't understand how I could have broken the sacred law. They taught me quite basic, plain and simple justice." I stopped talking for a moment, and then added: "We have a view of the world, but Animals have a sense of the world, do you see?"

She lit another cigarette.

"And what's become of them?"

"They're dead."

I pulled the Wolf mask further down my face.

"They had their games that involved playing tricks on each other for fun. If one of them found a long-forgotten bone, and the other one didn't know how to get it off her, she'd pretend a car was coming down the road that had to be barked at. Then the first one would drop the bone and race to the road, unaware that it was a false alarm."

"Really? Like people."

"They were more human than people in every possible way. More affectionate, wiser, more joyful . . . And people think they can do what they want to Animals, as if they're just things. I think my Dogs were shot by the hunters."

"No—why on earth would they do that?" she asked anxiously.

"They say they only kill feral Dogs that are a threat to wild Animals, but it's not true. They come right up to the houses."

I wanted to tell her about the vengeance of Animals, but I remembered Dizzy's warnings not to tell everyone my Theories. Now we were standing in darkness and couldn't see each other's faces.

"That's nonsense," she said. "I'll never believe he shot a dog."

"Is there really such a big difference between a Hare, a Dog and a Pig?" I asked, but she didn't answer.

She got into the car and promptly drove off. It was a large, swanky Jeep Cherokee. I recognized it. I wondered how such a small, fragile woman coped with such a large vehicle, and I went back inside, because it was starting to rain again.

His cheeks comically flushed, Oddball was dancing with a stout woman in Kraków folk costume, and looked perfectly happy. I watched him. He moved gracefully, without exaggeration, calmly leading his partner. And I think he saw me looking at him, because suddenly he spun her around with panache. But he'd obviously forgotten how he was dressed, and it was a funny sight—two women dancing, one huge, the other tiny.

After this dance the results of the vote for the best costume were announced. The winners were a husband and wife from Transylvania, dressed as toadstools. The prize was a field guide to mushrooms. We came second, and were awarded a mushroom-shaped cake. We had to dance together in front of everyone as Little Red Riding Hood and the Wolf, after which we were completely forgotten. Only now did I have a glass of vodka, and a strong urge to have fun came over me—yes, I'd even have been happy for them to strike up "Hey Falcons" again. But Oddball wanted to go home now. He was worried about Marysia, whom he had never left alone for long; after all, she'd been traumatized by her experience of Big Foot's shed. I told him I was committed to driving the President home. Most men would have stayed to keep me company in this difficult task, but not Oddball. He found someone who also wanted to leave the party early, the attractive Gypsy, I think it was, and disappeared in a not entirely gentlemanly fashion. Oh well, I'm used to doing difficult things on my own.

—✖—

At dawn I had that dream again. I went down to the boiler room and there they were—my Mother and Grandmother. Both in summer dresses, flowery ones, both with handbags, as if they were off to church and had lost their way. They avoided my gaze when I began to reproach them.

"What are you doing here, Momma?" I asked angrily. "How's it possible?"

They were standing between a stack of wood and the boiler, absurdly stylish, though the patterns on their dresses looked washed out and faded.

"Get out of here!" I shouted at them, but suddenly my voice stuck in my throat. I could hear shuffling noises and rising whispers coming from the garage.

I turned in that direction and saw that there were lots of people over there: men, women and children, in strangely festive clothing that had faded and gone gray. They had the same restless, terrified look in their eyes, as if they didn't know what they were actually doing here. They were streaming in from somewhere in a swarm, crowding in the doorway, unsure whether they could come in. They were whispering to each other incoherently, and shuffling their boot soles against the stone floor of the boiler room and the garage. Pressing from behind, the crowd kept pushing the front rows forward. I was seized with sheer terror.

I felt for the handle behind me and very quietly, doing my best not to draw attention to myself, I slipped out of there. Then, my hands trembling with fear, I spent a long time bolting the boiler-room door.

—✕—

When I woke up, the anxiety brought on by this dream was still intense. I didn't know what to do with myself, and I thought the best thing I could do would be to go and see Oddball. The Sun had not yet fully risen, and I hadn't had much sleep. A gentle mist floated over everything, just about to change into dew.

Oddball opened the door to me, looking sleepy. He couldn't have had a proper wash: the red spots that I'd made for him the day before with lipstick were still on his cheeks.

"What's up?" he asked.

I didn't know what to say.

"Come in," he muttered. "So how did it go?"

"Fine. Perfectly all right," I replied concisely, knowing that Oddball likes concise questions and concise answers.

I sat down, and he set about making coffee. First he spent a long time cleaning the machine, then poured the water from a measuring jug, and I noticed that he never stopped talking. It was very strange to see him so animated. Świętopełk, who talks and talks.

"I've always wanted to know what you keep in that drawer," I said.

"Here you are," he said, opening it to show me. "Be my guest— nothing but essential items."

"Just like me in the Samurai."

The drawer silently slid open at a gentle tug of his finger. In dapper gray compartments lay some very neatly arranged kitchen Utensils. A rolling pin, an egg whisk, a tiny battery-powered milk beater, and an ice cream spoon. And also some Utensils that I couldn't identify—some long spoons, spatulas, and strange hooks. They looked like surgical Instruments for complicated operations. It was plain to see that their owner took extraordinary care of them—they were polished and put away in the right places.

"What's this?" I asked, picking up some wide metal pincers.

"Those are tongs for removing cling film when it sticks to the roller," he said, and poured the coffee into cups.

Then he reached for a small whisk, used it to whip the milk into snowy froth and poured it onto the coffee. From the drawer he took out a set of circular stencils and a small container of cocoa powder. For a while he wondered which pattern to choose, and finally picked a little heart shape. Then he sprinkled cocoa powder onto it, and lo and behold, a brown cocoa heart appeared on the snowy foam on my coffee. He smiled broadly.

Later that day I thought about his drawer again, that peeping into it brought me total calm, and that I would really like to be one of those useful Utensils.

By Monday everyone knew the President was dead. The women who had come to clean the firehouse had found him on Sunday evening. Apparently one of them had suffered shock and had ended up in the hospital.

— ✖ —

To the Police,

I realize that for some very important reason the Police are not in a position to answer letters from the public (not just the anonymous ones). Without going into those reasons, I shall take the liberty of referring you once more to the topic that I brought up in my previous letter. But I would not wish the Police nor anyone else to be ignored in this manner. The citizen whom the public services ignore is in a way condemned to nonexistence. Yet it would be a mistake to forget that he who has no rights is not bound by any duties.

I am pleased to inform you that I have managed to obtain the date of birth of the deceased Mr. Innerd and to draw up his Horoscope (without the time, unfortunately, which makes my cosmogram less precise), and have found an extremely interesting fact in it, which fully confirms the Hypotheses that I presented to you previously.

Thus it appears that at the moment of his death the victim had transiting Mars in Virgo, which according to the best principles of traditional Astrology has many analogies with fur-bearing Animals. At the same time his Sun in Pisces indicates the weakest parts of the body, such as the ankles. So it looks as if Mr. Innerd's death was accurately forecast in his radix Horoscope. Therefore, were the Police to take note of the findings of Astrologers, many people could be protected from misfortune. The configuration of the planets clearly tells us that the perpetrators of this cruel Murder were fur-bearing Animals, most probably Foxes, either wild ones or runaways from the farm (or both acting in collusion), that somehow managed to drive the victim into the snares people had been setting there for years. He was caught in a particularly cruel type of trap, known as a "gibbet," and had hung in the air for some time.

This discovery leads us straight to a general conclusion. The Police should check exactly where each of the victims had Saturn. Then they will find that each one had Saturn in an animal sign; the President additionally had it in Taurus, which heralds a violent death by suffocation caused by an Animal . . .

> Please find enclosed a newspaper cutting about the
> reported sightings of a certain as yet unidentified Animal,
> seen in the Opole region, which is said to kill other Animals
> with a blow of its paw to the chest. Recently on television I
> saw a video recorded on a cell phone, in which a young
> Tiger was clearly visible. All this has been happening in the
> Opole region, and thus not far away from us. Perhaps they
> are Animals that escaped from a zoo, managed to survive
> the floods and are now at liberty? In any case the matter is
> worth investigating, especially since, as I have noticed, the
> local population is gradually yielding to pathological fear,
> if not panic.

As I was writing this letter, someone knocked timidly at my door. It was the Writer, the Gray Lady.

"Mrs. Duszejko," she said from the threshold. "What's going on around here? Have you heard?"

"Please don't stand in the doorway, there's a draft. Come inside."

She was wearing a knitted cardigan, almost floor length. She came in, taking tiny little steps, and sat down on the edge of a chair.

"So what will become of us?" she asked dramatically.

"Are you afraid Animals are going to kill us too?"

She bristled.

"I do not believe in your theory. It's absurd."

"I thought that you, as a Writer, had an imagination and a capacity for conjecture, and were not closed to ideas that at first glance seem improbable. You should know that everything possible to be believed is an image of the truth," I concluded by citing Blake, and it seemed to make an impression on her.

"I'd never have written a single line if I didn't have my feet firmly on the ground, Mrs. Duszejko," she said in the tone of an official, and then added in a softer tone: "I cannot imagine it. Would you please tell me—was he really suffocated by cockchafers?"

I bustled about making tea. Black tea. Let her know what Tea is.

"That's right," I said. "He was covered in those Insects, they'd gone into his mouth, his lungs, his stomach, his ears. The women said he was crawling with Beetles. I didn't see it, but I can perfectly well imagine it. *Cucujus haematodes* everywhere."

She gave me a penetrating stare. I couldn't interpret that look.

I served the tea.

XIV.

The Fall

The Questioner who sits so sly
Shall never know how to Reply.

Early in the morning they came for me and said I must make a statement. I replied that I'd do my best to drop in during the week.

"You don't understand," replied a young policeman, the one who used to work with the Commandant. Since his death he'd been promoted and was now in charge of the police station in town. "You're coming with us now, to Kłodzko."

In view of his tone of voice, I did not protest. I merely locked the house and took a toothbrush and my pills with me just in case. The last thing I needed was to have an Attack and fall ill there.

As it had been pouring with rain for two weeks and there was a flood, we drove the long way round, on the asphalt, where it was safer. When we were descending into the valley from the Plateau, I saw a herd of Deer; they were standing still, gazing without fear at the police jeep. Joyfully I realized that I didn't recognize them—it must be a new herd that had come across from the Czech Republic to graze on our luscious green mountain pasture. The Policemen weren't interested in the Deer. They didn't speak, either to me or to each other.

I WAS GIVEN A MUG OF INSTANT COFFEE WITH POWDERED CREAM and the interview began.

"You were going to drive the President home? Is that right? Please tell us in detail, moment by moment, what exactly did you see?"

And plenty more questions of this kind.

There wasn't much to tell, but I tried my best to be precise about every detail. I said I had decided to wait for the President outside because inside it was noisy. Nobody was bothering with the buffer zone anymore, and everyone was smoking inside, which was having a very bad effect on me. So I sat down on the steps and gazed at the sky.

After the rain Sirius had appeared, and the handle of the Big Dipper had risen . . . I wondered whether the stars can see us. And if they can, what might they think of us? Do they really know our future? Do they feel sorry for us? For being stuck in the present time, with no chance to move? But it also crossed my mind that in spite of all, in spite of our fragility and ignorance, we have an incredible advantage over the stars—it is for us that time works, giving us a major opportunity to transform the suffering, aching world into a happy and peaceful one. It's the stars that are imprisoned in their own power, and they cannot really help us. They merely design the nets, and on cosmic looms they weave the warp thread that we must complete with our own weft. And then a curious Hypothesis occurred to me—maybe the stars see us in the same way as we see our Dogs, for example—having greater awareness than they do, at some points in time we know better what's good for them; we walk them on leads so they won't get lost, we sterilize them so they won't senselessly reproduce, we take them to the vet for medical treatment. They don't understand where this comes from, why it happens, for what purpose. Yet they yield to us. So maybe we too should yield to the influence of the stars, but in the process we should arouse our human sensitivity. That's what I was pondering, as I sat on those steps in the dark. And when I saw that most of the people were coming out, and either on foot or in cars were heading off, I went inside to remind the President that I was going to drive him home. But he wasn't there, or anywhere else. I checked the toilets and walked around the firehouse. I also asked all the inebriated mushroom pickers where he'd got to, but nobody was capable of giving me a sensible answer. Some were still humming "Hey Falcons," others were finishing off the beer, flouting the rules by drinking it outside. So I assumed someone must have taken him home already, but I simply hadn't noticed. And I'm still sure it was a reasonable supposition. What harm could possibly come to him? Even if he'd fallen asleep in a drunken state among the burdocks, the Night was warm and he wasn't in any danger. Nothing suspicious occurred to me, so I fetched the Samurai and we went home.

"Who is the Samurai?" asked the policeman.

"A friend," I replied, in keeping with the truth.

"Surname please."

"Samurai Suzuki."

He was put out, but the other one smiled to himself.

"Please tell us, Mrs. Duszeńko . . ."

"Duszejko," I corrected him.

". . . Duszejko. Do you have any suspicions as to who might have had a reason to do harm to the President?"

I was surprised.

"You don't read my letters. I explained it all in there."

They exchanged glances.

"No, but we're asking a serious question."

"And I am giving you a serious reply. I wrote to you. In fact, I still haven't received an answer. It's bad manners not to answer letters. According to article 171, paragraph one of the Penal Code, persons under interrogation should be allowed to express themselves freely within the defined limits for the purpose of the task in hand, and only then may one pose questions aimed at supplementing, explaining or verifying their statements."

"You're right," said the first one.

"Is it true that he was entirely covered in Beetles?" I asked.

"We cannot answer that question. For the good of the inquiry."

"But how did he die?"

"We're asking the questions, not you," said the first one, and the second added: "The witnesses who saw you talking to the President during the party said you were standing on the steps."

"That's right, I was reminding him that I'd be taking him home because his wife had asked me to. But he didn't seem fully able to focus on what I was saying. So I thought I'd better simply wait until the ball ended and he was ready to leave."

"Were you familiar with the Commandant?"

"Of course I was. You know that perfectly well," I said to the young one. "Why on earth ask, if you know? Isn't it a waste of time?"

"What about Anzelm Innerd?"

"His name was Anzelm? I never would have guessed. I met him

once near here, on the little bridge. He was with his girlfriend. That was a while back, about three years ago. We had a brief conversation."

"What about?"

"Just a general chat, I can't remember. That woman was there, she can confirm it all."

I knew that the Police like to have everything confirmed.

"Is it true that you behaved aggressively during the hunting here, in the locality?"

"I would say that I behaved angrily, not aggressively. There's a difference. I expressed my Anger because they were killing Animals."

"Did you make death threats?"

"Anger can prompt one to utter various words, but it can also make one fail to remember them afterward."

"There are witnesses who have stated that you shouted, and I quote"—at this point he glanced at the papers spread on the desk—"'I'll kill you, you (obscenity), you'll be punished for these crimes. You have no shame, you're not afraid of anything. I'll beat your brains out.'"

He read it dispassionately, which I found amusing.

"Why are you smiling?" asked the second one in a wounded tone.

"I find it comical that I could have said such things. I'm a peaceful person. Perhaps your witness is exaggerating?"

"Do you deny that you appeared before the magistrate's court on a charge of overturning and destroying hunting pulpits?"

"No, I wouldn't dream of denying it. I paid a fine in court. There are documents to prove it."

"What aren't there documents for?" asked one of them, imagining he was posing a trick question, but I think I evaded it quite cleverly by saying: "For many things, sir. In my life and in yours. It's impossible to record everything in words, let alone official documents."

"Why did you do it?"

I gave him a look as if he had fallen from the moon.

"Why are you asking me about something you know perfectly well?"

"Please answer the questions. It must be included in the transcript."

By now I was entirely relaxed.

"Aha. So, once again: I did it so that no one would shoot at Animals from them."

"How come you have such precise knowledge of certain details of the murders?"

"Such as?"

"To do with the President, for instance. How did you know the insect was"—he looked at his notes—"*Cucujus haematodes?* That's what you told the Writer."

"Oh, did I? It's a common Beetle in these parts."

"So how do you know that? From that ento . . . the insect fellow who stayed with you in the spring?"

"Perhaps. But above all from Horoscopes, as I have already explained. Horoscopes contain everything. All the smallest details. Even how you're feeling today, or your favorite color for underwear. You just have to know how to read it all. The President had very bad aspects in the third house, which is the house of small Animals. Including Insects."

The Policemen couldn't stop themselves from exchanging meaningful looks, which to my mind was impolite. In their line of work nothing should surprise them. I continued with complete self-confidence; by now I knew they were a pair of bunglers.

"I have been practicing Astrology for many years, and I have extensive experience. Everything is connected with everything else, and we are all caught in a net of correspondences of every kind. They should teach you that at police training college. It's a solid, old tradition. From Swedenborg."

"From whom?" they asked in unison.

"Swedenborg. A Swede."

I saw that one of them noted the name down.

THEY TALKED TO ME LIKE THIS FOR TWO MORE HOURS, AND THAT afternoon they presented me with a forty-eight-hour detention order and a warrant to search my house. Feverishly I wondered if I had left any dirty underwear out on view.

That evening I was handed a shopping bag, and I guessed it was from Dizzy and Good News. There were two toothbrushes in it (why two? For morning and evening perhaps?), a nightdress, very luxurious and sexy (Good News must have dug it out of the new stock), some candy and a volume of Blake translated by someone named Fostowicz. Dearest Dizzy.

For the first time in my life I ended up in a purely physical prison, and it was a very difficult experience. The cell was clean, poor and dismal. When the door was locked behind me, I was seized with panic. My heart thumped in my chest and I was afraid I'd start to scream. I sat down on the bunk bed and was afraid to move. At this point it occurred to me that I would rather die than spend the rest of my life in a place like this. Oh yes, without a doubt. I didn't sleep all night—I didn't even lie down. I just sat in the same position until morning. I was sweaty and dirty. I felt as if the words I had spoken that day had soiled my tongue and mouth.

SPARKS COME FROM THE VERY SOURCE OF LIGHT AND ARE MADE OF the purest brightness—so say the oldest legends. When a human Being is to be born, a spark begins to fall. First it flies through the darkness of outer space, then through galaxies, and finally, before it falls here, to Earth, the poor thing bumps into the orbits of planets. Each of them contaminates the spark with some Properties, while it darkens and fades.

First Pluto draws the frame for this cosmic experiment and reveals its basic principles—life is a fleeting incident, followed by death, which will one day let the spark escape from the trap; there's no other way out. Life is like an extremely demanding testing ground. From now on everything you do will count, every thought and every deed, but not for you to be punished or rewarded afterward, but because it is they that build your world. This is how the machine works. As it continues to fall, the spark crosses Neptune's belt and is lost in its foggy vapors. As consolation Neptune gives it all sorts of illusions, a sleepy memory of its exodus, dreams about flying, fantasy, narcotics and books. Uranus equips it with the capacity for rebellion; from now on that will be proof of the memory of where the spark is from. As the spark passes the rings of Saturn, it becomes clear that waiting for it at the bottom is a prison. A labor camp, a hospital, rules and forms, a sickly body, fatal illness, the death of a loved one. But Jupiter gives it consolation, dignity and optimism, a splendid gift: things-will-work-out. Mars adds strength and aggression, which are sure to be of use. As it flies past the Sun, it is blinded, and all that it has left of its former, far-reaching consciousness is a small, stunted Self, separated from the rest, and so it will remain. I imagine it like this: a small torso, a crippled being with its wings torn off, a Fly tormented by cruel children; who knows how it will survive in the Gloom. Praise the Goddesses, now Venus stands in the way of its Fall. From her the spark gains the gift of love, the purest sympathy, the only thing that can save it and other sparks; thanks to the gifts of Venus they will be able to unite and support each other. Just before the Fall it catches on a small, strange planet that resembles a hypnotized Rabbit, and doesn't turn on its own axis, but moves rapidly, staring at the Sun. This is Mercury, who gives it language, the capacity to communicate. As it passes the Moon, it gains something as intangible as the soul.

Only then does it fall to Earth, and is immediately clothed in a body. Human, animal or vegetable.

That's the way it is.

I WAS RELEASED THE NEXT DAY, BEFORE THOSE UNFORTUNATE forty-eight hours had elapsed. All three of them came to fetch me, and I threw myself into their arms as if I had been in another world for years and years. Dizzy had a cry, while Good News and Oddball sat stiffly in the back of the car. They were plainly horrified by what had happened, far more than I was, and in the end I was the one who had to comfort them. I asked Dizzy to stop at the shop, and we bought ice cream.

But on the whole, from the time of my brief stay in custody I became very absentminded. I couldn't come to terms with the fact that the policemen had searched my house, and from then on I sensed their presence everywhere—they'd rummaged in the drawers, in the wardrobes and the desk. They hadn't found anything, for what could they have found? But order had been disturbed, peace destroyed. I drifted about the house, incapable of any work. I kept talking to myself, and realized that there was something wrong with me. My large windows attracted me—I stood in them, unable to tear my gaze from what I could see—rippling russet grasses, their dance in the invisible wind, the instigator of that motion. And shimmering patches of green in all shades too. I'd become pensive and would be lost in thought for hours at a time. I put down my keys in the garage, for instance, and couldn't find them for a week. I burned the kettle. I'd take vegetables out of the freezer and only rediscover them once they were shriveled and past their best. From the corner of my eye I could see how much movement there was in my house—people coming and going, from the boiler room upstairs and into the garden, then back again. My Little Girls running joyfully through the hall. Momma sitting on the terrace drinking tea. I could hear the clink of the teaspoon striking the cup and her long, sad sighs. It only went quiet when Dizzy came; and he was almost always with Good News, as long as she didn't have a delivery of goods the next day.

When my pains intensified, one day Dizzy called for an ambulance. Apparently I had to go to the hospital. It was a good time for an ambulance to come—August, the road was hard and dry, the weather was beautiful and—praise the planets—I had had my morning shower and my feet were nice and clean.

Now I was lying in the ward, strangely empty, with open windows, through which came aromas from the allotments—of ripe tomatoes, dry grasses, burning stalks. The Sun had entered Virgo, who was starting her autumn tidying and was already stocking up for the winter.

They came to see me, of course, but nothing makes me feel more uncomfortable than being visited in the hospital. I really don't know what to do with myself. Every conversation in this unpleasant place becomes unnatural and forced. I hope they didn't think badly of me for telling them to go home.

Ali the dermatologist often came and sat on my bed. He'd drop in from the next ward, bringing me well-thumbed magazines. I told him about my bridge in Syria (I wonder if it's still there?), and he told me about his work with itinerant tribes in the desert. For some time he had been a doctor for nomads, and had traveled with them, examining and treating them. Always on the move. He himself was a nomad. He had never stayed at any hospital for more than two years before something had suddenly started to make him itch and feel restless, so he'd try for another job in another place. The patients who had overcome all sorts of prejudices and finally come to trust him would be abandoned—one day a sign would appear on the door of his consulting room to say that Doctor Ali was no longer there. Naturally, his roving lifestyle and his ethnic origin doomed him to the interest of various special services—as a result his phone was always bugged. Or so at least he claimed.

"Do you have any Ailments of your own?" I once asked him.

Oh yes, he did. Every winter he suffered from depression, and the room at the workers' hostel that the local authority had assigned him deepened his melancholy even more. He had one valuable object that he had acquired through years of work—it was a large lamp that emitted rays similar to sunlight, and was thus designed to raise the spirits. He often spent the evening exposing his face to this artificial

Sun, while mentally wandering the deserts of Libya or Syria, or perhaps Iraq.

I wondered what his Horoscope was like. But I was too sick to do the calculations. This time I was in a bad way. I lay in a darkened room, suffering from a severe light allergy; my skin was red and blistered, stinging as if it were being slashed by tiny scalpels.

"You must avoid Sunlight," he warned me. "I've never seen skin like yours before—you are *crated* for life underground."

He laughed, because for him it was unimaginable—he was entirely geared toward the Sun, like a sunflower. Whereas I was like white chicory, a potato sprout—I should spend the rest of my life in the boiler room.

I admired him for the fact that—so he said—he only ever owned as many things as he could pack into two cases at the drop of a hat, in less than an hour. I resolved to learn this skill from him. I promised myself that as soon as I came out, I'd practice. A backpack and a laptop, that should suffice for any Person. Like this, wherever he ended up, Ali was at home.

This drifter physician reminded me that we should never make ourselves too comfortable in any particular place, in which case I had probably gone too far with my house. Doctor Ali gave me a jalabiya—a white ankle-length shirt, with long sleeves, that buttoned up to the neck. He said the white color acts as a mirror, reflecting rays of light.

IN THE SECOND HALF OF AUGUST my condition grew so much worse that I was taken to Wrocław for tests, which didn't really bother me. In a semiconscious state for days on end, I anxiously fantasized about my sweet peas, worrying that I should be tending the sixth generation, or else the results of my research would cease to be valid and once again we would assume that we don't inherit our life experience, that all the sciences in the world are a waste of time, and that we're incapable of learning anything from history. I dreamed that I called Dizzy, but he didn't answer the phone because my Little Girls had just given birth to children, and there were lots and lots of them on the floor in the hall and the kitchen. They were people, a completely new race of people brought forth by Animals. They were still blind—they hadn't yet opened their eyes. And I dreamed I was looking for my Little Girls in the big city; in the dream I still had hope, but it was a stupid hope, so painful.

One day the Writer came to see me at the hospital in Wrocław to comfort me politely and to gently inform me that she was selling her house.

"The place has changed," she said, offering me some mushroom pancakes from Agata.

She said she felt bad vibes there, she was afraid at night, and had lost her appetite.

"It's impossible to live in a place where things like that happen. Those dreadful murders have brought various minor deceptions and improprieties to light. It turns out I've been living among monsters," she said fretfully. "You are the only honest person in the whole place."

"You know what, I was planning to give up caring for the houses next winter anyway," I said, confused by the compliment.

"A wise decision. You'd be better off in a warm country . . ."

". . . without the Sun," I added. "Do you know of any such place, apart from the bathroom?"

She ignored my question.

"There's already a 'for sale' announcement in the paper for my house," she said, and paused for thought. "Anyway, it was too windy there. I couldn't bear the constant howling of the wind. It's impossible to concentrate with something rustling, whistling and murmuring in your ear all the time. Have you noticed how much noise the leaves make on the trees? Especially on the poplars—frankly it's intolerable. They start in June and they go on shaking until November. It's a nightmare."

I had never thought about it.

"They interrogated me, did you know?" she said indignantly, suddenly changing the subject.

I wasn't at all surprised, because they had interrogated everyone. This case was now their priority. What a ghastly word.

"And? Were you any help to them?"

"You know what, sometimes it seems to me we're living in a world that we fabricate for ourselves. We decide what's good and what isn't, we draw maps of meanings for ourselves . . . And then we spend our whole lives struggling with what we have invented for ourselves. The problem is that each of us has our own version of it, so people find it hard to understand each other."

There was some truth in what she said.

As she was saying good-bye, I rummaged in my things and handed her a deer trotter. As she took off the paper wrapping, her face twisted into a scowl of revulsion.

"What on earth is this? For the love of God, Mrs. Duszejko, what are you giving me?"

"Please take it. It's a bit like the Finger of God. It has entirely dehydrated, it doesn't smell."

"What am I supposed to do with it?" she asked in dismay.

"Put it to good use."

She wrapped the trotter up again, hesitated in the doorway, and was gone.

I spent ages pondering what the Gray Lady had said. And I think it tallies with one of my Theories—my belief that the human psyche evolved in order to defend us against seeing the truth. To prevent us from catching sight of the mechanism. The psyche is our defense system—it makes sure we'll never understand what's going on around us. Its main task is to filter information, even though the capabilities of our brains are enormous. For it would be impossible to carry the weight of this knowledge. Because every tiny particle of the world is made of suffering.

—✖—

So first I came out of prison. Then I came out of hospital. There can be no doubt I was battling with the influences of Saturn. Yet in August it moved far enough to cease to create a negative aspect, and so we spent the rest of the year like a good family. I lay in a darkened room, Oddball tidied and ran the house, while Dizzy and Good News cooked and did the shopping. Once I was feeling better, we made another trip to the Czech Republic, to the extraordinary shop where we visited Honza and his books. We had dinner with him twice, and held our own miniature conference on Blake, without any EU grants or support.

Dizzy found a short video on the Internet. It lasts no more than a minute. A handsome Stag attacks a hunter. We see it standing on its hind legs, striking the Man with its front hooves. The hunter falls over, but the Animal doesn't stop, it stamps on him in a fury, it doesn't give him a chance to crawl away on his knees. The Man tries to protect his head and to escape from the enraged Animal, but the Stag keeps knocking him down again.

The scene has no end—we don't know what happened afterward, either to the hunter or the Stag.

Lying in my dark room, in the middle of the summer, I watched this video over and over again.

XV.

Saint Hubert

The Bleat the Bark Bellow & Roar
Are Waves that Beat on Heavens Shore.

My Venus is damaged, or in exile, that's what you say of a Planet that can't be found in the sign where it should be. What's more, Pluto is in a negative aspect to Venus, and in my case Pluto rules the Ascendant. The result of this situation is that I have, as I see it, Lazy Venus syndrome. That's what I call this Conformity. In this case we're dealing with a Person whom fortune has gifted generously, but who has entirely failed to use their potential. Such People are bright and intelligent, but don't apply themselves to their studies, and use their intelligence to play card games or patience instead. They have beautiful bodies, but they destroy them through neglect, poison themselves with harmful substances, and ignore doctors and dentists.

This Venus induces a strange kind of laziness—lifetime opportunities are missed, because you overslept, because you didn't feel like going, because you were late, because you were neglectful. It's a tendency to be sybaritic, to live in a state of mild semiconsciousness, to fritter your life away on petty pleasures, to dislike effort and be devoid of any penchant for competition. Long mornings, unopened letters, things put off for later, abandoned projects. A dislike of any authority and a refusal to submit to it, going your own way in a taciturn, idle manner. You could say such people are of no use at all.

Perhaps if I had made an effort, I would have gone back to school in September, but I couldn't summon the strength to pull myself together. I was sorry the children had lost a whole month's teaching. But what could I do? I was aching all over.

I couldn't return to work until October. By then I felt so much better that I organized an English club twice a week, and helped my pupils to make up for the lost lessons. But it was impossible to work normally. In October children started being excused from my lessons because preparations were at full steam for the opening and consecration of a newly built chapel. It was to be consecrated to Hubert on his saint's day, November 3. I refused to let the children go. I'd rather they learned a few more English words than the lives of the saints by heart. But the young headmistress intervened.

"You're exaggerating. There are certain priorities," she said, sounding as if she didn't believe in what she was saying.

To my mind, the word "priority" is just as ugly as "cadaver" or "cohabitee," but I really didn't want to quarrel with her, either about excusing the children or about words.

"Naturally you'll be at the consecration of the chapel, won't you?" she said.

"I'm not a Catholic."

"It doesn't matter. We're all Catholics by culture, whether we like it or not. So please come."

I wasn't prepared for this particular argument, so I said nothing. The children and I made up for the missing lessons at the afternoon club.

DIZZY WAS INTERROGATED TWICE MORE, AND FINALLY WAS GIVEN notice to quit his job by mutual agreement. He was only going to work until the end of the year. He was given some vague justification, staff reductions, cutbacks, the usual excuses. People like Dizzy are always the first to be eliminated. But I think it had something to do with his statements. Was he a suspect? Dizzy wasn't bothered about it. He had already decided to become a translator. He planned to live off translating Blake's poetry. How wonderful—to translate from one language to another, and by so doing to bring people closer to one another—what a beautiful idea.

He was also conducting his own inquiry, and no wonder— everyone was anxiously waiting for the Police to make new discoveries, revelations that would put an end to this string of deaths once and for all. For this purpose he even went to see Mrs. Innerd and the President's wife, and tracked the murder victims' movements as much as he could.

We knew that all three had died from a heavy blow to the head, but it wasn't clear what sort of Tool could have inflicted it. We speculated that it may just have been a piece of wood, a thick branch perhaps, but that would have left specific evidence on the skin. Instead it looked as if a large object with a hard, smooth surface had been used.

On top of that, the Police had found trace amounts of Animal blood at the point of impact, probably from a Deer.

"I was right," I insisted once again. "It's the Deer, you see?"

Dizzy was tending toward a Hypothesis that the murders must be to do with settling scores. It was a known fact that the Commandant was on his way back from Innerd's house that evening, and that Innerd had given him a bribe.

"Maybe Innerd caught up with him and tried to take back the money, so they tussled, the Commandant fell, then Innerd took fright and dropped the idea of looking for the cash," said Dizzy pensively.

"But who murdered Innerd?" asked Oddball philosophically.

To tell the truth, I liked the concept of evil people who eliminate each other, in a chain.

"Hmm, maybe it was the President?" fantasized Oddball again.

It looked as if the Commandant had been covering up Innerd's crimes. But whether the President had anything to do with it, we had no idea. If the President killed Innerd, then who killed the President? The motive of revenge on all three of them was a possibility, and in this case too it was probably to do with business dealings. Could the gossip about the mafia be true? Did the Police have any proof of it? It was highly possible that other policemen were mixed up in these sinister practices too, and that was why the inquiry was making such slow progress.

I had stopped talking about my own Theory. Indeed, I'd just been exposing myself to ridicule. The Gray Lady was right—people are only capable of understanding what they invent for themselves and feed on. The idea of a conspiracy among people from the provincial authorities, corrupt and demoralized, fitted the sort of story the television and the newspapers reveled in reporting. Neither the newspapers nor the television is interested in Animals, unless a Tiger escapes from the zoo.

— ✖ —

The winter starts straight after All Saints' Day. That's the way here; the autumn takes away all her Tools and toys, shakes off the leaves—they won't be needed anymore—sweeps them under the field boundary, and strips the colors from the grass until it goes dull and gray. Then everything becomes black against white: snow falls on the plowed fields.

"Drive your plow over the bones of the dead," I said to myself in the words of Blake; is that how it went?

I stood in the window and watched nature's high-speed house-work until dusk fell, and from then on the march of winter proceeded in darkness. Next morning I fetched out my down jacket, the red one from Good News's shop, and my woolen hats.

The Samurai's windows were coated in hoarfrost, still young, very fine and delicate, like a cosmic mycelium. Two days after All Saints' I drove to town, with the aim of visiting Good News and buying some snow boots. From now on one had to be prepared for the worst. The sky hung low, as usual at this time of year. Not all the votive candles at the cemeteries had burned out yet, and through the wire fence I could see the colored lights flickering in the daytime, as if with these feeble little flames people were trying to assist the Sun as it weakened in Scorpio. Pluto had taken control of the World. It made me feel sad. Yesterday I had written emails to my gracious employers to say that this year I would no longer be taking on the task of caring for their houses in winter.

I was on my way before I remembered that today was November 3, and that there would be celebrations in town for Saint Hubert's Day.

Whenever some dubious rip-off is organized, they always drag children into it from the very start. I remember them doing the same thing to us for the communist-era May 1 parade. Long, long ago. Now the children were obliged to take part in the Kłodzko County Children and Young Adults' Creative Arts Contest, on the theme "Saint Hubert as the model modern ecologist," and then in a show about the life and death of the saint. I had written a letter on this matter to the education board in October, but I hadn't had an answer. I regarded this—like so many things—as scandalous.

There were lots of cars parked along the road, which reminded me about the mass, and I decided to go into the church to see the result of the lengthy autumn preparations that had caused so much harm to my English lessons. I glanced at my watch, and realized the mass had already started.

I happen to have occasionally entered a church and sat there in peace a while with the people. I've always liked the fact that people can be together in there, without having to talk to one another. If they could chat, they'd instantly start telling each other nonsense, or gossip, they'd start making things up and showing off. But here they sit in the pews, each one deep in thought, mentally reviewing what has happened lately and imagining what's going to happen soon. Like this, they monitor their own lives. Just like everyone else, I would sit in a pew and sink into a sort of semiconscious state. My thoughts would move idly, as if coming from outside me, from other people's heads, or maybe from the heads of the wooden angels positioned nearby. Every time, something new occurred to me, something different from what I would have thought at home. In this way the church is a good place.

Sometimes I have felt as if I could read the minds of the other people in here if I wanted to. On several occasions I seemed to hear other people's thoughts: "What pattern should we have for the new wallpaper in the bedroom? Is the smooth kind better, or the kind that's stamped with a subtle design? The money in my account is earning too little interest, other banks give better rates, first thing on Monday I must check their offers and transfer the cash. Where does she get her money from? How can she afford the things she's wearing? Maybe they don't eat, they just spend all their income on her clothes . . . How much he's aged, how gray he's gone! To think he was once the best-looking man in the village. But now what? He's a wreck . . . I'll tell the doctor straight—I want a sick note . . . No way, I shall never agree to anything of the kind, I won't be treated like a child . . ." And would there be anything wrong with such thoughts? Are mine any different? It's a good thing that God, if he exists, and even if he doesn't, gives us a place where we can think in peace. Perhaps that's the whole point of prayer— to think to yourself in peace, to want nothing, to ask for nothing, but simply to sort out your own mind. That should be enough.

But after the first few pleasant moments of relaxation the same old questions from childhood always came back to me. Probably because I'm a little infantile by nature. How can God be listening to all the prayers in the entire world simultaneously? And what if they contradict each other? Does he have to listen to the prayers of all these bastards, devils and bad people? Do they pray? Are there places where this God is absent? Is he at the Fox farm, for instance? And what does he think about it? Or at Innerd's slaughterhouse? Does he go there? I know these are stupid, naive questions. The theologians would laugh at me. I have a wooden head, like the angels suspended from the vault of the artificial sky.

But I was prevented from thinking by the insistent, unpleasant voice of Father Rustle. It always seemed to me that as he moved, his dry, bony body, covered in baggy, dark skin, rustled slightly. His cassock brushed against his trousers, his chin against his dog collar, and his joints creaked. What sort of creature of God was he, this priest? He had dry, wrinkled skin, and there was a little too much of it everywhere. Apparently he used to be obese, but he'd been cured of it surgically, by letting them remove half his stomach. And now he'd grown very thin, perhaps that was why. I couldn't help thinking he was entirely made of rice paper, the kind that's used to make lamp shades. To me he was like an artificial creature, hollow on the inside, and flammable too.

EARLY IN JANUARY, WHEN I WAS STILL PLUNGED IN THE BLACKEST despair because of my Little Girls, he had visited me on his traditional new-year round of the parish. First his acolytes had called by, in white surplices on top of warm jackets, boys with red cheeks, which undermined their gravity as emissaries of the priest. I had some halva, which I liked to nibble from time to time, so I broke off a piece for each of them. They ate it, sang some songs, and then went outside.

Father Rustle appeared, walking fast and out of breath; without shaking the snow from his boots he entered my little dayroom, stepping straight onto the rug. He sprinkled the walls with his aspergillum, dropped his gaze and recited a prayer, then quick as blinking, placed a holy picture on the table and perched on a corner of the sofa. He did it all at lightning speed—my eyes could barely keep up with him. It looked to me as if he didn't feel at ease in my house and wanted to leave as soon as possible.

"A cup of tea, perhaps?" I asked shyly.

He refused. For a while we sat in silence. I could see the altar boys having a snowball fight outside.

Suddenly I felt an absurd need to nestle my face into his wide, starched sleeve.

"Why do you weep?" he asked in that strange, impersonal priest's slang, in which they say "trepidation" instead of "fear," "attend" instead of "take notice," "enrich" instead of "learn" and so on. But not even that could stop me. I went on crying.

"My Dogs have gone missing," I said at last.

It was a winter afternoon, Gloom was already pouring into the dayroom through the small windows, and I couldn't see the expression on his face.

"I understand your pain," he said after a pause. "But they were just animals."

"They were my only loved ones. My family. My daughters."

"Please do not blaspheme," he bristled. "You cannot speak of dogs as your daughters. Don't weep anymore. It's better to pray—that brings relief in suffering."

I tugged at his lovely clean sleeve to draw him to the window, and showed him my graveyard. The gravestones stood sadly, covered with snow; a small lantern burned on one of them.

"I'm already reconciled to the fact that they're dead. They were probably shot by hunters, did you know?"

He didn't answer.

"I wish I could have buried them at the very least. How am I to mourn them without even knowing how they died and where their bodies are?"

The priest twitched nervously.

"It's wrong to treat animals as if they were people. It's a sin—this sort of graveyard is the result of human pride. God gave animals a lower rank, in the service of man."

"Please tell me what I should do. Perhaps you know, Father?"

"You must pray," he replied.

"For them?"

"For yourself. Animals don't have souls, they're not immortal. They shall not know salvation. Please pray for yourself."

THAT'S WHAT CAME BACK TO MY MIND, THIS SAD SCENE FROM almost a year ago, when I didn't yet know what I know now.

The mass was still in progress. I took a seat quite near the exit, next to the third-year children, who were looking rather quaint, by the way. Most of them were dressed as Does, Stags and Hares. They had masks made of cardboard and were growing impatient to perform in them. I realized the performance would take place straight after the mass. They obligingly made room for me. So there I sat among the children.

"What sort of show will it be?" I whispered to a girl from 3A with the lovely name Jagoda.

"How Saint Hubert met the deer in the forest," she said. "I'm playing a hare."

I smiled at her. But in fact I couldn't understand the logic: Hubert, not yet a saint, is a ne'er-do-well and a wastrel. He adores hunting. He kills. And one day, during the hunt, he sees Christ on the cross, on the head of a Deer that he is trying to kill. He falls to his knees and is converted. He realizes how badly he has sinned until now. From then on he stops killing and becomes a saint.

How does someone like that become the patron saint of hunters? I was struck by the fundamental lack of logic in it all. If Hubert's followers really wanted to emulate him, they would have to stop killing. But if the hunters have him as their patron, they're making him the patron saint of the sin he used to commit, from which he broke free. Thus they're making him the patron saint of sin. I had already opened my mouth and was drawing air into my lungs in order to share my doubts with Jagoda, but I realized this was not the time or place for a debate, especially as the priest was singing very loud and we couldn't hear each other. So I simply set up a Hypothesis in my mind, that the point here was appropriation via antithesis.

The church was full, not so much because of the schoolchildren who had been herded in here, but a large number of quite unfamiliar men who were filling the front pews. Everything went green before my eyes because of their uniforms. There were yet more of them standing to the sides of the altar, holding drooping colored flags. Even Father Rustle was festive today, but his baggy, gray face looked ponderous. I couldn't sink into my favorite state and abandon myself to contemplation as usual. I was anxious and worked up, and felt as if I were gradually slipping into a state where vibrations began to run around inside me.

Someone touched me gently on the arm and I looked round. It

was Grześ, a boy from the senior class, with lovely, intelligent eyes. I taught him last year.

"Did you find your dogs?" he whispered.

Instantly I was reminded of how last autumn his class had helped me to put up notices on fences and at bus stops.

"No, Grześ, unfortunately not."

Grześ blinked.

"I'm very sorry, Mrs. Duszejko."

"Thank you."

Father Rustle's voice broke the cold silence, with only a light scattering of foot-scraping and throat-clearing, and everyone shuddered, moments later to fall to their knees with a rumble that rolled to the very vault.

"O Lamb of God . . ." The words thundered overhead, and I heard a strange noise, a faint thudding sound from all directions—it was people beating their own chests as they prayed to the Lamb.

Then they started heading for the altar, moving out of the pews with their hands folded and their gaze lowered, repentant sinners, and soon there was a scrum in the aisle, but they all had more goodwill than usual, so without exchanging glances they made way for each other, looking deadly serious.

I couldn't stop wondering what they had in their bellies. What they had eaten today and yesterday, whether they had already digested the ham, whether the Chickens, Rabbits and Calves had already gone through their stomachs yet.

The green army in the front rows had also stood up and was moving down the pew to the altar. Father Rustle was now coming along the railing, accompanied by an altar boy, feeding them their next bit of meat, this time in symbolic form, but nevertheless meat, the body of a living Being.

It occurred to me that if there really was a Good God, he should appear now in his true shape, as a Sheep, Cow or Stag, and thunder in a mighty tone, he should roar, and if he could not appear in person, he should send his vicars, his fiery archangels, to put an end to this terrible hypocrisy for once and for all. But of course no one intervened. He never intervenes.

The shuffling of feet was getting quieter by the moment, and finally the cluster of people gradually went back to their pews. In silence, Father Rustle solemnly began to wash the vessels. It occurred to me that he could do with a small dishwasher, the kind that fits one set of tableware; he'd only have to press a button and there'd be more time for his sermon. He climbed into the pulpit, straightened his lacy sleeves—the image of them from a year ago in my dayroom came back to me again—and said:

"I am delighted that we can consecrate our chapel on this happy day. I am all the more pleased to be taking part in this valuable initiative as chaplain to the hunters." Silence fell, as if everyone wanted to spend some time digesting in peace after the feast. The priest looked around the gathered assembly and continued:

"As you know, dear brothers and sisters, for some years I have been guardian of our brave hunters. As their chaplain I bless the hunting headquarters, organize meetings, administer the sacraments and send off the deceased to the 'eternal hunting grounds'; I also take care of matters relating to the ethics of hunting and do my best to provide the hunters with spiritual benefits."

I began to fidget restlessly, as the priest continued:

"Here in our church the beautiful chapel of Saint Hubert occupies one aisle. There is already a holy figure on the altar, and soon the chapel will also be adorned by two stained-glass windows. One will show the stag with the radiant cross that, according to legend, Saint Hubert met while hunting. The other window will show the saint himself."

The congregation turned their heads in the direction indicated by the priest.

"And the people who initiated this new chapel," the priest went on, "are our brave hunters."

All eyes now turned toward the front rows. Mine too—reluctantly. Father Rustle cleared his throat and was plainly getting ready for a very solemn speech.

"My dear brothers and sisters, hunters are the ambassadors and partners of the Lord God in the work of creation, in caring for game animals, in cooperation. Nature, among which man lives, needs help in order to flourish. Through their culls the hunters conduct the correct policy. They have built and regularly stock"—at this point he took a discreet peep at his notes—"forty-one feeding racks for roe deer, four storage feeders for red deer, twenty-five scatterers to feed pheasants and one hundred and fifty salt-licks for deer . . ."

"And when the Animals come to feed they shoot at them," I said aloud, and the heads of the people sitting nearest turned reprovingly in my direction. "It's like inviting someone to dinner and murdering them," I added.

The children were looking at me with eyes wide open, in terror. They were the same children whom I taught—class 3B.

Busy with his oration, Father Rustle was too far away to have heard me. He stood in the pulpit, tucked his hands into the lacy sleeves of his surplice and raised his eyes to the church vault, where stars painted long ago were starting to peel.

"In the current hunting season alone they have prepared fifteen tons of concentrated feedstuff for the winter period . . ." he went on. "For many years our hunting association has been buying and releasing pheasants into the environment, for the purposes of paid shoots for tourists, which supplement the association's budget. We cultivate the customs and traditions of hunting, with a selection process and oath-taking for new members," he said, and there was a note of pride in his voice. "We conduct the two most important hunts of the year, on Saint Hubert's day, today, and on Christmas Eve, according to tradition and with respect for the rules of hunting. But our chief desire is to experience the beauty of nature, to nurture the customs and traditions," he ardently continued. "There are still a lot of poachers, who disregard the laws of nature and kill animals in a cruel way with no respect for hunting law. You observe that law. Nowadays, fortunately the concept of hunting has changed. We are no longer seen as people who just want to shoot everything that moves, but as people who care about the beauty of nature; about order and harmony. In recent years our dear hunters have built their own hunting lodge, where they often meet to discuss the topics of culture, ethics, discipline and safety while hunting, and other issues of interest to them . . ."

I snorted with laughter so loud that now half the church turned to look at me. I was almost choking. One of the children handed me a paper tissue. At the same time I could feel my legs starting to stiffen, and the nasty numbness coming on, which made me move my feet, then my calves—if I didn't do it, in seconds a terrible force would blast through my muscles. I thought I was having an Attack, and it also occurred to me that it was a very good thing. Yes, quite, if you please, I'm having an Attack.

Now it seemed clear to me why those hunting towers, which do after all bear a strong resemblance to the watchtowers in concentration camps, are called "pulpits." In a pulpit Man places himself above other Creatures and grants himself the right to their life and death. He becomes a tyrant and a usurper. The priest spoke with inspiration, almost elation:

"Make the land your subject. It was to you, the hunters, that God addressed these words, because God makes man his associate, to take part in the work of creation, and to be sure this work will be carried through to the finish. The hunters carry out their vocation of caring for the gift from God that is nature consciously, judiciously and sagaciously. May your association thrive, and may it serve your fellow man and all of nature . . ."

I managed to get out of the row. On strangely stiff legs I walked almost right up to the pulpit.

"Hey, you, get down from there," I said. "That's enough."

Silence fell, and with satisfaction I heard my voice echoing off the vault and aisles, becoming strong; no wonder one could be carried away by one's own oration here.

"I'm talking to you. Can't you hear me? Get down!"

Rustle stared at me with his eyes wide open, terrified, his lips quivering, as if, taken by surprise, he were trying to find something suitable to say. But he couldn't do it.

"Well, well," he kept saying, not exactly helplessly, nor aggressively.

"Get down from that pulpit this instant! And get out of here!" I shouted.

Then I felt someone's hand on my arm and saw that one of the men in uniform was standing behind me. I pulled away, but then a second one ran up and they both grabbed me firmly by the arms.

"Murderers," I said.

The children were staring at me in horror. In their costumes they looked unreal, like a new half-human, half-animal race that was just about to be born. People began to murmur and fidget in their seats, whispering to each other indignantly, but in their eyes I could also see sympathy, and that enraged me even more.

"What are you gawping at?" I cried. "Have you fallen asleep? How can you listen to such nonsense without batting an eyelid? Have you lost your minds? Or your hearts? Have you still got hearts?"

I was no longer trying to break free. I let myself be calmly led out of the church, but right by the door I turned and shouted at all of them: "Get out of here. All of you! Right now!" I waved my arms. "Go away! Shoo! Have you been hypnotized? Have you lost your last dregs of compassion?"

"Please calm yourself. It's cooler here," said one of the men once we were outside. Trying to sound threatening, the other one added: "Or we'll call the Police."

"You're right, you should call the Police. There's an incitement to Crime going on here."

They left me and closed the heavy door to stop me from coming back into the church. I guessed that Father Rustle was continuing his sermon. I sat down on a low wall and gradually came to. My Anger passed, and the cold wind cooled my burning face.

Anger always leaves a large void behind it, into which a flood of sorrow pours instantly, and keeps on flowing like a great river, without beginning or end. My tears came; once again their sources were replenished.

I watched two Magpies that were frolicking on the lawn outside the presbytery, as if trying to entertain me. As if saying, don't be upset, time is on our side, the job must be done, there's no alternative . . . Curiously they examined a shiny chewing-gum wrapper, then one of them picked it up in her beak and flew away. I followed her with my gaze. They must have had a nest on the presbytery roof. Magpies. Fire-raisers.

— ✖ —

Next day, although I had no classes, the young headmistress called and asked me to come to the school that afternoon once the building was empty. Without being asked, she brought me a mug of tea and cut me a slice of apple cake. I knew what was in the wind.

"I'm sure you understand, Janina, that after what happened . . ." she said, sounding concerned.

"I'm not 'Janina,' I've asked you not to call me that before," I corrected her, but perhaps it was pointless. I knew what she was going to say—she was probably trying to boost her own self-confidence with these formalities.

". . . OK, Mrs. Duszejko."

"Yes, I know. I'd rather you and the children listened to me and not the hunters. The things they say are demoralizing for the children."

The headmistress cleared her throat.

"You've caused a scandal, and what's more you did it in church. Worst of all, it happened in front of the children, for whom the person of the priest, and the place where it occurred, should be special."

"Special? All the more reason for preventing them from listening to such things. You heard it yourself."

The young woman took a deep breath, and without looking at me, said: "Mrs. Duszejko, you're wrong. There are certain rules and traditions that are inherent in our lives. We can't just reject them out of hand . . ." It was plain to see that she was girding her loins now, and I knew what she was going to say.

"But I don't want us to reject them, as you put it. It's just that I refuse to let anyone encourage children to do evil things or teach them hypocrisy. Glorifying killing is evil. It's as simple as that."

The headmistress rested her head in her hands and replied in a soft voice: "I have to terminate your contract. You must have guessed that already. It'd be best if you applied for sick leave for this term— that will be a nod in your direction. You've already been unwell, so now you can extend your sick leave. Please understand me, I have no other course of action."

"What about English? Who's going to teach English?"

She turned red.

"Our religious instruction teacher studied at a language school," she said, casting me a strange look. "In any case . . ." She hesitated before going on. "Rumors have reached me before now of your unconventional teaching methods. Apparently you burn candles, some sort of fireworks during lessons, then other teachers complain about a smell of smoke in the classroom. The parents are afraid it's something satanic, Satanism. Perhaps they're just simple people . . . And you give the children strange things to eat. Durian-flavored candy, for instance. What on earth is that? If any of them were poisoned, who'd be responsible? Have you ever stopped to think?"

These arguments of hers devastated me. I'd always done my best to surprise the children in some way, to excite their interest. Now I could feel all the strength draining out of me. I had lost the will to say anything more. I hauled myself to my feet and left the room without another word. From the corner of my eye I saw her nervously shuffling the papers on her desk; her hands were shaking. Poor woman.

I had everything I needed in the Samurai. Falling before my eyes, the Twilight was in my favor. It always favors people like me.

— ✖ —

Mustard soup. It's quickly made, without much effort, so I had it ready in time. First we heat a little butter in a frying pan and add some flour, as if we were going to make a béchamel. The flour sucks up the melted butter beautifully, then gorges on it, swelling with satisfaction. At this point we flood it with milk and water, half and half. That's the end of the frolics between flour and butter, unfortunately, but gradually the soup appears; now we must add a pinch of salt, pepper and caraway to this clear, still-innocent liquid, bring it to the boil and then switch off the heat. Only now do we add the mustard in three forms: whole-grain French Dijon mustard; smooth brown mustard or the mild, creamy kind; and mustard powder. It's important not to let the Mustard boil, or else the soup will lose its flavor and go bitter. I serve this soup with croutons, and I know how much Dizzy likes it.

The three of them arrived together, and I wondered what sort of a Surprise they had for me; perhaps I had an anniversary of some kind—they were in such a serious mood. Dizzy and Good News had lovely winter jackets, identical, and it occurred to me that they really could make a fine couple, both so small and beautiful, like fragile snowdrops growing by the path. Oddball seemed gloomy, and spent ages shifting from foot to foot, rubbing his hands together. He had brought a bottle of chokeberry brandy, his own home produce. I never liked his homemade alcoholic drinks; in my view he skimped on the sugar and his liqueurs always had a bitter aftertaste.

By now they were sitting at the table. Still frying the croutons, I looked at them all together, maybe for the last time. That's exactly what crossed my mind—that it was time to part. Suddenly I saw the four of us in a different way—as if we had a lot in common, as if we were a family. I realized that we were the sort of people whom the world regards as useless. We do nothing essential, we don't produce important ideas, no vital objects or foodstuffs, we don't cultivate the land, we don't fuel the economy. We haven't done any reproducing, except for Oddball, who does have a son, even if it's just Black Coat. So far we've never provided the world with anything useful. We haven't come up with the idea for any invention. We have no power, we have no resources apart from our small properties. We do our jobs, but they are of no significance for anyone else. If we went missing, nothing would really change. Nobody would notice.

Through the silence of the evening and the roar of the fire in the kitchen stove I heard sirens howling somewhere below, carried here from the village on a furious wind. I wondered whether they could hear this ominous sound too. But they were talking in hushed voices, leaning toward each other, calmly.

As I was pouring the mustard soup into ramekins, I was overcome by such strong emotion that my tears began to flow again. Luckily they were too involved in their conversation to notice. I stepped back to put the pan down on the worktop under the window, from where I watched them furtively. I saw Oddball's pale, sallow face, his gray hair politely combed to one side and his freshly shaved cheeks. I saw Good News in profile, the beautiful line of her nose and neck, and a colored scarf wrapped around her head, and I saw Dizzy's shoulders, small and hunched, in a hand-knitted sweater. What's going to become of them? How will these children cope?

And how will I cope? After all, I'm like them too. My life's harvest is not the building material for anything, neither in my time, now, nor in any other, never.

But why should we have to be useful and for what reason? Who divided the world into useless and useful, and by what right? Does a thistle have no right to life, or a Mouse that eats the grain in a warehouse? What about Bees and Drones, weeds and roses? Whose intellect can have had the audacity to judge who is better, and who worse? A large tree, crooked and full of holes, survives for centuries without being cut down, because nothing could possibly be made out of it. This example should raise the spirits of people like us. Everyone knows the profit to be reaped from the useful, but nobody knows the benefit to be gained from the useless.

"There's a glow down there, in the village," said Oddball, standing by the window. "Something's on fire."

"Sit down. I'll serve the croutons," I said, once I had assured myself that my eyes were dry. But they wouldn't come to the table. They were all standing by the window, in silence. And then they looked at me. Dizzy with real anguish, Oddball with disbelief, and Good News furtively, with a sorrow that broke my heart.

Just then Dizzy's phone rang.

"Don't answer it," I cried. "It's via the Czech Republic, you'll pay through the nose."

"I can't not answer, I'm still working for the Police," replied Dizzy, and said into the phone: "Yes?"

We looked at him expectantly. The mustard soup was going cold.

"I'll be right there," said Dizzy, and a wave of panic swept over me at the thought that everything was lost, and now they'd be leaving forever.

"The presbytery's on fire. Father Rustle is dead," said Dizzy, but instead of leaving, he sat down at the table and started mechanically drinking the soup.

I have Mercury in retrograde, so I'm better at expressing myself in writing than in speech. I could have been a pretty good writer. But at the same time I have trouble explaining my feelings and the motives for my behavior. I had to tell them, but at the same time I couldn't tell them. How was I to put it all in words? Out of sheer loyalty I had to explain to them what I had done before they found out from others. But Dizzy spoke first.

"We know it's you," he said. "That's why we came today. To make a decision."

"We wanted to take you away," said Oddball in a sepulchral tone.

"But we didn't think you'd do it again. Did you do it?" said Dizzy, pushing aside the half-drunk soup.

"Yes," I said.

I put the pan back on the stove and took off my apron. I stood before them, ready for Judgment.

"We realized when we heard how the President died," said Dizzy quietly. "The beetles. Only you could have done that. Or Boros, but Boros had gone long ago. So I called him to check. He couldn't believe it, but he admitted that some of his valuable pheromones had indeed gone missing, for which he had no explanation. He was in his forest and he had an alibi. I spent a long time wondering why, what on earth you had in common with someone like the President, but then I guessed it must have a connection with your Little Girls. Anyway, you've never hidden the fact that they hunted, have you? All of them. And now I can see that Father Rustle hunted too."

"He was their chaplain," I whispered.

"I had some suspicions earlier, when I saw what you carry about in your car. I've never told anyone about it. But are you aware of the fact that your Samurai looks like a commando vehicle?"

Suddenly I felt myself losing the power in my legs, and I sat down on the floor. The strength supporting me had left me, evaporated like air.

"Do you think they'll arrest me? Are they going to come for me now and shut me in prison again?" I asked.

"You've murdered people. Are you conscious of that? Are you aware?"

"Easy now," said Oddball. "Easy."

Dizzy leaned forward, grabbed me by the shoulders and shook me.

"How did it happen? How did you do it? Why?"

On my knees, I shuffled over to the sideboard, and from under the wax cloth I pulled the photograph I'd taken from Big Foot's house. I handed it to them without looking at it. It was etched in my brain, and I couldn't forget the tiniest detail.

XVI.

The Photograph

The tygers of wrath are wiser than the horses of instruction.

It was all plain to see in the photograph. The best proof of a Crime that one could possibly imagine.

There stood the men in uniforms, in a row, and on the grass in front of them lay the neatly arranged corpses of Animals—Hares, one beside another, two Boars, one large, one smaller, some Deer and then a lot of Pheasants and Ducks, Mallards and Teals, like little dots, as if those Animals' bodies were a sentence written to me, and the Birds formed a long ellipsis to say "this will go on and on."

But what I saw in the corner of the picture almost caused me to faint, and everything went dark before my eyes. You didn't notice, Oddball, you were occupied with Big Foot's dead body, you were saying something while I was fighting my nausea. Who could have failed to recognize that white fur and those black patches? In the corner of the picture lay three dead Dogs, neatly laid out, like trophies. One of them was unfamiliar to me. The other two were my Little Girls.

The men cut proud figures in their uniforms, smiling as they posed for the photograph. I had no trouble identifying them. In the middle was the Commandant, and beside him the President. On the other side stood Innerd, dressed like a commando, and next to him was Father Rustle in his clerical collar. Then the head of the hospital, the fire chief, and the owner of the gas station. The fathers of families, exemplary citizens. Behind this row of VIPs, the helpers and beaters were standing slightly to one side; they weren't posing. There was Big Foot, turned three-quarters facing, as if he had been holding back, and had only run into the picture at the last moment, and some of the Moustachios with armfuls of branches for the large bonfire they were about to make. If not for the corpses lying at their feet, one might have thought these people were celebrating a happy event, so self-satisfied did they look. Pots of hunter's stew, sausages and kebabs skewered on sticks, bottles of vodka cooling in buckets. The masculine odor of tanned hide, oiled shotguns, alcohol and sweat. Gestures of domination, insignia of power.

I had fully memorized every detail at first glance, without having to study it.

Not surprisingly, above all I felt relief. I had finally found out what had happened to my Little Girls. I had been searching for them right up to Christmas, until I lost hope. I had been to all the tourist hostels and asked people; I had put up notices. "Mrs. Duszejko's dogs are missing—have you seen them?" the children from school were asking. Two Dogs had vanished into thin air. Without trace. Nobody had seen them—and how could they, considering they were dead?

Now I could guess where their bodies had gone. Someone had told me that Innerd always took the leftovers from hunting to the farm and fed them to the Foxes.

Big Foot knew about it from the very start and he must have been amused by my distress. He saw me calling them, in desperation, and walking all the way to the other side of the border. He never said a word.

That fateful night he had made himself a meal of the Deer he'd poached. To tell the truth, I have never understood the difference between "poaching" and "hunting." Both words mean killing. The former in a covert, illegal way, the latter openly, within the full majesty of the law. And he had simply choked on one of its bones. He met a well-deserved Punishment. I couldn't help thinking of it like that—as a Punishment. The Deer punished him for killing them in such a cruel way. He choked on their flesh. Their bones stuck in his throat. Why didn't the hunters react to Big Foot's poaching? I don't know. I think he knew too much about what went on after the hunting, when, as Father Rustle would have us believe, they devoted themselves to ethical debate.

So while you were looking for a phone signal, Świętopełk, I found this photograph. I also took the Deer's head, to bury the remains in my graveyard.

At dawn, by the time I went home after that dreadful Night of dressing Big Foot, I knew what I had to do. Those Deer we saw outside the house had told me. They chose me from among others—maybe because I don't eat meat and they can sense it—to continue to act in their Name. They appeared before me, like the Stag to Saint Hubert, to have me become the punitive hand of justice, in secret.

Not just for the Deer, but for other Animals too. For they have no voice in parliament. They even gave me a Weapon, a very clever one. Nobody guessed a thing.

I FOLLOWED THE COMMANDANT FOR SEVERAL DAYS, AND IT GAVE me satisfaction. I observed his life. It wasn't interesting. I discovered for example that he often went to Innerd's illegal brothel. And he drank nothing but Absolut vodka.

That day as usual I waited for him on the road to come back from work. I drove after him, and as usual he didn't notice me. Nobody takes any notice of old women who wander around with their shopping bags.

I waited a long time outside Innerd's house for him to emerge, but there was rain and wind, so finally I felt too cold and went home. However, I knew he'd come via the Pass, taking the side roads, because they were sure to have been drinking. I had no idea what I was going to do. I wanted to talk to him, to stand face-to-face with him—on my terms, not his, like at the police station, where I had been an ordinary suppliant, a tedious madwoman who's hopeless at everything, pathetic and laughable.

Perhaps I wanted to give him a fright. I was dressed in a yellow waterproof cape. I looked like a large gnome. Outside the house I noticed that the plastic shopping bag in which I had brought the Deer's head home and which I had then hung on the plum tree had filled with water and frozen solid. I unhooked it and took it with me. I don't know if I took it with the intention of using it. One doesn't think about such things at the time when they're happening. I knew

Dizzy was due to come that evening, so I couldn't wait long for the Commandant. But just as I reached the Pass, along came his car, and I took that to be a sign too. I stepped into the road and waved my arms. Oh yes, he did have a fright. I pulled off my hood to show him my face. He was furious.

"What do you want now?" he shouted at me, leaning out of the window.

"I want to show you something," I said.

I had no idea what I was going to do. For a moment he hesitated, but as he was fairly drunk, he was in the mood for an adventure. He got out of the car and unsteadily walked a short way after me.

"What do you want to show me, woman?" he asked.

"It's to do with Big Foot's death." I said the first thing that entered my mind.

"Big Foot?" he asked dubiously, and then instantly realized who that meant, and burst into spiteful laughter. "Yes, indeed, he really did have enormous feet."

Intrigued, he followed me, taking several paces to the left, toward the undergrowth and the well.

"Why didn't you tell me you shot my Dogs?" I asked, suddenly turning to face him.

"What do you want to show me?" he said angrily, trying to maintain control. He was the one who was going to ask the questions.

I pointed my index finger at him like a pistol barrel and prodded him in the belly.

"Did you shoot my Dogs?"

He laughed, and immediately relaxed.

"What are you on about? Do you know something that I don't?"

"Yes," I said. "Answer my question."

"It wasn't me who shot them. It may have been Innerd, or the parish priest."

"The priest? He hunts?" I was speechless.

"Why shouldn't he? He's the chaplain. He hunts like anything."

His face was puffy, and he kept adjusting his trouser belt. It never occurred to me that he had money there.

"Turn around, woman, I want to take a piss," he said suddenly.

We were standing right by the well when he started scrabbling at his fly. Without thinking at all, I positioned myself with the bag of frozen ice as if for throwing the hammer. My only fleeting thought was: "This is *die kalte Teufelshand*"—oh yes, where is that from? Didn't I tell you that the sport I won all the medals for was hammer throwing? I came second in the national championships in 1971. So my body adopted the familiar position and gathered all its strength. Oh, how wise the body is. I could say it was my body that made the decision, it took the swing and struck the blow.

I just heard a crack. For a few seconds the Commandant remained upright, swaying, but the blood immediately began to pour down his face. The cold fist had struck him on the head. My heart was thumping and the roar of my own blood was deafening me. My mind was a blank. I watched as he fell beside the well, slowly, softly, almost gracefully, his belly blocking the opening. It didn't take much effort to push him in. Really.

And that's all. I didn't stop to think about it. I was sure I had killed him, and it seemed quite all right. I had no pangs of conscience. I only felt great relief.

There was one other thing. In my pocket I had the Finger of God, the Deer's trotter, one of the four I'd found in Big Foot's house. I had buried the head and the other three feet, but I had kept this one for myself. I don't know why. I made prints with it in the snow, lots of them, chaotically. I thought they'd still be there in the morning to imply that the Deer had been here. But no one saw them except you, Dizzy. Water poured from the sky that night and wiped out all the prints. That was a Sign too.

I went home and set about making our supper.

I know I had a lot of luck, and that was what emboldened me. For surely it means I'd chanced upon a good moment, a time when I had the permission of the Planets? How come nobody intervenes to stop all the evil that's rife everywhere? Is it like with my letters to institutions? They should answer, but they don't. Don't we demand this sort of intervention convincingly enough? One can put up with the petty things that hardly cause any discomfort, but not with senseless, ubiquitous cruelty. It's perfectly simple—if other people are happy, we're happy too. The simplest equation in the world. As I drove to the Fox farm with the Cold Fist, I imagined I was triggering a process that would reverse everything evil. That Night the Sun would enter Aries and an entirely new year would begin. For if evil created the world, then good must destroy it.

And so I set off to see Innerd on purpose. First I called him and said we must meet; I said I had seen the Commandant just before his death and he'd told me to deliver something. Innerd agreed at once; at the time I didn't know the Commandant had had some money on him, but now I can see that Innerd was hoping to get it back. I said I would come to his farm once he was alone there. He agreed. He was shocked by the Commandant's death.

Earlier that day, in the afternoon, I had prepared a trap—I'd taken some wire snares from Big Foot's shed. I'd removed them so many times before that I knew very well how they worked. You choose a young, springy tree and bend it to the ground; then you pin it down by trapping it under a solid branch. You attach a wire noose to it. When the Animal gets caught in the noose, it starts to struggle, and the tree straightens, breaking the Animal's neck. I hid the wire noose among the ferns after making the effort to bend a medium-sized birch tree.

None of the employees ever stayed at the farm at night, the lights were switched off, and the gate was locked. That evening the gate was open. For me. We met inside, in his office. He smiled when he saw me.

"Do I know you from somewhere?" he said.

He can't have remembered our encounter on the bridge. No one remembers meeting old biddies like me.

I said we must go outside, that's where I had the thing from the Commandant, I hid it in the forest. He took his keys and his jacket and followed me. Once I was leading him through the wet ferns, he started to grow impatient, but I played my role well, replying to his insistent questions in monosyllables.

"Oh, it's here," I finally said.

He looked around uncertainly and cast me a glance as if he had only just understood.

"What's here? There's nothing here."

"Here," I said, pointing, and he took that one step forward, putting his foot in the noose. It must have looked comical from the outside—he did what I said, like a child at preschool. I was assuming that my trap would break his neck, just like a Deer's. That's what I wanted to happen, because he'd fed my Little Girls' bodies to the Foxes. Because he hunted. Because he stripped Animals of their skin. I think it would have been a perfectly fair Punishment.

Unfortunately, I'm no expert on Murder. The wire caught around his ankle, and as the tree sprang straight, it merely knocked him over. He fell and howled with pain—the wire must have cut into his skin, possibly the muscle too. I had my backup plan, involving the shopping bag. This time I had prepared it deliberately, in the freezer. The ideal murder Weapon for an old woman. Old girls like me always go about with plastic bags, don't they? It was simple—I hit him with all my might as he tried to get up, once, twice, maybe more. After each blow I waited a while to see if I could still hear him breathing. Finally he went quiet. I stood over the dead body in silence and darkness, my mind a blank. Once again I felt nothing but relief. I extracted his keys and passport from his jacket, pushed the body into the clay pit and covered it with branches. I quietly returned to the farm and went inside.

I wish I could forget what I saw there. Weeping, I tried to open the cages and chase out the Foxes, but then I discovered that Innerd's keys only fitted the first hall, which led into the others. For ages I searched desperately for the remaining keys, delving in the contents of closets and drawers, until at last I found them. I told myself I wouldn't leave this place until I had freed the Animals. It took a long time for me to open all the cages. The Foxes were bewildered, aggressive, dirty, sick, and some had wounds on their legs. They didn't want to leave the cages—they weren't familiar with freedom. When I waved my hands at them they growled. Finally I came up with an idea—I fully opened the door to the outside world and withdrew to my car. And later it turned out they had all escaped.

On my way home I threw away the keys, and after memorizing the date and place of his birth, I burned Innerd's passport in the boiler room. I did the same with the shopping bag, though I try not to burn waste plastic.

I got home without being noticed. Once I was in the car I couldn't remember a thing. I felt exhausted, my bones ached, and I spent the whole evening vomiting.

Sometimes the memory came back to me. I wondered why Innerd's body hadn't been found yet. I fantasized that the Foxes had eaten him, picked his bones clean, and then dragged them about the forest. But they hadn't touched him. He went moldy, which in my judgment is proof that he was not a human Being.

From then on I carried all my Tools about in the back of the Samurai. A bag of ice in the portable cooler, a pickax, a hammer, nails, even some syringes and my glucose. I was ready for action at any moment. I wasn't lying when I kept insisting it was Animals taking revenge on people. That was the truth. I was their Tool.

But will you believe me when I say I didn't do it entirely consciously? I instantly forgot what had happened, as if there were some powerful Defense Mechanisms protecting me. Perhaps I should ascribe it to my Ailments—quite simply, from time to time I was not Janina, but Bellona or Medea.

I don't know how and when I took Boros's bottle of pheromones. He called me later to ask about it, but I didn't confess. I said he must have lost it, and expressed my sympathy for his absentmindedness.

So when I said I would take the President home, I already knew what was going to happen. The stars had started their countdown. I only had to follow them.

He was sitting against a wall, dumbly staring into space. When I came into his field of vision I didn't think he had noticed me at all, but he coughed and said in a sepulchral tone: "I feel unwell, Mrs. Duszejko."

This Man was suffering. "Unwell" didn't just apply to his present physical state after overindulging in drink. He was ill in general, which brought him closer to me.

"You shouldn't overdo it with alcohol."

I was ready to carry out my sentence, but hadn't yet taken the final decision. It occurred to me that if I was in the right, everything would fall into place and I'd know exactly what to do.

"Help me," he wheezed. "Take me home."

It sounded sad. I felt sorry for him. Yes, I should take him home, he was right. Release him from himself, from the rotten, cruel life he led. This was the Sign, I understood it at once.

"Wait here a moment, I'll be right back," I said.

I went to the car and took the bag of ice from the cooler. A chance witness might have thought I was going to make him a cold compress for a migraine. But there weren't any witnesses. Most of the cars had driven off by now. Someone was still shouting at the front entrance; I could hear raised voices.

In my pocket I had the little bottle that I had taken from Boros.

When I returned he was sitting with his head tilted backward, crying.

"If you're going to drink that much, one day you'll have a heart attack," I said. "Let's go."

I took him under the arm and dragged him to his feet.

"Why are you crying?" I asked.

"You're so kind . . ."

"I know," I replied.

"What about you? Why are you crying?" he said.

That I didn't know.

We walked into the forest. I kept pushing him further among the trees; only once the lights of the firehouse were hardly visible did I let him go.

"Try to vomit, it'll make you feel better at once," I said. "And then I'll send you home."

He glanced at me with an absent gaze.

"What do you mean, you'll 'send' me home?"

I patted him reassuringly on the back.

"Go on, throw up."

He rested against a tree and leaned forward. A trickle of saliva streamed from his mouth.

"You want to kill me, don't you?" he wheezed.

He started to cough and hawk, but then I heard a gurgling noise, and he vomited.

"Oh," he said, ashamed.

That was when I gave him a little of Boros's pheromones to drink in the bottle cap.

"You'll feel better right away."

He drank it without batting an eyelid, and started to sob.

"Have you poisoned me?"

"Yes," I said.

And then I was sure that his time had come. I wrapped the handles of the shopping bag around my hand, and twisted my body to take the very best swing. I hit him. I struck him on the back and neck, he was much taller than I am, but the blow was so mighty that he sank to his knees. And again it occurred to me that things fall into place just as they're meant to. I hit him once again, this time with success. Something cracked, he groaned and fell to the ground. I had the feeling he was grateful to me for this. In the dark I positioned his head to make sure his mouth was open. Then I poured the rest of the pheromones onto his neck and clothing. On the way back, I threw the ice under the firehouse, and hid the shopping bag in my pocket.

That's exactly how it happened.

THEY SAT MOTIONLESS. THE MUSTARD SOUP HAD GONE COLD LONG ago. Nobody said a word, so I threw on my fleece, left the house and walked toward the Pass.

From the direction of the village I could hear sirens howling; their plaintive, mournful sound was carried on the wind across the entire Plateau. Then it all went silent. I just saw the lights of Dizzy's car driving into the distance.

XVII.

The Damsel

Every Tear from Every Eye
Becomes a Babe in Eternity,
This is caught by Females bright
And return'd to its own delight.

Dizzy must have called by early that morning, while I was still sleeping off my pills. How else could I have slept after what had happened? I hadn't heard him knocking. I didn't want to hear anything. Why hadn't he stayed longer? Why hadn't he tapped on the window? He must have wanted to tell me something important. He'd been in a hurry.

I stood on the porch, confused, but all I saw lying on the doormat was the volume of Blake's letters, the one we had bought in the Czech Republic. Why had he left it here for me? What was he trying to tell me? I opened the book and leafed through it vacantly, but no scrap of paper fell out, nor did I notice any message.

The day was dark and wet. I could hardly drag my feet along. I went to make myself some strong tea, and only then did I see that one page of the book was marked with a blade of grass. I read the text, a passage we hadn't worked on yet, from a letter to Richard Phillips, subtly underlined in pencil (Dizzy hated scribbling in books): "I read in the *Oracle and True Briton* of Octr 13, that"—and here Dizzy had added in pencil "a Mr. Black Coat"—"a Surgeon has with the Cold Fury of Robespierre caused the Police to seize upon the Person & Goods or Property of an Astrologer & to commit him to Prison. The Man who can Read the Stars often is oppressed by their Influence, no less than the Newtonian who reads Not & cannot Read is oppressed by his own Reasonings & Experiments. We are all subject to Error: Who shall say that we are not all subject to Crime?"

It took about ten seconds for the penny to drop, and then I felt faint. My liver responded with a dull, intensifying pain.

I had started to stuff my things and my laptop into my backpack when I heard the engine of a car, or rather at least two cars. Without a second thought, I grabbed it all and ran downstairs into the boiler room. Briefly I thought that maybe Momma and Grandma would be waiting there for me again. And my Little Girls. Perhaps that would have been the best solution for me—to join them. But nobody was there.

Between the boiler room and the garage there was a small hiding place for the water meters, cables and mops. Every house should have a hiding place like that in case of Persecution and War. Every house. I squeezed in there with my backpack and laptop under my arm, in my pajamas and slippers. My stomach was aching more and more.

First I heard knocking, then the creak of the front door and footsteps in the hall. I heard them coming up the steps and opening all the doors. I heard the voices of Black Coat and the young policeman who used to work with the Commandant and had interviewed me later. But there were other, unfamiliar ones too. They spread about the entire house. They tried calling me, "Citizen Duszejko! Janina!" and actually that was quite enough reason for me not to want to respond.

They went upstairs—they were sure to be bringing in mud—and visited every room. Then one of them started coming downstairs, and moments later the door into the boiler room opened. Someone came in and took a good look around, peeping into the larder too, and then went through to the garage. I felt a rush of air as he passed by, only centimeters away from me. I held my breath.

"Where are you, Adam?" I heard from above.

"Here!" he shouted back right by my ear. "There's no one here."

Someone upstairs cursed. Obscenely.

"Brr, what a nasty place," said the one in the boiler room to himself, switched off the light and went upstairs.

I could hear them standing in the hall, talking. They were conferring.

"She must have simply cleared out . . ."

"But she left the car. Odd, isn't it? Did she go on foot?"

Then Oddball's voice joined them, out of breath, as if he had followed the Police at a run.

"She told me she was going to Szczecin to visit a friend."

Where did he get that idea from? Szczecin! How funny!

"Why didn't you tell me before, Dad?"

No answer.

"To Szczecin? She has a friend there? What do you know, Dad?" asked Black Coat pensively. It must have been painful for Oddball to have his son drilling him like that.

"How's she going to get there?" A lively discussion began, and I heard the voice of the young policeman again: "Oh well, we were too late. And we were pretty close to catching her at last. She took us in for a long time. And to think how many times we had her within our grasp."

Now they were standing in the hall, and even at this distance I could smell that one of them had lit a cigarette.

"We must call Szczecin at once to find out how she might have got there. By bus, by train, hitchhiking? We must issue an arrest warrant," said Black Coat.

And the young policeman said: "We're hardly going to need an antiterrorist squad to find her. She's a crazy old woman. Round the twist."

"She's dangerous," said Black Coat.

They left the house.

"We must seal this door."

"And the one downstairs. All right, then. Come on," they said to each other.

Suddenly I heard Oddball's ringing voice.

"I'll marry her when she gets out of jail."

And at once Black Coat angrily replied.

"Have you totally lost your marbles out here in the wilds, Dad?"

THERE I STOOD, SQUEEZED INTO THE CORNER, IN TOTAL DARKNESS, for a good while after they had gone, until I heard the roar of their car engines. After that I waited another hour or so, listening to the sound of my own breathing. I no longer had to dream. I really was in the boiler room, as in my dreams, in the place where the Dead came. I thought I could hear their voices somewhere under the garage, deep inside the hill, a great underground procession. But it was the wind again, whistling as usual on the Plateau. I crept upstairs like a thief and quickly dressed for the journey. I only took two small bags—Ali would have been proud of me. Of course there was a third way out of the house too, through the woodshed, and I slipped out that way, leaving the house to the Dead. I waited in the Professor's outhouse until it grew dark. I only had the essential items with me—my notebooks, Blake, my medicine and the laptop containing my Astrology. And the Ephemerides of course, in case I were to end up on a Desert Island in the future. The further I moved away from the house across the shallow, wet snow, the more my spirits lifted. From the border I looked back at my Plateau, and remembered the day when I first saw it—I'd been delighted, but hadn't yet sensed that one day I would live here. The fact that we don't know what's going to happen in the future is a terrible mistake in the programming of the world. It should be fixed at the first opportunity.

By now the valleys beyond the Plateau lay in dense Gloom, and from up here I could see the lights of the larger towns—Lewin and Frankenstein far away on the horizon, and Kłodzko to the north. The air was pure and the lights were twinkling. Here, higher up, night had not yet fallen, the sky in the west was still orange-and-brown, still growing darker. I wasn't afraid of this darkness. I walked ahead, toward the Table Mountains, tripping over frozen clods of earth and clumps of dry grass. I felt hot in my fleeces, my hat and scarf, but I knew that as soon as I crossed the border I wouldn't need them anymore. It's always warmer in the Czech Republic, nothing but southern slopes.

And just then, over on the Czech side, Venus, my Damsel, shone out above the horizon.

She was growing brighter by the minute, as if a smile had risen on the dark face of the sky, so now I knew I had chosen a good direction and was heading the right way. She glowed in the sky as I safely crossed the forest and imperceptibly stepped across the border. She was guiding me. I walked across the Czech fields, constantly moving in her direction, as she descended lower and lower, as if encouraging me to follow her over the horizon.

She led me as far as the highway, from where I could see the town of Náchod. I walked down the road in a light and happy mood—whatever happened now, it would be Right and Good. I felt no fear at all, though the streets of the Czech town were empty now. But what is there to be afraid of in the Czech Republic?

So when I stopped outside the bookshop, not knowing what would happen next, my Damsel was still with me, though out of sight behind the rooftops. And then I found that despite the late hour there was someone in the shop. I knocked, and Honza opened the door to me, not in the least surprised. I said I needed a place for the night.

"Yes," he said, letting me in without asking any questions.

A FEW DAYS LATER BOROS CAME TO FETCH ME, BRINGING SOME clothes and wigs that Good News had thoughtfully prepared for me. Now we looked like an elderly couple on our way to a funeral, and in a sense it was true—we were going to my funeral. Boros had even bought a lovely wreath. This time he had a car, though borrowed from some students, and he drove it fast and assertively. We made a lot of stops at parking areas—I really was feeling ill. The journey was long and tiring. When we reached our destination, I couldn't stand on my own feet, so Boros had to carry me over the threshold.

———————

Now I live at the Entomologists' research station on the edge of the Białowieża Forest, and since I've been feeling a little better, each day I try to go on my short round. But I find it hard to walk now. Besides, I haven't much to keep an eye on here, and the forest is impenetrable. Sometimes, when the temperature rises and oscillates close to zero, sluggish Flies, Springtails and Gall Wasps appear on the snow—by now I have learned their names. I also see Spiders here. I have learned, however, that most Insects hibernate. Deep inside their anthill, the Ants cling to each other in a large ball and sleep like that until spring. I only wish people had the same sort of confidence in each other. Perhaps because of the different air and my recent experiences, my Ailments have grown worse, so I spend most of my time just sitting and gazing out of the window.

Whenever Boros appears, he always comes with interesting soup in a thermos flask. Personally, I haven't the strength to cook. He also brings me newspapers, encouraging me to read them, but they prompt my disgust. Newspapers rely on keeping us in a constant state of anxiety, on diverting our emotions away from the things that really matter to us. Why should I yield to their power and let them tell me what to think? I trot around the little house, treading paths this way and that. Sometimes I don't recognize my own footprints in the snow and then I ask: who could have come this way? Who made these footprints? I think it's a good Sign not to recognize oneself. But I am trying to complete my Investigations. My own Horoscope is the thousandth, and I often sit over it, doing my best to understand it. Who am I? One thing's for sure—I know the date of my death.

I think of Oddball, and that this winter he'll be alone on the

Plateau. And I think about the concrete I poured—will it withstand the frost? How will they all survive yet another winter? The Bats in the Professor's cellar. The Deer and the Foxes. Good News is studying in Wrocław and is living in my apartment. Dizzy's there too—it's easier for two to live together. And I'm sorry I failed to bring him round to Astrology. I often write to him through Boros. Yesterday I sent him a little story. He'll know what it's about:

A medieval monk and Astrologer—in the days before Saint Augustine forbade the reading of the future from the stars—foresaw his own death in his Horoscope. He was to die from the blow of a stone that would fall on his head. From then on he always wore a metal cap beneath his monk's hood. Until one Good Friday, he took it off along with the hood, more for fear of drawing attention to himself in church than for love of God. Just then a tiny pebble fell on his bare head, giving him a superficial scratch. But the monk was sure the prediction had come true, so he put all his affairs in order, and a month later he died.

That is how it works, Dizzy. But I know I still have plenty of time.

AUTHOR'S NOTE

The epigraphs and quotations in the text are from *Proverbs of Hell*, *Auguries of Innocence*, *The Mental Traveller* and the letters of William Blake.

Father Rustle's sermon is a compilation of genuine sermons by hunt chaplains sourced from the Internet.

My thanks to the Netherlands Institute for Advanced Study (NIAS) for the opportunity for peaceful, productive work. And to Andrew Leader for his very generous grant toward the cost of translation.

Olga Tokarczuk—Nobel Prize laureate, winner of the Man Booker International Prize—doesn't merely cross borders, she soars over them. In a dozen path-breaking books of virtuosic range, she melds fiction and philosophy, reimagines history, upends genre in ways that surprise, delight, and provoke. Her work opens new chambers in our interior lives.

Whether constellating our love affair with motion (*Flights*) or tracing the rise and fall of an eighteenth-century cult leader (*The Books of Jacob*), with each foray she crafts new kinds of vessels for storytelling. Readers of more than forty languages discover through her writing ways to keep our wonder and our humanity alive in a world growing ever more complex and entwined. Lyrical, playful, and "marvelously weird" (*The New York Times Book Review*), Tokarczuk is a star whose genius burns bright and will beckon to readers for generations to come.